PRAISE FOR THE DURRANT WALLACE MYSTERIES

"First-rate . . . keeps readers wondering whodunit until the very end."
—*Mysterious Reviews*

"Legault knows his history, and that's what makes this novel shine."
—*The Globe and Mail*

"A whopping good tale of adventure and murder in the frozen tundra of western Canada . . . a riveting and winning history mystery."
—*The Hamilton Spectator*

"A suspenseful plot that draws us in and keeps us hooked."
—*Alberta Views*

"A historical mystery that stands proud among the best of the genre . . . Legault's intimate knowledge of these mountains and their history brings Durrant and Holt City alive . . . Time well spent."
—*Rocky Mountain Outlook*

"Legault knows there's a fine balance between developing rich characters and leaving enough mystery to maintain interest until the next adventure." —*Calgary Herald*

"For those looking for a glint of Canadian history set in a more riveting narrative . . . *The End of the Line* combines the guilty pleasure of a page-turning murder mystery with the brain food found in Pierre Berton's history books." —*Avenue Magazine*

"Legault does a good job developing this rich character while never allowing the suspense of the story to flag." —*Quill & Quire*

THE THIRD RIEL CONSPIRACY

STEPHEN LEGAULT

TouchWood
Editions

TouchWood Editions
touchwoodeditions.com

LIBRARY AND ARCHIVES CANADA CATALOGUING IN PUBLICATION
Legault, Stephen, 1971–
The third Riel conspiracy / Stephen Legault.

(A Durrant Wallace mystery)
Issued also in electronic formats.
ISBN 978-1-927129-85-2

1. Riel Rebellion, 1885—Fiction. I. Title. II. Series :
Legault, Stephen, 1971– . Durrant Wallace mystery.

PS8623.E46633T55 2013   C813'.6   C2012-906788-1

Editor: Frances Thorsen
Proofreader: Vivian Sinclair
Design: Pete Kohut
Cover image: Pete Kohut
Author photo: Dan Anthon

Canadian Patrimoine   Canada Council Conseil des Arts   BRITISH COLUMBIA
Heritage canadien   for the Arts   du Canada   ARTS COUNCIL

We gratefully acknowledge the financial support for our publishing activities
from the Government of Canada through the Canada Book Fund, Canada
Council for the Arts, and the province of British Columbia through the
British Columbia Arts Council and the Book Publishing Tax Credit.

RECYCLED
Paper made from
recycled material
FSC   FSC® C103567

The interior pages of this book have been printed on 100% post-consumer
recycled paper, processed chlorine free, and printed with vegetable-based inks.

1 2 3 4 5 17 16 15 14 13

PRINTED IN CANADA

For Jenn, Rio, and Silas
For Sharon and Ernie
For the part of the story that remains untold

Author's Note to Readers

The Third Riel Conspiracy is a work of fiction. While I've taken pains to see that it conforms as much as possible to actual events and motivations of the Northwest Resistance of 1885, attentive readers will note many deviations from the historical record. The investigation undertaken by Sergeant Durrant Wallace of the North West Mounted Police and his companions is based on the real timeline and events of the period, but I've taken liberties with many of the characters who took part in this piece of Canadian history. Louis Riel, Sam Steele, Leif Crozier, Edward Dewdney, and others all played a part in the Northwest Resistance, but their appearance in this work is purely fictional.

This mystery novel is intended to entertain and provoke an interest in the actual occurrences that led up to the Battle of Batoche and the events that transpired afterward. Consider it a starting point from which you can launch your own investigation into the dramatic history of Western Canada.

A note on language: Throughout, some characters refer to the Métis as half-breeds or savages. This reflects the predilection of the times and not my or the publisher's point of view.

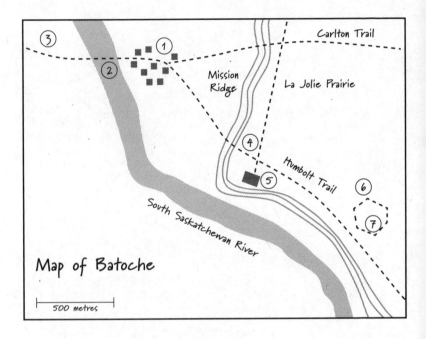

Map of Batoche

|—— 500 metres ——|

1. Batoche
2. Ferry
3. To Dakota Camp
4. Church
5. Cemetery
6. Zareba
7. Jasper Diver's body

PART ONE
BATOCHE

ONE

THE ZAREBA

WITH THE TUMULT OF RIFLE fire echoing in the distance, Reuben Wake found his kit, stowed in a latched compartment in his wagon. He took up the oilcloth-wrapped package where his Colt revolver had been placed and unrolled the canvas; the pistol wasn't there. Instead, a heavy stone fell to the earth at his feet.

Wake looked around as if he might find the Colt nearby, but it was nowhere to be seen. He scratched his greasy head with his free hand, pushing his leather cap up as he did.

That's when he heard the hammer of a pistol being cocked.

Wake froze. Everything became very still. He felt the wind on his face, still strong from the east, and he thought he could smell the stew the cooks had prepared for lunch.

"Turn around." The voice was behind him.

Reuben Wake hesitated.

"Faites-le maintenant." Do it now.

As Wake began to turn, a pistol was pressed to his forehead.

"What the hell—" Wake's mouth was suddenly dry.

"Long live Riel." The man pulled the trigger and the cartridge exploded. Wake closed his eyes but no bullet reached him. It was a misfire, and the gunman cried out as gunpowder burned his hand.

Wake, startled and in a panic, spun to flee as his would-be killer recocked and fired again. This time the bullet found its mark, breaching Wake's temple and ending his life instantly.

MAY 12, 1885. BATOCHE, NORTH WEST TERRITORIES.
EARLIER IN THE DAY.

The battle raged all morning, but Reuben Wake had been left behind.

At first light the commander of the North West Field Force,

General Frederick Middleton, broke camp and led his soldiers to La Jolie Prairie to rout the despicable half-breeds. The rest of the field force, nearly eight hundred men, was to attack the Métis defences at the Mission Ridge, high above the village of Batoche. The intent was to crush the rebellion between the Métis, their Indian conscripts, and the Dominion of Canada.

Wake had been with Middleton on the previous day when the general first approached the broad plain of La Jolie Prairie. Recently Wake had become a teamster, and he owned a livery stable in Regina. When war had broken out in the North West Territories, he was only too happy to enrol. At sixty-two, he was too old to join the infantry, so he put his skills with horses to work as a foreman tending the stock. On the third day of fighting he had been left with the mounted infantry's horses at La Jolie Prairie. Despite the cover of a dense grove of aspens, he had been wounded in the arm and ordered by the company's doctors to rest. Now, on the fourth day of the battle, he was inside the zareba, the field force's defensive structure set high above the Saskatchewan River.

The zareba was roughly rectangular and spanned several hundred yards. With walls built from packing crates, upturned wagons, and earthen berms, the African-inspired enclave was cloistered around a fetid pool. Outside its hastily constructed walls, the zareba was ringed with deep rifle pits—not unlike those used by the half-breeds—set along the Humboldt Trail. Since the first day of the Battle of Batoche, it had been home to the North West Field Force.

Staying behind angered Wake. Riel's savages were running out of ammunition and had taken to loading their guns with every-thing from melted-down coins to silverware. Wake surmised that the fighting would soon be over. He could smell the powder from the Winnipeg Field Battery, its guns firing from its position just outside the haphazard walls of the encampment. Its target was the village of Batoche. A strong wind blowing from the east meant that Wake couldn't hear the field guns and Captain Howard's magnificent Gatling gun firing at the Jolie Prairie. Reports came into the zareba on a regular basis, telling of the action.

Reuben Wake had been spoiling for a fight and now he wasn't going to get it. General Middleton's plan was to crush the rebellion this very day with a swift attack on two fronts. His force would feint along the skirmish line of La Jolie Prairie, and Colonel Van Straubenzie would charge the defences along the Mission Ridge and sweep down on Batoche. Wake made his way to the western entrance of the encampment to get a view of the action. Overhead the prairie sky was slate grey, the clouds featureless, their bellies pan-flat in all directions. He stood on a crate to see beyond the entrenchments. Behind him, several of the wagons of the field force were organized in a rectangle that formed the inner defence of the encampment. Here his lads tended to the horses, the cook and his swampers prepared meals for the soldiers, and the handful of deserters and prisoners were put to work.

As he stood watching the field guns firing, he heard a shout from the northwest and managed to heave himself up onto the top of the wall. There he spied a great host of men riding toward the zareba, the general in the lead.

"It's Middleton!" a man from the field battery shouted, "come back from the Jolie Prairie!"

"I wonder if he got his prize?" Wake shouted back. He speculated if Louis Riel, General Gabriel Dumont, and the other traitors had been killed or captured. When the men came into view, Wake could tell by their dour expressions that they had not been victorious. Middleton looked to Wake like a man who had just eaten something rank. His face was grim, and he pressed his horse to the entrance of the zareba. Wake jumped down in time to catch up to the animal and took the reins from the general's hands.

The stout commander was silent as the rest of his company rode in around him. Other teamsters took the horses into the makeshift corral. Middleton didn't say a word but instead strode off toward his private carriage.

Another member of the infantry dismounted next to Wake. "Did things fare poorly at La Jolie Prairie?" asked Wake.

The man shook his head and spat on the ground. "It was our forces at the Mission Ridge that missed their signal to advance. Middleton lacked the fortitude to press his advantage without the coordinated attack in place."

"The Métis remain dug in?"

"Greatly diminished, and doing little more than throwing pots and pans." The solider handed the reins of his mount to another teamster. "But yes, they still hold the Mission Ridge and the skirmish line along the St. Laurent Road."

Wake led the mare to the stable amid the commotion and disorder of the returning mounted infantry. He could hear the hullabaloo as more men fell back to the zareba, the day's momentum lost. Wake's frustration boiled. All his life he had harboured an unaccountable bigotry toward the half-breeds. To him, these sons and daughters of Frenchmen and Indians were the ruin of the young nation, and he had made a long career of causing them pain. Fuming, he passed the reins of Middleton's mare to a young stableboy, instructing him to keep her at the ready as the general might not yet be done for the day. He walked out of the stable and circled the encampment again. When he passed the northern quarter, he saw Middleton standing by his lodgings. Colonel Van Straubenzie of the 10th Battalion Royal Grenadiers was at attention before him. Middleton was dressing him down for failing to mount the direct attack that was supposed to come when he heard Middleton's guns.

Wake paused and leaned on a nearby wagon to adjust his sling. He could hear Van Straubenzie explain that with the wind he had not heard the sound of the Gatling gun. Van Straubenzie asked what the general's orders for the field force were for the rest of the day. "Take them as far as you please," said Middleton, dismissing the colonel with a wave of his hand. Van Straubenzie marched toward the company of foot soldiers gathered at the entrance of the zareba. Wake followed.

All might not be lost. Wake might yet get a chance to kill a half-breed in this battle. He simply needed to get out of the zareba and look for his chance. He'd already had an opportunity once on this campaign and had made good use of it. But killing one half-breed wasn't enough for Reuben Wake. He wanted more. Given the opening, he would try for the greatest prize in this war: the so-called prophet himself.

At the compound gate where Van Straubenzie's officers were gathered, the colonel was issuing hurried orders. A great hurrah went up from the men. Several hundred of them mounted their horses and charged out of the zareba, heading toward the Métis skirmish line at the top of the hill above Batoche. In the distance, the Winnipeg Field Battery opened fire again.

Men raced for their horses, and Wake, not wanting to be caught standing still, ran against the surge toward the corral to muster the mounts. Nobody wanted to miss the action. Near the centre of the camp, the kitchen was in chaos. Men dropped their tin plates and grabbed their Winchesters, making for the Mission Ridge. In no time, the men who had retreated from La Jolie Prairie that morning had regrouped and were charging across the open ground between the encampment and the village of Batoche.

That's when Middleton appeared, calling for his horse. Wake found the mare and snatched the reins from the stableboy's hands in time to present them to the commander himself. And with that the general was gone. Wake stood again in the relative quiet of the zareba. To hell with the doctor's orders. This would be his last chance to kill a dirty Indian, and he wasn't going to be sitting on his ass while the others had all the fun. He would retrieve his pistol from where he had stowed it while in hospital and get in on the action. And should Riel be captured alive, Wake still had a job to do.

TWO

DISPATCH FROM STEELE

Durrant Wallace stood in the rain, a stream of water pouring from his hat's curled brim. It spilled down onto the front of his heavy oilskin coat. The dim flicker of oil lamps cast the only illumination on muddy Stephen Avenue, Calgary's main street. Durrant receded like a shadow into a doorway next to the Stockman's Bar and watched the entrace of the busy saloon.

The night had started off with sleet driving in from the foothills of the Rocky Mountains. Around midnight the North West Mounted Police sergeant felt the temperature shift, and the ice turned to rain. It was all the same to Durrant Wallace. Wet was wet and cold was cold. The ache that had settled into his game left leg and burned in his right hand felt as if it might paralyze him. In the ten months since Durrant Wallace had returned from Holt City, Calgary had grown by more than five hundred souls, and more were arriving on the banks of the Bow and Elbow Rivers daily. What had started as a crossroads on the cattle trail from Fort Benton, Montana, in 1881 had grown into a sprawling town of tents, tipis, clapboard shacks, and even a few streets boasting wooden homes with porches.

While Calgary had selected its first chief of police that very year, the Mounted Police still kept the peace along the Canadian Pacific Railway, intercepting illegal whiskey and upholding the laws of the Dominion of Canada. With the outbreak of war in the North West Territories, more settlers and farmers were crowding into the city's confines.

Durrant Wallace, a veteran of the celebrated March West in 1874, was among those who had been left behind at the outbreak of war. It came as no surprise to him.

Superintendent Sam Steele, now a major in the militia of General Strange, had delivered the news personally. When the tensions between the half-French, half-Indian Métis and a handful of full-blood Indian bands loyal to Riel had erupted into violence on March 19, Steele had been called away from his post near Golden, British Columbia. Riel had declared a provisional government in the Saskatchewan Territory. He had written to the Government of Canada and threatened to "commence without delay a war of extermination upon all those who have shown themselves hostile to our rights."

All winter, rumours had been spreading up and down the North West Territories that such an act was inevitable. When it finally happened, Steele and the other men of the North West Mounted Police were called together to serve as scouts for a company of men that would march north from Calgary and then east from Fort Edmonton to confront the rebels. Steele had stepped off the train at Calgary's new station to a cheering crowd. Durrant had approached him late that evening at the barracks in Fort Calgary. Now, standing in the driving rain, he recalled the meeting with his superior.

"YOU ASKED TO see me, sir?" Durrant held his sealskin hat in his left hand, his deformed, frostbitten right hand leaning on his silver-handled cane. He was dressed in the scarlet serge he rarely wore during regular undertakings. Durrant reported daily to Sub-Inspector Dewalt, Fort Calgary's deputy commander, but it was to Steele that Durrant owed his allegiance.

"Good of you to come, Sergeant. Sit if you like. I see you've given up with the crutch."

"Yes, sir, except in the worst weather."

"And the cane?"

"A gift from Garnet Moberly. He came by it after our time in Holt City. It seems that its previous owner felt a certain indebtedness to Mr. Moberly, who had no need for it."

"Indeed." Steele stood and placed his reading glasses on the ledger laid open on the desk. He trimmed the wick on the oil lamp, and the sparse room brightened. Steele could see the scars that marred Durrant's countenance, a grim reminder of his having been left for dead on the prairie during the bitter winter of 1881.

"I can't take you with me, Durrant."

Durrant tried not to betray his disappointment.

"General Strange, who is leading the Alberta Field Force, will have nothing to do with it and Sub-Inspector Dewalt says he can't spare you. I know that you and Dewalt have never seen eye to eye," continued Steele.

"He did everything in his power to *prevent* my reinstatement after my . . . *convalescence*," Durrant said. "If he had had his way, I'd still be collecting the post and taking the census. I'd be an errand boy."

"*I* ruled that day, and the decision to reinstate was mine. You earned it. But he's your superior officer at Fort Calgary. If General Strange was on side, it would be another matter. He doesn't know you as I do, Durrant."

"I understand. Thank you for delivering the news in person, sir. Better to hear it from you than from Dewalt." Durrant stood and turned to go.

"Durrant," said the superintendent, his eyes bright in the light of the lamp. Durrant stopped and looked back. "I'll find a way to get you into this. I promise you that. It's just not going to be with the Scouts."

"I appreciate that."

"Don't thank me, Sergeant. Louis Riel and Gabriel Dumont are powerful, intelligent, and driven men, not to be trifled with. These ranchers and policemen I'll be leading know this country, and are handy with their Winchesters, but the boys that are coming by train from Toronto, Montreal, and Halifax are not soldiers. Blood may well be spilled. I just hope that cooler heads prevail."

"I wouldn't count on it, Superintendant."

"Nor would I, Durrant."

IT HAD TAKEN Steele just two days to assemble his Scouts, but he had to wait for General Strange to form up his regulars, so it was more than a week before the entire Alberta Field Force could march north to Fort Edmonton. Once they had left, there was only a handful of North West Mounted Police left to watch over the rough city.

At long last the man Durrant had been waiting for emerged. He yelled a good night to his companions in the bar and staggered down the muddy street.

Durrant watched a moment and then, his crutch under his right arm for support, stepped down into the road and carefully crossed to the wooden plank sidewalk on the far side. The mud pulled at his prosthetic and the rain threatened to flatten him, but he reached the other side.

The man he was following turned into a boarding house at the end of Stephen Avenue. Durrant picked up his pace and reached the door of the two-storey building in time to observe the man tromping up the stairs.

Durrant entered and made for the staircase. The crutch was a clumsy and noisy tool, so he set it by the door and limped carefully to the steps. Practice and patience had brought back much of his former mobility, and a recent visit to the NWMP hospital in Regina to have the prosthetic adjusted had given him more trust in the leg's stability.

As he mounted the stairs, he reached inside his dripping coat, retrieved his Enfield Mk II, and held it at his side. His thumb worried the hammer. He listened a moment and heard a door close. Quietly ascending the stairs, he peered down the long hallway that ran the length of the building. There were four doors on either side. Enough light reached the hallway through a window at the top of the stairs that Durrant could make out the muddy tracks left by the man.

Durrant waited. He wanted to catch the man sleeping to avoid the possibility of a violent end to this pursuit. The fellow had arrived from Fort Benton, Montana, a week before with a string of horses to sell. He was known to have a reputation for settling his disputes with a pistol. There were rumours that he was also involved with selling illegal whiskey on the Blackfoot reserve. Drawing a silent breath, Durrant stepped noiselessly toward the closed door, his pistol still pointing at the floor as his right hand tried the door handle. To his surprise, it turned easily: he had expected to find the door locked. With minimal effort he pushed it open and scanned the room, the Enfield pistol levelled at the gloom.

There was no one in the bed. Durrant could smell tobacco and the sweet stench of whiskey along with something else, a tang that caused him to catch his breath. The sparse room appeared empty. Durrant stepped inside and closed the door, checking to be sure his foe wasn't hiding behind it. That's when he saw the armoire resting behind the door, and he quickly brought his pistol back up. He carefully stepped to one side of its double doors and, fearing a blast of buckshot, flipped the latch on the closet and threw the doors open. It was empty.

Behind him, the bed and its frame seemed to leap from the floor. The room filled with bedsheets, mattress, and steel frame, all colliding with Durrant. As he was thrown forward against the armoire, Durrant caught sight of the man leaping to his feet from beneath the bed and making for the door. The heavy mattress and frame momentarily pinned Durrant against the closet as the man fled, crashing down the hall toward the stairs. With his pistol held before him, Durrant rushed as quickly as he could to the stairs. He caught sight of the man jumping the last six steps and running for the exit door. The flight of stairs was difficult for Durrant and he felt his heart sink when he thought his prey might slip away into the storm.

Cursing himself, he reached the parlour and hop-stepped for the door. He got there in time to see the pursued man slip in the mud and land on his back on Stephen Avenue. The man gripped a Colt pistol in his hand. Durrant stood in the door, his own pistol aimed at the prone figure.

"Police! Drop the gun!" he commanded. The din of the rain swallowed up his words so he yelled, "You're wanted for horse stealing. Drop it!"

The man was getting to his feet, his body soaked with rain and dripping with mud, but he made no move to throw down his weapon.

"Last chance. Drop the gun. I've got you dead to rights." His left hand level with his eye, Durrant stared down the steel barrel of the Enfield, its forward sight aimed squarely at the man's heaving chest.

The man made as if to raise his pistol, and Durrant shifted his sight and pulled the trigger. The Enfield's explosion was consumed by the storm. Wallace's shot found its mark on the man's right arm and his pistol dropped into the muddy street. The man bent and gripped his wound.

"Welcome to the Dominion of Canada. You're under arrest."

THERE WAS THE expected confrontation at the North West Mounted Police fort. Durrant stood in the lockup, his prisoner behind bars in the adjoining room and his supervisor, his uniform hastily pulled on, standing before him. Sub-Inspector Raymond Dewalt had been sleeping when Durrant rode into the compound of the fort. Durrant's prisoner was in shackles and was led by a short rope tethered to the pommel of his saddle. The constable on night watch had roused Dewalt, and once the prisoner was behind bars the sub-inspector confronted Durrant. "What were you doing going after this man alone, Wallace?" Dewalt hissed.

"I saw my chance and I took it, sir."

"You could have gotten yourself killed! Or worse, you could have killed a civilian with your reckless behaviour. I thought you and I were clear that there was to be no discharge of a firearm within the limits of the town of Calgary."

Durrant broke open the rotating cylinder of the Colt pistol he had taken from his prisoner and emptied the cartridges from it onto the table. "Someone forgot to tell that to our man back there."

"Don't play smart with me, Sergeant. We're not on the open range here; it would have been just as easy for you to wait until morning when we could have sent constables to arrest your man as he took his breakfast."

Durrant snapped the cylinder closed. "Inspector, our men here in Calgary are stretched thin. Nobody knows that better than you. With the rebellion and fears that the Cree might strike along the frontier, our constables are at their wits' end trying to cover the territory and keep the peace in this town. If I'd waited for there to be a contingent of men, this ruffian might have slipped back across the border. He might see that Calgary is an easy place to profit from thievery and moonshining. I saw the chance and I took it."

Dewalt watched the sergeant lock the pistol in a desk drawer and wipe his hands on his coat. "You could have been killed," the sub-inspector protested weakly. "How would I explain that?"

"Your troubles with me would have been over."

DURRANT STOOD IN the fort's jail. The doctor had just left and the prisoner was looking angrily at the sergeant, cradling his bandaged right arm with his left hand. "What's your name?" Durrant asked.

"I ain't telling you a goddamned thing."

Durrant looked around as if to inspect the cell. "Who are you stealing horses with?" The prisoner sat staring at Durrant through the bars. "You come up from Fort Benton country. We've got a report from Fort Macleod that you trailed twenty head of horses through there ten days ago. We've got half a dozen men in this area who say that you sold them horses under false pretenses. Forged papers from a breeder in Pincher Creek."

"You got nothing to hold me on. And you shot up my arm!"

Durrant continued. "There's a bunch of men in this town that are pretty riled up about parting with their cash and getting stolen horses in return. Buck Stilton is one of them. Maybe you don't know Buck, but he's one tough customer. Last year he punched a man in a bar fight so hard that he split the man's skull right open. Buck doesn't like to be messed with. I've told Mr. Stilton that you're here and he's wondering if he might see you about those horses you sold him. Mr. Stilton says he'd like to have a conversation about getting his money back."

Durrant stepped closer to the bars and dangled a set of keys. He slid one of them into the lock of the cell door and opened it.

"What are you doing?" asked the prisoner.

"You said I got nothing to hold you on."

"Yeah?"

"So I figured I'd let you go."

"What the . . ." The prisoner sat down on his bunk.

"Don't you want to go?"

The man looked pale as a winter day. "My name is Bud Ensley. I got a right to a lawyer in the Dominion Territory, I think."

Durrant's face grew dour. "I know that name—Ensley. You and me, I believe we got history."

THE SUN ROSE over the NWMP barracks and Durrant Wallace was still sitting in the guardroom. When Durrant had been stationed at Fort Walsh in the late '70s, Jeb Ensley was a notorious whiskey runner who had been running contraband up from Fort Benton, Montana, through the Wild Horse and Onefour region along the Medicine Line and up into the Cypress Hills. Ensley was part of a gang of outlaws, retired Civil War vets, and hired killers. After the arrival of the Mounted Police in 1874, the gang had fled back across the border but hadn't abandoned the lucrative trade in whiskey with the Indians of the Dominion. Bud Ensley, now in Fort Calgary's lock-up, was Jeb's kid brother.

In the winter of 1881, Jeb Ensley and several other men had been trying to take whiskey and rum and other contraband to the Indians throughout the North West Territories. They had already killed one man—a Hudson's Bay Company factor—when he refused to trade with them. The North West Mounted Police were tracking Jeb across the Cypress Hills. Durrant Wallace was closing in and in his customary fashion had thrown caution to the wind in order to pursue his quarry. Ensley and his gang had ambushed him, shooting his horse and wounding Durrant in the gun battle. It had nearly cost him his life; instead, he'd lost his left leg and much of the use of his right hand. Ensley and the others had disappeared after that. It was thought they had left Montana and headed south for Oklahoma, or even Texas. Now Durrant had his best lead in almost five years as to the whereabouts of the man who had attempted to kill him.

There was a knock, and the door pushed open. Durrant saw young John, who had replaced him in attending to the post and wire service. "Sergeant Wallace?"

"What is it, John?"

"A wire for you. From Superintendent Steele."

"Bring it here, son." The boy looked at Durrant's hand on his pistol, and Durrant lifted it and waved him over. John crossed the floor and handed Durrant the cable.

"There's been a fight at Fish Creek, sir. Have you heard?"

"Yes, read it in the papers yesterday."

"Ten men killed and forty-three wounded! Middleton hisself nearly got shot!"

"Middleton walked right into it. If the Métis hadn't run out of ammunition, it would have been far worse."

"What do you think will happen?"

"Middleton's got good men under his command. He got beat at Fish Creek. It won't happen again, so long as he doesn't split his forces and walk into another ambush."

"You want me to wait for a reply from you to Superintendant Steele?" the boy asked.

"No, if a response is needed, I'll send it myself."

"Thank you again, Sergeant Wallace."

"Everything is going to be okay, John. You'll see. Hell, Steele's Scouts will have restored some peace to the territories before June arrives."

"Yes, sir!" The boy seemed to brighten. He turned and left, closing the door behind him.

Durrant watched him go and then unfolded the wire correspondence. He decoded it as he read:

> To Sergeant Durrant Wallace.
> From Sam Steele, Commanding, via Fort Edmonton.
> Urgent.
> Sergeant Wallace, havoc on the trail to Batoche.
> Disaster at Fish Creek has resulted in delays. Forces stretched thin. In need of men who can parley with Cree. Proceed at once to intercept Middleton's forces to aid in the restoration of peace.

Steele had kept his promise.

DURRANT WAS STANDING before Sub-Inspector Dewalt. "He hasn't told me where his older brother Jeb is now," said Durrant. "He has told me enough that I can deduce he's back in Montana, either in Fort Benton or down in the Judith Basin."

The deputy commander of the fort had shaved and straightened his uniform and was sitting at his desk with a cup of black coffee, regarding Wallace with a weary expression. "You don't expect me to license a trip across the Medicine Line now so you can track down this phantom, do you?"

Durrant felt his pulse quicken. "No, sir—"

"Good." Dewalt cut him off. "You said it yourself last night. We're stretched thin."

"Yes, sir." Durrant was holding the cable from Steele in his hands.

"Then what *do* you want, Sergeant?"

"Hold him. Make sure he's not allowed out on bail. The magistrate will surely see that this man is a flight risk. If he's allowed to post a bond, he'll be on the Macleod Trail before you can take the shackles off him."

"And just how long am I supposed to hold him?"

"Until I get back," Durrant said, his eyes betraying some mirth.

Dewalt put his coffee down. "Back from where exactly, Sergeant?"

Wallace stepped forward and handed the cable to his superior. "The Saskatchewan Territory, sir."

THE MORNING'S PROMISE was spoiled, as the afternoon began grey and threatened more rain. Durrant Wallace used the hated crutch to make his way through the streets toward a familiar address three blocks east of Stephen Avenue. He was anticipating the visit, but he wasn't looking forward to the parting.

He had already wired Steele, who was riding east with his Scouts and the Alberta Field Force for Fort Pitt. When he arrived, he would learn that Durrant was on his way to Batoche. Durrant guessed he could make double time if he travelled light and alone.

Durrant was eager to be on his way. He'd won his assurance from Dewalt that Bud Ensley would be held for as long as was possible; that was the best he could hope for from the sub-inspector. Durrant felt the tear of priorities in his chest. While he wanted nothing more than to strike out immediately for Fort Benton in search of Jeb Ensley and his crew, he owed his service to the Crown and to the Dominion, and now he had been called back into action. He aimed to fulfill that duty.

He came to a row of houses that bordered a broad woodland along the banks of the Bow River. The homes had been constructed in 1884, the year after the railway came through town. No tar-paper shacks or flophouses for navvies, these homes had porches and parlours and families living in them. He stood a moment on the street, regarding a yet unpainted house. He had to prepare his words carefully.

"What are you doing standing out on the street, Sergeant Wallace?" His preparation was truncated by a voice from a second-storey window.

Durrant looked up to see Charlene Louise Mason, a mischievous smile on her face, leaning on her arms and looking down at him. He recalled the first time he had seen her, disguised as a mute stableboy and hiding from her estranged and violent husband. Fooled by her masquerade, Durrant had taken her on as aide-de-camp when he had travelled to the end of steel the previous spring to investigate a murder there. Despite her deception, which had nearly cost both of their lives, they had become close in the intervening year.

"Charlene, you are nothing but trouble to me." His face betrayed a smile. "Come down here, please, and let me have a word with you."

She closed the window and a moment later was at the door. "Do come in, sir." Her eyes were bright.

"I've got mud on my boots," Durrant pointed out.

"Well, then, use the horn there to pull them off and be careful not to get any on your trousers." Durrant did as he was told and stepped into the house. "Is Mr. Lloyd at home?" he asked.

"He's at the I.G. Baker Company store. I expect him home a little later in the afternoon."

"Very well, I'd like a word with him too—"

"You'll be having words with a great many people it seems," Charlene laughed. "Would you like tea? Or shall I make you coffee?"

"Coffee would be good, please. I haven't slept yet."

"Durrant, I swear, you need someone just to make certain you remember to eat and sleep!"

"Well, young John is a help, but he's a poor substitute for my lad Charlie."

"Well, Charlie goes by Charlene these days, sir, and you're the one who hired me off to the Lloyds to keep house. I would have been just as happy working for Paddy at the stables at the fort, like when you found me. At least then I could have looked in on you from time to time."

"Didn't seem proper." Durrant was still standing, watching Charlene grind coffee and put the pot on the stove.

"What do you know of proper, Sergeant Wallace?" Charlene poured him a cup of coffee and offered it with a slice of bread and honey. "What is it that you've come to tell me, Durrant?"

"Steele has sent a wire. I'm to leave for the Saskatchewan Territory tonight. I'll be catching the 6:05 east train."

"I shall have to get packing!"

Durrant sipped his coffee. "Not this time, Charlene. It's to war I go."

THEY HAD ARGUED for nearly an hour. Argued as only Charlene Louise Mason could. She could be the most persistent, stubborn woman in the world, thought Durrant. In the end, by sheer force of his masculinity, he had carried the day, and when they parted she had been distant.

Derek Lloyd had come home before Durrant left and given his assurance that he would keep a watchful eye on Charlene. Without the disguise of a stableboy, she was vulnerable. Durrant's greatest anxiety was that her husband might find her before Durrant Wallace could find *him*.

DURRANT HEARD THE whistle sound when the train crossed the Bow River, slowing to enter the town. In a moment the platform was filled with steam and a few passengers arriving from Canmore, Banff, and the recently renamed Laggan, formerly Holt City.

Durrant gathered his haversack. Wrapped in a tarp, the barrel of his Winchester protruded from the top of the bag. Young John ran up, breathless. The lad had weaved his way through passengers and railway workers to reach Durrant and was now red-faced and bending over to catch his breath. He held out a cable for Durrant.

> To Sergeant Durrant Wallace.
> From Leif Crozier, Assistant Commissioner, Prince Albert Division, NWMP.
> Urgent.
> Have learned of Superintendant Steele's request of you to lend assistance to Scouts there. Colonel Otter suffered defeat at Cut Knife to Poundmaker. Withdrew to Battleford. All are held up in the NWMP Fort. Do not attempt to reach Batoche via Battleford. Poundmaker's Cree control region. Remain at Fort Calgary.

Durrant looked from the paper to John, who was regaining his breath. Behind him the pullman porter yelled, "All aboard!"

"Tell Dewalt the train had already left." Durrant handed the cable back to John. Then he threw his bag in the door of the train and hauled himself up with his left hand. The train began to move forward, and young John and Calgary slowly disappeared in a plume of steam and black smoke.

THREE

RUMOUR AND GOSSIP

Durrant Wallace rode north and east from the train depot at Swift Current. He had procured a horse from the NWMP detachment and, freshly outfitted, was making his way across country. On the evening of May 12, just at sundown, Durrant came to the place where the Humboldt Trail drove down off the steps of the Saskatchewan and crossed the swollen river. The scene on the far side of the dell was like a dark dream. The town of Batoche lay in ruins. Buildings were pocked with holes and several fires burned in the tall dry grass along the banks of the river. Beyond, on a high sloping hill above the town, more fires smouldered and Durrant could see what looked like a church and rectory amid the grey haze.

Durrant considered the scene. At first he could not determine which side had emerged victorious after what had been four days of fighting, but one thing was clear: the battle was over. He could see soldiers of the Dominion flying their colours from several of the remaining buildings and then he knew that General Middleton's troops had carried the day. While his first impression was that of relief that the bloodshed was over, he also felt disappointed that he had not be able to stand shoulder to shoulder with his fellow Mounted Police and countrymen.

As he had so often done before, Durrant put the spurs to his horse not knowing what perils lay on the road ahead. When he reached the river he boarded the ferry and rode it across the Saskatchewan. He could not know that while the war might be over for the men he met on the other side, for him it had just begun.

BATOCHE WAS SET on a broad plain along a bend in the Saskatchewan River. It consisted of a dozen buildings laid out along the Humboldt Trail. Here and there were bodies of Métis men cut down during the final hours of the battle.

Soldiers gathered up wounded men from both sides of the confrontation and began the process of clearing debris from the town. Durrant recognized a few men from the ranks of the North West Mounted Police and spoke with those he had served with over his eleven years on the force. The mood was celebratory but restrained, and Durrant soon learned why. Already questions were being asked by those who had participated in the battle: why had so many good men been lost on both sides of the conflict? What had they died for?

He rode up the steep slope of the Mission Ridge, off the flood plain and into the woods near the church and the rectory. The ridge had been the scene of some of the heaviest fighting. The fields had been burned and the cemetery trampled. The rifle pits the Métis had constructed as defensive battlements lay empty.

Middleton's encampment was a mile from the church. Durrant took note of the soldiers on the road and the artillery used to shell the village. The Gatling gun, on loan from its manufacturer in the United States, was still being watched over by its operator.

Dismounting as he approached the encampment, Durrant presented his credentials to the sentry. A company of men was being assembled to pursue Riel and Dumont, who had fled after the battle. Other soldiers were sitting around smouldering fires, eating and smoking, while teamsters were attending to horses and their tack. It was loud and smelled of woodsmoke and sweat, and the acrid taste of gunpowder still tainted the air.

Durrant found a teamster and arranged to leave his horse. Shouldering his haversack, he set off to forage for a hot meal, however meagre. He was surprised to hear his name called as he passed by a tent erected on dry ground near the entrance to the compound. Dr. Saul Armatage emerged, wiping his bloody hands on an operating gown.

Durrant adjusted his pack and reached out his left hand as the man approached.

"What the hell are you doing here, Durrant?" the doctor demanded, but he was smiling when he said it.

Durrant looked around as if asking himself the same question. "I just arrived, coming on Steele's orders."

"Late to the party by about three hours."

"Are there many dead?"

"Nine on our side, including Captain John French. He led the charge into Batoche this very afternoon. I wish you had been here to see it, Durrant. It was quite the show. Old Middleton making haste to catch up and lead his men."

Durrant looked saddened. "How many dead on both sides?"

"Twenty-five on the battlefield . . ."

"You say twenty-five *on* the battlefield."

"Yes, that's right."

"The way you say that, Saul . . ."

The sun was down and the camp was dark. Lamps were being lit to cast illumination on the final hours of the long day. "Yes, it is a peculiar thing. Men died on the field of battle, but just a few hours ago, we found a man dead right here, inside the zareba."

"A sniper? I noticed that the banks of the Saskatchewan would prove hard to defend against."

"We did have some trouble from the Dakota Sioux along the riverbanks the first night. Peppered the camp with rifle fire throughout the eve of the ninth. Nobody could get a wink of sleep. This man wasn't shot by a sniper. He was a teamster, was taken at point-blank range and died where he fell. He was murdered, Durrant. We have a man in irons for it."

AFTER SUNDOWN, THE temperature was near freezing. Durrant

Wallace, Saul Armatage, and a dozen other men sat around a fire. "Tell me what you can about this murder, Saul. I can see it's playing on your mind," said Durrant.

Saul took a branding iron and moved the coals of the fire around, sending a shower of sparks up to circle above them in the night sky. "The dead man's name is Reuben Wake. He was a foreman with the teamsters. Yesterday he came back from the skirmish at Jolie Prairie with a bullet in his right arm." Saul paused to indicate the flesh on his own bicep where the man had been wounded. "I dug the bullet out and patched him up but forbid him from joining in today's affair. He was likely to cause his own death, not being able to handle a horse or a gun." Saul immediately regretted his choice of words. Durrant shifted awkwardly.

"He was pretty miffed about being sidelined, mind you. He kept ranting about wanting to get back in the mix with the half-breeds. Today, after the first offensive failed and Middleton came back to stew, I saw Wake milling about the camp. When the charge was signalled this afternoon, he was still in the zareba, but with all the artillery fire and shooting, nobody heard the shot that killed him. He was found about three o'clock. As I understand it, a search was conducted by a number of men here in the camp and a Métis deserter named La Biche was put in irons. I'm told he still had the murder weapon on his person: Wake's own Colt Navy revolver, with two rounds fired."

"You weren't in the compound at that time, Saul?"

"When Middleton finally mustered his own company and moved on Batoche, I went along and set up a field hospital in the town itself. I was there until about an hour before you arrived."

"So what is it that's troubling you, then?"

"Besides the fact that a man has been murdered in the first place, it's that the killer was found so swiftly, and still in possession of the weapon that did the deed. It just doesn't sit well with me. If you killed a man and intended to get away with it, wouldn't you dispose of the weapon?"

"Maybe he was holding it as a trophy?" Durrant eyed the other men around the fire. "What do we know about the murdered man?"

"I know very little of him. Mr. Wake had lived in Regina for some years and he owned a livery stable, but I don't know much else."

"What about you men?" Durrant motioned to the men warming themselves by the fire. "Who knew this man Reuben Wake?"

He watched their faces in the firelight. They kept their eyes down. One man spit a stream of tobacco juice into the fire, and it sizzled on the logs burning there. "*Nobody* here knew this man?"

"There are two hundred in the service of the horses," replied a grenadier from Winnipeg. "How could we know each and every one?"

Again the group fell silent. Durrant watched as the men shuffled. "Your silence says more than your words."

"You've not changed one bit, Durrant," said a man walking into the circle of light. He was tall and broad in the shoulders and stout around the waist. He wore the heavy field coat and cape of the North West Mounted Police. Several of his comrades moved aside so he could sit on a wooden plank bench.

"I should say *you* have!" Durrant stood and limped to the man, extending his hand. "It's good to see you, Tommy."

"And you, Durrant. I heard about your business at the end of the line last spring. It was good to know that the old Sergeant Wallace had finally returned to service."

Durrant returned to his seat and turned to Saul. "Tommy Provost was one of the lads who plucked me from the Cypress Hills in '81."

"I remember now." Saul shook a finger at Provost. "It's you I have to thank for all this grief in my life."

"Don't blame me, Doctor." Provost packed tobacco into his pipe.

"I had heard you had left Fort Walsh, but I lost track of you after that," said Durrant.

"I did. I went to work for Commissioner Irvine in Regina when it was seen fit to move headquarters there."

"That would explain the nobleness of your stature and the

heartiness of your girth," said Durrant, and several of the men laughed.

"Laugh if you like, Durrant. It's a good bit of work, and I get to keep my eye on things clear across the territories. As I'm getting on, it's nice not to have saddle sores each and every day."

"And yet here we are."

"I couldn't resist the temptation for one last adventure."

"They found you a uniform that fit?" teased Durrant.

"We just let the old one out a little around the waist." Tommy patted his tummy. "And sewed on a couple more bars ..." He indicated the flashings on his sleeve demonstrating the rank of staff sergeant.

"He outranks you, Sergeant Wallace." Saul exaggerated a cautionary tone. "Best mind your manners."

"Don't I always? So, Staff Sergeant, I suppose, given your posting so close to the top of the echelon in Regina, you must have known this fellow Reuben Wake?"

"I know *of* him. There's a difference," said Provost.

"Then what do you have to tell?"

"Just rumour and gossip is all."

Durrant looked around the circle of men by the fire. "It may well come to pass that this man's death was simply an unfortunate side story to the rebellion, but I for one should like to know for certain before we send a man to hang. It may be just gossip, but there is almost always a shadow of the truth in every story. Let it be told."

Tommy Provost looked at his comrades. Most of the men looked down at their feet or into the flames. "Well," he confided, "I heard it told that Reuben Wake—" He paused. Durrant's eyes rested none too gently on him. "I heard it told that Wake had his way with a girl out by Dumont's Crossing. This tale got repeated among the soldiers here at Batoche; the man whose daughter Wake molested was held up with Riel before the fighting got under way."

"You think that this man somehow managed to learn of this foul deed and took it upon himself to slip into the zareba and kill Mr. Wake with his own pistol?" asked Durrant.

"It's possible," answered another man. "If a man set his mind to it he could easily slip into the zareba."

"Even a man of Métis complexion?" asked Durrant.

"We have many Métis here among us. Not all have taken up arms with Riel. Some in fact are here among our own field force."

Durrant's face registered astonishment at the story. "Does any man here know the name of the father? It wasn't this man in irons, this Terrance La Biche?" The men shook their heads.

Saul Armatage spoke. "His name was Lambert. Jacques Lambert. I too have heard this story, and I can tell by your tone of voice, Sergeant, where this is going."

"Indeed," said Durrant. "It troubles me that the dead man, Wake, may have brought this trouble on himself through his actions at Dumont's Crossing. If this story was so well known, why wasn't he arrested?"

"Don't be so incredulous, Durrant. It's not so strange, is it?" asked Provost. "There was a lot of looting happening along the trail up from the Qu'Appelle where we decamped nearly a month and a half ago now. Some of the men took to ransacking the homes and farms of the Métis along the way, looking for food and blankets. After the affair at Fish Creek, I think some of the men bore a grudge. Maybe Mr. Wake was one of them."

Durrant watched his old friend. "Tommy, you and I have a long history. We rode west together in '74. We served together at Walsh. I owe you my life. We've both been lawmen for more than a decade now, though I suppose each of us has been sidelined in his own way these last few years. I can tell you that a man who has his way with a girl in this manner isn't exacting revenge. This isn't some passing fancy that he up and decides to undertake: it's bred in his bones and he's just looking for the excuse." Durrant paused and let that settle in. "So the gossip is that Reuben Wake had his way with a Métis woman as his revenge for the killing at Fish Creek—"

"Not so much a woman as a young girl." Provost looked at his boots. "Story is that she was just thirteen. That's all I've heard of it. Rumour spreads like wildfire on the prairie, and it may be that this story got to the ears of the girl's pappy."

"The man you have in custody has no relation to this girl?" asked Durrant.

"Not that any can tell," Provost said. "I've not spoken to the man, and likely won't get the chance," and by that Durrant knew he meant he didn't want to. "From what I understand, and again this is just hearsay, he hasn't said a word by way of confession. He was found in possession of Wake's pistol, and two cartridges fired from it. One of them is in Wake's brain."

"So we don't know what this man La Biche's motive might have been?"

Provost shook his head.

"What else do we know of Reuben Wake?" asked Durrant.

"That's all we know." Provost looked at Durrant across the lick of flames.

"Well, as we can't ask the corpse himself, I suppose we'll have to ask others this question and see what answers might arise." Durrant stood with some difficulty and took up his crutch and his rifle.

"Might as well leave it alone," another man cautioned. "Dead is dead and all the questions in the world ain't going to bring this fellow back to the living."

"You might be right. From what you chaps tell me, there may have been more than one who wanted Reuben Wake dead, and if that's the case, then Mr. La Biche may face the gallows for a crime he didn't commit. That doesn't sit well with me, and I hope it doesn't sit right with you, Staff Sergeant." Durrant was looking now at Tommy Provost.

"It doesn't, but I don't think you or I will get much say in the matter."

The rest of the circle was silent. Durrant looked at Saul and signalled with a nod that he wanted a word. The two men stepped away from the fire and into the icy night air. "What do you make of this, Saul?"

"It's too simple to lay the blame on this La Biche fellow. I should like to know at least what his motive was before we go and hang him."

"I should like to find this Jacques Lambert and ask him of his whereabouts this afternoon. Where are these men now?" Durrant asked.

"Terrance La Biche is locked in a makeshift stockade here in the compound and under guard. Sub-Inspector Dickenson won't let you see him."

"Who is this Dickenson?"

"He's with F Division out of Regina; he's taken control of the prisoner and won't let others near the man. Refused me access to assess his health."

Durrant rubbed his whiskers, wondering what it was that made a man turn into a horse's ass as soon as he reached the rank of sub-inspector. "What of Lambert?"

"He's in the infirmary. This man I *have* attended to. He was captured yesterday along the banks of the river, below our camp. I believe he may have tried to kill himself."

"First I'll look in on La Biche, and then you and I will visit Lambert."

Saul shook his head. "I suppose it wouldn't be the first time you've tried to pull rank on a superior officer, Durrant. Be careful. Powerful emotions have been stirred up with this rebellion. The fighting might be over at Batoche, at Duck Lake and Fish Creek, but the feud smoulders all around. There is something in the death of Reuben Wake that makes me fear that all of the blood over Riel's rebellion has yet to be spilled."

The conversation returned to a congenial tone as the men began swapping stories of their adventures. Saul slapped the side of his leg. "I almost forgot to mention it, Durrant. Garnet is here!"

"He is!"

"He arrived two days ago. He's formed up with the Surveyors Intelligence Corps, a bunch of men from the Dominion Land Survey who took up the call at the outbreak of trouble. They have proven themselves quite useful in a pinch, helping out today at La Jolie Prairie, and then on the final charge into the village."

"Is Garnet safe?"

"Who knows? When Riel and Dumont fled during the last minutes of the battle, Garnet took a group of men in pursuit. He could be halfway to Montana by now for all I know."

"It will be good to see him once more. I hope that I shall."

"You know how Garnet is; one moment he's there, the next he's gone. He'll be glad to see you, I'm sure. And he'll be very interested in the discovery of this body in the zareba today. You know how he is: all questions of means, motive, and opportunity."

FOUR

THE INQUIRY BEGINS

MAY 13, 1885. BATOCHE.

He was there when Durrant awoke. Durrant lay curled in a blanket on the cold ground inside the zareba. There was a fire kindled and Garnet Moberly was sitting on an upturned crate, his Martini-Henry rifle cradled in his lap and his twin Webley revolvers holstered over a thick canvas coat. His face was partially obscured by the wide-brimmed hat favoured by the Surveyors Intelligence Corps.

"There's coffee," he said when Durrant stirred. "It's fresh."

Durrant was cold through to his bones. He'd been sleeping rough with just a pair of wool blankets for the last ten nights, having travelled light since leaving the train at Swift Current. If he was surprised to find Garnet at his side that morning, Durrant didn't show it.

"Coffee would be good." Durrant sat up stiffly. Garnet used a rag to lift the blackened pot from the flames and poured a cup of thick coffee for Durrant, who let the heat of the tin cup warm him. "It's good to see you, Garnet." Durrant placed his Enfield and his snub-nosed British Bulldog revolver next to him as he pulled his prosthetic from under the blankets. "Mind if I warm my leg before I put it on?"

"Not at all, lad."

"I take it you and your men didn't locate Riel last night?"

"We were close. We tracked his party north, but around two o'clock we were relieved by a group of Scouts who know this area better. If he's not in our hands by nightfall, my men and I will take up the hunt once more.

"I fear I might be getting a little old for this sort of thing. When Art Wheeler put out the call for men I couldn't help but join up.

I was at Rogers Pass proving out the line that Rogers surveyed. A wire was sent to Eagle Summit and one of the lads came up the pass to report the news, and I made for Fort Calgary."

"When did you pass through Calgary?"

"May 1."

"I had just left. Did you see Charlene?"

"I wasn't there but a few hours while Wheeler formed us up into a company and we were on the tracks once again."

"I'm worried about her."

"She's fine," Garnet said paternally. He watched as Durrant slipped from under his blankets, rolled up his left pant leg and affixed his leg. "You're looking quite well, Sergeant."

"The prosthetic fits better now. It doesn't worry the nub so much anymore. I can walk without the crutch much of the time. I use that cane you gave me most days."

"You've discovered its secret?"

"I have indeed, though I've not had call to use it."

"Not yet, but knowing you, I suspect you will."

Saul Armatage arrived, holding a heavily laden cloth and wearing his wool travelling suit and overcoat. They sat by the fire and ate potatoes with the skin on them and slabs of bacon with biscuits and drank more of Garnet's coffee.

"Is what I hear true? There has been a murder in the zareba, and a Métis deserter has done the deed?" asked Garnet while he finished his breakfast. Durrant and Saul retold what they had learned of the deceased man the previous evening. When they finished, Garnet said, "This Reuben Wake character certainly sounds like he was worth the bullet."

"It's all just conjecture at this point," cautioned Durrant.

"*You're* going to investigate, *aren't* you?" Garnet's tone suggested both amusement and inevitability.

"I should like to get to the bottom of some things."

"Such as what, if any, motive did this Terrance La Biche have?

Who else besides the father of the molested girl might have wanted Reuben Wake dead?" said Saul.

"How was it that this La Biche, who was supposedly under guard, managed to sneak away at the height of the battle, find Wake's very own pistol and kill him with it, and then sneak back into the cookery?" added Garnet.

Durrant agreed. "I'm very curious about what motive Mr. La Biche might have had. If he hadn't taken up arms but was merely tending to his cattle, as we have heard, one might assume that he didn't hold with Riel and Dumont. If that was the case, then why kill a teamster under the command of the Dominion?"

"And why this *particular* teamster?" asked Garnet.

"If the rumour of . . . rape . . . is true"—Durrant looked down at his hands uncomfortably—"and if this girl's father is here in this very camp, also under guard, did he slip his bonds?"

Saul added, "The murdered man was shot in the head at point-blank range. How is it possible that a Métis who was a foe of the deceased was able to walk right up to him and pull the trigger?"

Durrant had been sitting on a crate. He stood up now, taking his crutch and tucking his armament into holsters and pockets. "These are all good questions, gentlemen, and I am grateful that you have deputized yourselves as aides in this investigation. I must go and face the unpleasant task of requesting an interview with Terrance La Biche from my superior, Sub-Inspector Dickenson. I should hope he is as not as obstreperous as all accounts suggest."

"And if he is?" asked Saul.

"Then I shall have to persuade him to the best of my ability."

DURRANT WALLACE FOUND Sub-Inspector Damien Dickenson inside a makeshift detention centre that had been fashioned inside the zareba. He was sitting on a round of wood, smoking a pipe and cleaning his Winchester.

"Good morning, Sub-Inspector," Durrant said as he made his way into the tight enclosure of wagons. He stopped and stood at attention.

Dickenson looked up. He was a ginger-haired man with a broad moustache and small blue eyes set close together on his round face. "Good mornin'."

"My name is Sergeant Durrant Wallace." He stood stiffly before the seated man.

"You're Mounted Police?"

"I am. Fort Calgary, sir."

"You don't wear the serge?"

"No, sir. I haven't in some time. The kind of work I do, it's better to conceal my purposes."

Dickenson looked at Durrant. "I know who you are—the infamous Sergeant Wallace." Dickenson stood and offered his hand. Durrant glanced down at his own game right hand, and Dickenson awkwardly switched to his left so that Durrant could shake it. "I didn't think you'd been assigned to the campaign, but here you are."

"Indeed, here I am, sir. It's a clandestine effort that's led me here to Batoche."

"Care for a seat, Sergeant?" Dickenson turned up another round of wood for Durrant to sit on. Durrant accepted, lying his rifle and crutch down beside him. "Did you see any action, Wallace?"

"Not to speak of. I made haste to reach Batoche, but didn't arrive in time to get into the fray. How did you fare?"

"Very well. I was able to do my part on the Mission Ridge. I was with Van Straubenzie and the others yesterday afternoon when the charge was ordered. We went hard for the Mission Ridge and swept all resistance away."

Durrant listened in silence.

"I don't care to seem rude, but what is your business here in the stockade?" asked Dickenson.

"I understand that you have a man named La Biche here in custody?"

Dickenson drew on his pipe. "The assassin? Yes, he's in that wagon there." He pointed with his chin.

"He got caught red-handed?"

"He was in possession of Reuben Wake's pistol."

"Did you catch the man yourself?"

"A man named Jasper Dire did. He's a volunteer in Major Boulton's Regina company."

"You've interviewed him?"

"I have."

"What did you learn?"

Dickenson regarded Durrant with a cool eye. He drew on his pipe, the smoke circling around his features a moment before he spoke. "He's a rebel. A half-breed. When it looked as if the battle was going against the Métis, he broke away from the cookery and sought out a man to kill. Even the score, I suppose."

"This is what he told you?"

"It's what happened. It's a simple matter of facts."

Durrant studied Dickenson's face. "How many others are being held here in the stockade that were arrested that day?" asked Durrant.

"Twelve men. Some others were captured and released after they laid down arms."

"How many men are being held here that were *not* captured in the fighting? Are there others like La Biche who surrendered?"

"One other—a Métis—who was found in the willows along the riverbank. He had a knife on his person."

"And what was he doing?" asked Durrant.

"He says he was just sitting. His name is Jacques Lambert. He's not well in the head. Cut his own wrists there on the banks of the river. Middleton's doctor had to bandage them. The man is under guard in the infirmary."

"Where is the murder weapon, Inspector?"

"We have it under lock and key. If Wake has any family, they'll get it after the trial."

Durrant knew from experience that, descendants or not, Wake's pistol would in all likelihood end up a trophy of Dickenson as soon as the gavel was dropped on Terrance La Biche.

"Would you mind if I spoke with La Biche?"

Dickenson took the pipe from his mouth. "I don't think that would be appropriate, Sergeant."

"As I see it, the case needs strengthening, sir. I don't want to tell you your business, but I fear that when this case goes to court the judge will throw it out. We need to establish a clear motive for this man's involvement in the death of Mr. Wake. We have to prove that there was some reason he sought out Reuben Wake instead of any other man in the zareba that day. Why not simply kill the cook? Why go to all the trouble of searching out Mr. Wake?"

Dickenson was regarding Durrant through a pall of pipe smoke. "I don't think we'll have to worry about the judge."

"If we get a *Regina* judge, that is."

Dickenson's small eyes narrowed so that they were mere slits in his round face. "You can have ten minutes."

TERRANCE LA BICHE was chained to the seat of a covered wagon. He was lying on his side on the floor, his hands shackled above his head, and was feigning sleep. "Mr. La Biche, I'm Sergeant Durrant Wallace of the North West Mounted Police. I'm here to ask you some questions."

"Then ask your questions."

"Would you rather not sit up here on the seat and talk like civilized men?"

"There is nothing civilized about this situation, Red Coat."

"Sir, you are under arrest for the murder of Reuben Wake. If you're found guilty, you will hang from the neck until dead. I thought you might appreciate a moment or two to plead your case."

The man looked up. He was dark-skinned, with a thick head of curly back hair and piercing eyes. He wore a thin coat over workclothes. He stood up, pulling on the chains, and sat on the bench. There was no blanket in the wagon.

Durrant stepped up into the wagon and sat down on the spring-loaded seat next to the Métis man, considering him for a moment. "Mr. La Biche, did you kill Reuben Wake?"

"You're the first one to ask. The others, they did not bother to ask this question." La Biche's accent had hints of both French and Cree.

"Did you kill him?"

"I did *not*. Doesn't mean that I didn't want to." La Biche leaned toward Durrant so that his face was just a few feet from the policeman's. "In fact, I was looking for a chance since getting myself caught on the very first day of fighting. But no such opportunity came my way."

"Let's back up a moment, Mr. La Biche. Tell me what happened on May 9, the first day of fighting."

"It wasn't the first time that we gave hell to General Middleton and his men. I was at Fish Creek, yes? That was the twenty-fourth of April. It was cold as hell. That's where this all started, this business with Wake.

"I was with General Dumont when we ambushed Middleton's men there. That old fool split his troops and had half of them marching up the west side while the other half marched on the east of the creek. It was easy for us to bear down on one column of his men without much risk to ourselves. General Dumont assigned me to lead a company of men who would pick off Dominion troops from the hillside. We worked our way around to try and flank these soldiers and that's when I saw Wake."

"You knew this man?"

"Of course I knew him. I had known him for many years. Known him and come to hate him!"

"After you saw Wake, what happened? Where was he?"

"He was minding the horses, just like he always done. Just with the horses. I recognized him right off, as he had been up to Batoche several times over the years. That is how I have come to know him: his trips here to Batoche. He had come in the guise of a friend, but soon we were to learn that it was all trickery.

"I simply couldn't believe my luck it was him. I wanted to kill that man right then. I broke off from my companions and made my way along Tourond's Coulée, trying to get close enough that I could shoot him right between his eyes. But I couldn't get a good shot at him, and I didn't want to reveal myself and miss. By the time I was in position, Middleton had found a scow and his second column was crossing the river. We'd killed ten and wounded more than forty, so the day belonged to us. Dumont ordered a retreat. I was the last to leave. Dumont ordered us to retreat to Batoche. It took General Middleton more than two weeks to pull himself together again." La Biche grinned.

"When Middleton finally reached Batoche, I was dug in just near a ravine and had a good shot at your Dominion soldiers as they came up through the trees. The whole time I was looking for Wake, but because he was with the horses, I couldn't find him. I knew I would have to do something if I was going to get close to him, so when the soldiers started to fall back to take their supper, I slipped out of my trench and headed up the Humboldt Trail. I got a bit of luck there and come across some cattle that had been spooked, so when I gave myself up I looked just like a farmer. Told the Dominion soldiers that took me that I was tired of Riel's religious ranting and that I didn't want to fight for him any longer. What do you think they did?" He laughed. "I think they were happier to see those cows than they were a deserter such as myself.

"They marched me back here and made me dig trenches all night, and the next day I got put in with the cooks. I kept trying to get away to find Wake, but he was always out tending to his horses. Until that last day." La Biche was suddenly serious.

"I saw that he got his arm shot up at La Jolie Prairie, and I knew that was going to be my chance. I had even put away a meat hatchet I was going to use to do the job. The battle cry went up and all the men were charging this way and that. I lost track of Wake. The next thing I know, there are these two men on me, dragging me away from the pots I was scrubbing and putting me in chains. Now here I am. And Wake is dead, but I didn't kill him."

"When they took you away, they said you had Wake's Colt in your possession."

"I didn't have a gun. How could I have gotten a gun? When I gave myself up they searched me. I was unarmed. I had the hatchet hidden in one of the stores, but like I have told you, I didn't get a chance to use it on the man."

"Where exactly did you stow it?"

"I had it hidden under a sack of flour in the cookery. Go and see for yourself."

"Sub-Inspector Dickenson has told me that you had Wake's pistol in your coat and that there were two rounds fired."

"I didn't have the pistol when the men came for me." He made an "empty" expression with his hands. "They took my coat from me when I was arrested. I slept last night with just this," he said, his fingers holding the light fabric of his tunic. "No blanket. Not even a hot meal, just one of those terrible biscuits. I didn't even get to eat that damned cow!"

"You knew Wake from before. You said that he'd been here over the last year?"

"He had been here several times. In fact, he was here when General Dumont and his companions went to Sun River, south of the Medicine Line, to bring our father, the prophet, home."

"What did Reuben Wake have to do with the business of bringing Riel back to Batoche?"

Suddenly Dickenson appeared in front of the wagon. There were two men with him, wearing the uniforms of the Regina volunteers of French's Scouts. "That will be enough questions, Sergeant. We've orders to move this man."

"I'll need just a few more minutes with him, Sub-Inspector."

"No, Sergeant, you'll not need just a few more minutes. He's my prisoner, and I will interrogate him now in my own way. I aim to learn what I can from this man about the whereabouts of Gabriel Dumont and Louis Riel and see what I can find out about further plots to assassinate our proud Dominion boys. Then he's for Regina and the noose."

"I assume, Sub-Inspector, that this man is to be transported to stand trial?"

"That's correct," Dickenson answered, stepping forward and unlocking La Biche. He grabbed the man's arm so hard that Durrant thought he might break it.

"Will you see that he is properly cared for? He hasn't had a meal or a blanket to sleep under. This man is *your* prisoner. You are responsible for his care. Do I make myself clear?"

"Sergeant, if you don't show respect for my rank I'll see that *you* are in irons too. This man is a traitor against the Crown and a murderer and will hang for his crime."

"That may well be so, but he will stand trial first or his blood will be on *your* hands. Mark my words." Durrant stayed seated on the bench of the wagon as Dickenson and the volunteers marched La Biche away.

REASONABLE DOUBT

"DID YOU EXAMINE THE BODY of Reuben Wake, Saul?" Durrant was standing in the hospital tent where Saul Armatage was about to operate on a man's leg. The soldier was propped up on his elbows, watching the undertaking. Saul was using what looked like a pair of pliers to pull a nail from deep in the man's shin.

"They ran out of ammunition, so they started shooting nails or anything else they could load in their guns," he explained. The patient winced as Saul pulled out the nail. A jet of blood followed, and Saul quickly applied pressure to the wound and dressed it. When he had finished, the soldier pulled on a pair of trousers and, using a stick for a crutch, made his way out of the tent.

"I saw the body. Pronounced him dead. Saw that he had a head wound, but there were ten others who were alive that I needed to attend to, so I didn't do an autopsy. You think something else killed Mr. Wake other than the bullet wound in his head? To me it seemed pretty obvious—"

"I don't know, Saul. But I can tell you this: I doubt very much that Terrance La Biche killed him. He wanted to, and that was his purpose in surrendering—to get close enough to Wake to murder him. I don't believe it was him that killed Wake. If La Biche had done the deed, he'd be telling everybody he met."

Saul took off his apron, hung it up, and walked to where Durrant stood at the door. He was still rubbing his hands.

"I don't suppose the body is still in your morgue?" asked Durrant.

"It should be. We've buried the dead from May 11, but not yet from yesterday. They're being sewn into blankets to be laid to rest today."

"Can we have a look?"

"Of course, Durrant. Shall we fetch Garnet first?"

DURRANT, SAUL, AND Garnet entered the morgue, a drab tent behind the hospital. There were five bodies laid out on the ground, and two young soldiers were sewing blankets over them. When the three men entered the tent, the soldiers looked up and then returned to their work.

"Which one of these is Reuben Wake?" asked Saul.

"Not sure," one of the soldiers replied.

Saul muttered under his breath and went to inspect the tags affixed to each corpse's shroud. He went through all five and then turned and looked at his colleagues.

Garnet stepped forward and withdrew a knife from his coat, bending to slit the stitching on the blankets. The soldiers looked on in disgust. "What the Sam Hill are you doing?"

Garnet looked up at the boys. "You're addressing a lieutenant in the Surveyors Intelligence Corps, gentlemen. I suggest you keep quiet until asked a question."

"He's not here," Saul said when all five mantles had been slit.

"Then where the hell is he?" asked Durrant.

"GENTLEMEN," SAID DURRANT as they left the tent, "I need to attend to a matter in the cookery. When I spoke with Mr. La Biche an hour ago he claimed that his coat was taken from him when he was arrested, which is where Wake's pistol was found. La Biche says he had put aside a meat hatchet of some sort to use on Wake. While I look into its whereabouts, I wonder if the two of you might make some discreet inquiries around the compound as to what might have happened to the corpse of Mr. Wake."

They agreed to gather again after they had completed their assigned tasks. Durrant found his way through the labyrinth of wagons and tents to where the central kitchen had been set up. While many of the regiments had their own cooks and kitchens, General Middleton's mounted infantry, and several other companies, shared a common scullery that occupied a tent set close to the general's quarters.

It was midafternoon as Durrant approached, and the kitchen was beginning to prepare the evening stew. Half a dozen men were cleaning pots from the lunch meal in a vat of water simmering over an open fire. Nearby three more were chopping onions, potatoes, and carrots, and another was butchering a cow. Durrant stepped into the gloom. The cook who was doing the rough work with the cow looked up.

"You missed lunch. Come back in two hours." He hacked at the carcass.

"I've eaten, thank you."

"What do you want? I got eight hundred mouths to feed—"

"I'm Sergeant Durrant Wallace of the North West Mounted Police. I want to ask you about Terrance La Biche."

The cook stopped hacking. "I've already told the other Red Coat about La Biche."

"I thought that I might save some embarrassment and clear up some of the facts. You had him working here with you?"

"He was there, with the other half-breeds, cleaning up." The cook pointed with his cleaver at the men washing pots.

"Did he do anything other than wash up?"

"Sometimes he helped with the meals."

"Yesterday, after the noonday meal, there was a general charge sounded. What was Mr. La Biche doing around that time?"

"He was doing the pots."

"It's been said that at about that time he was able to leave your watch and make his way across the compound and kill Reuben Wake."

"That's what they said when they come to take him away."

"Did Mr. La Biche not leave the kitchen around that time?"

The cook was silent.

"He did," said one of the men cutting potatoes.

The cook glared at him, then looked back at Durrant. "He said he had to use the lavatory. I'm not going to make him soil his trousers."

"I'm not here to question how you manage your kitchen or how you watch over those whose charge you have been given. I'm trying to establish if Mr. La Biche had the opportunity to kill Mr. Wake."

"He left for a moment. He'd been well behaved the last three days. Never tried to run off so I let him go to the lavatory. I didn't think nothing of it."

"How long was he gone?"

"Just five minutes, if that."

Durrant looked around. The man cutting potatoes had returned to his work. Was five minutes long enough to cross the zareba, find the Colt pistol, and then find Wake and shoot him in the head? "Had he had other unescorted absences the day before yesterday?"

"He didn't," said the cook quickly.

Durrant looked around at the others. "Any of you men notice Mr. La Biche sneaking off?" They all shook their heads. Durrant turned back to the cook. The carcass next to him was nearly cleaved clean to the bone. "I wonder if you might show me your stores. I want to inquire after something Mr. La Biche has told me."

Behind the kitchen was a heavily laden wagon, its forks lying on the muddy earth. The cook, who stood six inches taller than Durrant, put a meaty hand on the box. "We keep most of the stores here."

Durrant scanned the contents. Laying his crutch against the side of the wagon, he used his left hand to haul himself into the wagon. The cook watched as Durrant disappeared inside. There were tins of coffee and crates of canned peaches and huge sacks of corn, flour, and beans. Bags of onions and potatoes were piled high. Durrant started shuffling the sacks about. The cook poked his head into the back of the cart. "Sergeant, what're you doing?"

Durrant shouldered a fifty-pound sack of flour aside and retrieved something that had been beneath it. He held it up for the cook to see and blew hard on it. A cloud of flour enveloped the back of the wagon. Durrant waved a meat hatchet back and forth in his hand. "Missing something?" he asked.

DURRANT WALKED ACROSS the zareba to the familiar compound where the teamsters managed the company's stock. There were several hundred horses mustered in the makeshift corrals, creating a giant open-air barn. Men shouting and horses whinnying made for a tremendous din. The air was rich with the tang of manure, which had been raked into a massive pile near one end of the corrals. Though the temperature was just above freezing, a cloud of flies buzzed over the steaming dung.

Durrant walked among the rows of stalls, minding his footing on the churned earth. After a few minutes of searching he asked one of the teamsters for directions, and with a sideways glance he was pointed to where Wake's body had been found.

Durrant knew he was in the right place: a tight grouping of wagons bore the same insignia, WAKE LIVERY AND BOARDING. He stopped and considered the scene. Here the wagons were configured in a tight square, creating a compact enclosure five or six yards across. Between two of the wagons a narrow passage led to the rest of the stables. Wake must have arranged his wagons in such a manner to provide the perception of protection, even within the walls of the zareba. The actions of a man who knew he had enemies? Or just a precaution during a time of war?

Durrant studied the ground in the narrow passage. He quickly found the place where Wake had fallen. Though the weather had been mostly grey over the last twenty-four hours, no rain or snow had sullied the earth, and he was able to see where the man had bled. Durrant stooped and examined the spot, looking beneath the wagons for anything the killer might have left behind. He could see nothing. He straightened and went inside the enclosure. There was a fire ring in the centre, and Durrant could easily see where several men had regularly bedded down. Some dirty dishes, a heap of cast-off bedding, and a few faggots of wood had been pushed under one of the wagons. Durrant examined the wagons and soon located a latch to a compartment above the running board of one. He popped it open and found little of interest—just a few personal items, including a comb, a straight razor, and a Bible. Durrant opened the book to see if there was an inscription, but there was nothing. He put the items back. He stepped on a small stone and looked down at it. It was a polished river rock, nothing out of the ordinary.

It seemed obvious that someone had known where Wake kept his personal effects, including his pistol. The killer had simply snuck into the enclosure, taken the Colt, and surprised Wake. Reports claimed that two cartridges had been fired from the Colt. Why two? Durrant wondered. Saul had mentioned only a single hole in the man's head. Without the corpse to examine, the question remained.

Why go to the trouble of stealing the man's pistol? With so many arms about, why not just use what was close at hand? Even Terrance La Biche had been able to secret away a sizable hatchet. Whoever had killed Reuben Wake must have intended on placing the pistol on La Biche, and that the plan from the start had been to frame him.

Durrant concluded his search having found more questions than answers.

SIX

FOG OF WAR

MAY 14, 1885.

It felt warmer to Durrant Wallace when he awoke for the second morning inside the zareba. Now he was meeting with Saul and Garnet over a morning meal. "While you slept the morning away"—Saul sat down on a stump and passed a plate of food to each of his friends—"I was able to ascertain that some of our host of men will decamp today. The company will send a contingent of men to join up with General Strange and Durrant's very own Sam Steele. They are to rendezvous with the general at Fort Pitt. Most of our company will remain behind to root out further troublemakers around Batoche."

"That gives us a little more time." Durrant drank his coffee and warmed his prosthetic by the fire. "Has La Biche been dispatched to Regina?"

"No. It's as if he were the pea in a shell game, though. He's being kept apart from the other prisoners. I have asked to see him to administer medical care, but have been told he's to be seen by General Middleton's personal surgeon and none other."

"Seems as if Sub-Inspector Dickenson is acting more than a little suspicious," said Durrant.

"Indeed. As of this morning, La Biche has been stowed in a wagon near to where the Regina companies have pitched their camp, close to the rank little pond that serves as our water source," said Saul, his eyebrow pitched at an angle to illustrate his displeasure with the prospect.

"This means we yet have an opportunity to learn more about our murdered man and those who may have wanted him dead," said Durrant.

Garnet winked at Saul. "My good Sergeant, it's as before. You simply can't accept the simple explanation, can you? Why not accept that this man La Biche had it in for Reuben Wake and found a way to do him in? You told us yourself that he'd gone to the lavatory at the very time that Reuben Wake was killed!"

"Surely you of all people would understand my reluctance to accept the simple explanation, Mr. Moberly. Wasn't it you who taught me to seek out a man's means, motive, and opportunity when making such an inquiry?"

"Did this man not have all three?" asked Garnet.

"He said that while he had the intent of killing Mr. Wake, he was not able to seize it."

"So there is some skulduggery afoot, then?" suggested Garnet.

"Do you believe the true murderer had access to La Biche's garment after his arrest?" asked Saul.

Durrant took a mouthful of breakfast and set his plate down on the grass. "If this man had killed Wake, why would he not simply confess to it, if he is so honest about his intent? He went to the trouble of putting aside a meat hatchet. We must determine what La Biche's motive might have been for allowing his own capture in the first place. He was on the verge of confessing this to me yesterday when we were interrupted. I aim to have another go at him this morning. Then we must set about learning who else wished to undertake this brazen act."

"There could well be many." Garnet dug his pipe from his pocket and packed down a plug of tobacco.

"This is certainly the case, my friend. We'll need to work together to learn all we can while we are still at the scene of the crime. Saul, are you able to free yourself of your service in order to help us out?"

"I don't see why not. All but the most minor wounds have been attended to now. What did you have in mind?"

"Well, there is the matter of the physical evidence that we must consider," said Durrant. "We're going to need to find out where

Mr. Wake's body is. We may have to track down, amid these eight hundred soldiers, who it was that disposed of the body and in such haste! We'll need to examine Mr. Wake's pistol to determine if in fact this was the weapon used to kill our man. Can you be of assistance with either of these tasks?"

"I have, despite my isolation in Regina before this endeavour, kept abreast of some new insights into the forensic sciences that may be of assistance. Matching the make and model of the weapon with the wound hasn't been perfected, but some advances have been made. Mind you, we don't have access to the records of the weapon's manufacturer here, and that will complicate matters. I can certainly tell you whether the bullet that caused the death of Mr. Wake was fired from a shotgun, a rifle, or a small- or large-calibre pistol. Durrant, we'll first have to find the body and get access to the weapon, currently under the watch of your overzealous colleague Sub-Inspector Dickenson."

"I will find a way to wrest it from Dickenson's grasp," said Durrant. "We have several angles to explore to find the body. We shall go to the cemetery at our earliest convenience and look to see if Mr. Wake has been consigned to that place. If need be we will go straight to the source and find the men who committed the corpse to the grave. Garnet and I will handle that. In the meantime, I aim to parley with Mr. La Biche, and others in the stockade, in order to learn all that I can about what motivated his course of action on the first day of battle. Let's convene again at the lunch hour. Gentlemen, we must use our wits here. I suspect that there is more to this murder than we can see at this time. There are those about our encampment who will interfere, possibly roughly, with our investigation."

IN THE EARLY morning light Durrant made his way across the zareba to where Saul Armatage had told him he might find La Biche. It was still cold enough that the muddy earth underfoot was nearly frozen. He located the spot near the squalid lake where La Biche was being held. Determining that the detainee was being guarded by a single man, he approached the wagon. "Good morning, Constable." Durrant stepped close to the wagon. The bleary-eyed young constable looked down at him from the seat. Durrant had had the foresight to fill a coffee cup before he walked over, and he handed it up to the tenderfoot. The constable gratefully accepted it. "I'm Sergeant Durrant Wallace. I'd like to interview the prisoner."

The young man straightened. "I'm sorry, sir, but Sub-Inspector Dickenson says that no one is to talk with the killer except his self."

"Is that so?"

"That's his orders to me."

"You pulled the morning shift, son?" Durrant changed tack. "Still cold enough last night—could see my breath this morning." The young man only nodded. His face was pale. "There's bacon this morning. Wouldn't it be nice to have a square meal? I'd be happy to sit in your stead for a few minutes while you found a plate. It was going fast last I looked."

"But—"

"Son, I've been Mounted Police for twelve years now. I've guarded more than my share of prisoners."

The young constable wavered, looking as if he might begin to drool at the prospect of bacon. "Anything happens to this man and it's my head that will be on the block." He looked around to see if he was being observed.

"I take responsibility."

"An yer not to have words with him," said the young man, and then added, "Sir."

"I'll just stand watch."

"A spot of breakfast might return some feeling to my fingers and toes," the young man conceded.

"Hurry along."

The constable disappeared toward the mess. Durrant pulled

himself up onto the seat of the wagon. Terrance La Biche was not there.

Durrant stepped down into the back of the covered buckboard. There was a set of chains for securing a prisoner, and a worn grey blanket was curled up in one corner. Durrant put his hand on the blanket. It felt warm to the touch, but he could not decide if that was simply the feel of the heavy wool or if it had been slept in and cast aside just recently.

He was holding the blanket in his hands when he looked up to see a face regarding him from behind the wagon. He instinctively put his left hand on his Enfield. It was Sub-Inspector Dickenson.

"I heard that you were a little jumpy, Wallace. Going to throw down on me?" The sub-inspector was grinning.

Durrant straightened. "Where is Mr. La Biche?"

"I think you are forgetting that I am a superior officer, Sergeant."

"Where is Mr. La Biche, *sir?*"

Dickenson laughed. "He's being attended to by Middleton's physician at the present moment. He seems to have come down with something of the flu."

"Sleeping out without a blanket will do that."

"As you can see, he has been furnished with one."

Durrant stepped down from the wagon and faced Dickenson. "You knew I was coming to speak with this man. You've moved him so that I can't question him."

Dickenson laughed. "Sergeant, you really do believe that there is some kind of malfeasance afoot, don't you? The simple fact is that this man was caught red-handed trying to kill Reuben Wake."

"He told me yesterday about his encounter with Wake at Fish Creek." Durrant tossed the blanket back into the wagon.

"He readily admits that his aim was to kill Reuben Wake, Wallace."

"What a man does in the heat of battle and what he does in cold calculation are two different things, Sub-Inspector. The facts don't add up to justify this man's arrest for murder. Charge him with conspiracy, if you must, but I believe that the real killer is still afoot, and may be still within our camp. There is too much that is circumspect to simply open and shut this case."

"You are deluding yourself, Sergeant. The matter is plain to see. La Biche freely admits to his effort at Fish Creek. He has told you that he was under the command of General Dumont when his forces ambushed us at Fish Creek on April 24. I was there. I saw it occur."

"Surely you confuse an act of war with attempted murder."

"No, Wallace, it is you who is confused. It was no act of war. This man who you seem to think is innocent, when seeing Wake holding fast to a team of quarter horses and carts, broke away from the fighting and on his own flanked our position. He took up a post high above the fray and took aim to do Mr. Wake in. I saw this with my very eyes. Had my company not fired a volley into the grass where he lay taking a bead, Mr. Wake would not have survived the Battle of Fish Creek, and would now be with the ten brave loyalists who were buried in that coulee."

Durrant pondered this information. He compared Dickenson's version of the Battle of Fish Creek with the tale told by Terrance La Biche. That the man wanted Wake dead and tried to kill him during the battle was obvious, but that Dickenson had witnessed this act and had previously said nothing seemed suspect.

"By La Biche's own account we know that he wanted Reuben Wake dead, Sub-Inspector. That is not in question. What is in question is whether he, or some other person, delivered the fatal shot here, in the zareba. While I do not doubt the veracity of your claim, there are others who had cause to see Wake murdered, and your interference in my efforts to unearth these other motives is very curious indeed. What is your stake in this matter? Why are you so determined to hold La Biche for this crime?"

Dickenson laughed. It was a harsh, staccato sound and it made Durrant think about a caged animal. "Sergeant Wallace, the only interference that I am posing is to your unauthorized and unbecoming intrusion into a case of murder you have no right to investigate. I suggest that if you wish to keep your stripes you go back to Fort Calgary at once. Maybe there you can find some gentle undertaking that won't tax your handicaps and result in you being ousted from the force." Dickenson's laughter trailed off and he fixed Wallace with a dark stare. "If you're not careful to mind your own business, Sergeant, you may find yourself knocked down to the rank of private before this campaign is through."

Dickenson strode off, leaving Durrant standing alone. It was time to investigate Sub-Inspector Dickenson's role in the death of Reuben Wake.

SEVEN

SINS OF THE FATHER

MAY 15, 1885.

They walked out the half-mile between the zareba and the cemetery on the Mission Ridge, overlooking the town of Batoche. It was early in the afternoon and the sky was light and there were birds flying through the groves of aspens in small flocks, dodging this way and that, all together as if one giant synchronized creature.

"We're not going to find him here." Garnet had his Martini-Henry over his shoulder and was aware that several of the Métis loyal to Riel had not been caught, including Gabriel Dumont.

"If we don't look here, then we can't eliminate it as a possibility." Durrant's voice betrayed his own resolution that the body of Reuben Wake would not be discovered in the cemetery on the Mission Ridge.

"It's a nice afternoon for a walk," said Saul, breathing deeply. "With the exception of a few hours on the last day of fighting when I set up a field station in the village, I haven't been outside of the zareba."

Garnet looked at him and said, "Marvellous country, this Saskatchewan Territory. Completely understandable why the Métis didn't want to give up their access to the Saskatchewan River. Without it, it would be tough to farm. Here we are," he said as they came upon the church.

"Looks like the mission didn't entirely miss the sting of battle." Durrant pointed with his cane at the corner of the building, where it had been raked by the Gatling gun on the first day of the struggle. The three men turned south at the church and followed a path down through a small ravine and up onto the plateau where the cemetery was cloistered, overlooking a broad bend in the South Saskatchewan River.

"Not a bad view if you have to suffer it for eternity," said Saul.

Durrant noted that the fence had been demolished and several of the headstones knocked to the ground during the fray. He set one right.

"Any sign of recent activity?" Durrant asked. Both of his companions shook their heads. "Let's look around in the trees. If someone was to bury our man Wake, and wanted to do it in secret, then it's unlikely that they'd line him up in a plot all neat and tidy."

The three men fanned out and searched through the woods. They found no evidence of recent digging except for several Métis rifle pits, each pocked and scarred by the heavy fire from the Dominion soldiers who had attacked along this bluff.

"No sign, Durrant," said Saul.

"His corpse could be just about anywhere," conceded Garnet.

Durrant looked at his two friends. "What are we to make of this disappearance?"

"It's bloody well odd," said Garnet. "The man's not been dead for thirty-six hours and someone has spirited away with his cadaver."

"It's certainly not normal battlefield procedure, and despite him being in charge of the horses, he would have been given a proper burial by the Dominion. Middleton won't be happy. He stands on ceremony."

"Would he have been taken back to Regina?" asked Durrant.

"Unlikely, unless someone did it clandestinely. There has been no official movement south since before the ninth of May. If someone did take him that way, it's for reasons passing my understanding," said Saul.

"Why would someone abscond with the corpse of Reuben Wake? With the case supposedly open and shut against our Mr. La Biche, why disappear with the body?" asked Durrant.

"Someone has something to hide, lads," said Garnet.

"We need to find out who, and what," concluded Durrant.

IT WAS MIDAFTERNOON when they walked back through the ravine and up the hill toward the rectory. They had missed the midday meal, and they were ready to retire to the zareba for a brief rest before resuming their inquiry when the door to the church burst open and a man in black robes came toward them. Garnet and Durrant each had their rifles aimed at the man before he could take two steps. Durrant held his Winchester 73 short-barrelled rifle with one hand. "Hold fast!" he called, and the man in black came to a stop, his face white and his eyes as big as saucers.

"State your business!" Garnet held his weapon easily against his shoulder, his face relaxed as he took careful aim.

"My business is God," said the man, holding out his arms in a gesture of supplication.

"If you are armed you'll have the privilege of meeting him," said Durrant, lowering the Winchester. "Step forward. Who are you?"

"My name is Father André Lefèbvre. I am a priest. I am assigned to the mission at St. Laurent, up that trail." He pointed over his shoulder at the track that headed north through La Jolie Prairie. "I am here in Batoche as I often am to minister to the Métis."

"Have you been here through the fighting?" Durrant asked, as Garnet lowered his rifle.

"I have, and for several weeks before. These are my people, and I had to watch over them."

"What can we do for you? You seem agitated, Father Lefèbvre," said Durrant.

"I got word that there were men in the woods robbing graves, so I meant to come out and put a stop to such wickedness."

"We're not grave robbers. We were searching for a recent burial, but we didn't find what we were looking for."

"The Métis are to be buried in a common grave over on the plain." The priest pointed toward the cemetery. He turned back to look at Durrant. "Who is it that you are looking for?"

Durrant looked at Saul and then at Garnet. "We're looking for a man who was murdered on the last day of fighting in the field force's encampment. His name was Reuben Wake." At the mention of the name the priest's face went pale, and he crossed himself. "You know this man?" asked Durrant, stepping forward.

"Que le Seigneur ait pitié! God have mercy on my soul. I know this man. He was the devil himself."

THEY SAT IN the church, the three inquisitors on a bench that had most recently been used as a gurney for the wounded, and Father Lefèbvre on their right. The room was warm and smelled of incense and pine. Though none said it, it felt good to be indoors and warm.

Durrant studied the priest. He guessed the man to be seventy, though he looked healthy. "Tell us about this man, the one you call the devil," commanded Durrant.

"He was as Lucifer," said the priest, shaking his head and clasping his hands before himself.

"So you say, but in what manner?"

The priest drew a deep breath. "I don't know how much I should tell you, to be honest. You are a Mounted Policeman, are you not? You have Terrance La Biche in chains. Mr. La Biche was a parishioner of mine, and a friend. He is a good man, honest and God-fearing, and I don't wish to impugn him with my words."

Durrant leaned forward and rested his forearms on his legs. He looked up at the priest. "Father, Mr. La Biche has told me that on May the ninth he allowed himself to be captured for the sole purpose of entering the zareba of the Dominion Field Force to kill Reuben Wake." The priest sat back and shook his head. "Do you doubt the veracity of my claim?"

"No. No, I do not."

"What I have not told you, sir, is that he insists that while he had every intention of killing Mr. Wake, he did not get his chance."

"He says that someone beat him to it," said Saul.

"What can you tell us that might support Mr. La Biche's story?" asked Durrant.

"Reuben Wake had *many* sins," the priest began. "He has been a man of trickery, evil deeds, and many crimes over his sixty years. Mr. La Biche has known of this man's foul nature for much of the last twenty years, but alas, La Biche is new to our congregation, and to Batoche, and so we have not had the benefit of his long history with this man to guide us. Despite this long list of complaints against Wake, I believe that it is the man's most recent act of deception and evil that would cause Mr. La Biche to wish to end his life.

"When Gabriel Dumont went to Sun River last May to call back his leader to advocate for the rights of the Métis, he took but a few trusted men with him. These were men who had been in the service of his cause for many years. The preparations were arduous, but when it came time to leave, the teamster for the journey could not be found. They searched everywhere, but he had disappeared.

"With time running short and other matters pressing on their minds, another man was asked to serve the mission. This was a man who had been in and around our community for some time, but that few in *this* area knew well. This was Reuben Wake.

"At the time, we knew him as a driver and agent who brought goods by wagon train to Batoche from Regina. He had proven himself trustworthy, and Dumont, in need of a man to handle the stock on the overland journey, brought this man into the fold for the mission to return Riel to the North West.

"Dumont and the others had more pressing concerns than the lineage of the teamster tending the horses: how they would get back and forth across the border, if the Red Coats ... if the Mounted Police would allow their passage, and what response they would get when they finally met with Riel in Montana. He had been in exile all these years. A schoolteacher, with a family! They never suspected that they had signed on an agent of the enemy whose sole purpose was to undermine their efforts, both in convincing Riel and in securing safe passage."

"Did they learn of Wake's true purpose?" Saul's excitement was apparent.

"Not until it was too late. They got as far as Sun River before they learned of Wake's ploy."

"What happened in Sun River?" asked Durrant.

"I'm not sure. Those who returned have vowed not to speak of it."

"Wake did not return to Batoche after that?" asked Durrant.

"No! All I know is that Riel and the others returned, and Wake was never seen here again, until he arrived with the Dominion soldiers. There were rumours . . ."

"What sort of rumours?"

"I don't know. Whispers, really, that something happened while Wake was in Sun River. But none have spoken of it. Terrance La Biche came to live among us late in July and *he* told us the story of Wake's long history of evil stretching to a time when Wake was an Indian Agent on the Dakota reserve. He had violent ways in Winnipeg and Regina."

"You don't know what might have transpired in Sun River, Father?"

"All I know is that Wake was apart from the mission to return Riel for some time, and when the party rode north with the prophet, Wake was no longer among them. Dumont never spoke of it, nor did the others."

Durrant sat up straight. "Is it possible, Father, that you take sides with La Biche and his fellow Métis because of how close you have come to be with them?"

"It is true, Sergeant, that I have come to love these people and can relate to their struggle. Time will tell if what has happened here on the banks of the Saskatchewan will mean anything to the future of this young nation. It may not. It may have all been in vain. If I were not a man of the cloth who viewed murder as a mortal sin against God, I may have walked into your zareba and killed Wake myself!"

The church was silent a moment, the words of Lefèbvre leaving the holy space completely still. There was a shout on the road outside the church that startled each of the men from their amazement. Durrant stood and went to the door. The priest was right behind him. In the fading light of the afternoon a small caravan of troops could be seen moving up through the forest from the village toward the church.

"Dear Lord, no!" said the father.

"What is it?" asked Garnet, moving behind the men in the doorway.

The priest broke from the portal and rushed to where the road lay. The column of troops passed. With them was a man with long, wavy hair, his beard in disarray but his stride measured and purposeful. The prisoner turned to regard the priest who was rushing toward him. He held up his hand in a gesture of greeting. The priest reached out and took the man's hand and kissed his fingers, and then, after he had passed, dropped to the ground to weep, his face buried in his hands.

"What the hell is going on?" Saul was behind them and could not see the road.

"It's Riel. He's been captured," said Garnet.

EIGHT

THE FIRST CONSPIRACY REVEALED

MAY 16, 1885. BATOCHE.

It was six o'clock when reveille was sounded in the camp. While the Battle of Batoche was won and the Métis defeated, Big Bear of the Plains Cree was still on the march. He held a dozen prisoners taken from Fort Pitt and Frog Lake who had to be rescued. General Middleton had given orders. In just a few days' time, the Dominion Field Force would break camp and begin to march toward Fort Pitt, where they would rendezvous with General Strange's Alberta Field Force and Sam Steele's Scouts. Before they could decamp, there was still much to be done to secure the township around Batoche and ensure that the Métis were hunted down and brought to trial.

As Durrant awoke, his first thought was, Where is Terrance La Biche? For two days now, Sub-Inspector Dickenson had been spiriting La Biche around the encampment, keeping him from plain sight. Soon the prisoner would be sent south along the trail to Regina. Durrant knew that if he was to have any chance to question the man again, it would be during this period of upheaval while the next phase of the campaign was planned. Durrant wondered, too, about Jacques Lambert, the Métis man who had been captured and was now being held in the hospital with cuts on his wrists. While all of his fellows had fled as the fighting came to a close, this man had been caught on the banks of the Saskatchewan below the zareba.

In the darkness Durrant pulled on his prosthetic and stood up stiffly. Garnet Moberly appeared from the gloom, two steaming cups of coffee in hand. Silently he handed one to Durrant. Garnet spoke first. "I am told that my company is to make for Fort Pitt in the coming days." Durrant said nothing. After a moment Garnet added, "You seem distracted."

"I am. I can't help but think about what Father Lefèbvre told us yesterday. The devil himself, he called Wake."

"It may simply be the spirit of the times," said Garnet.

"I don't think so. Certainly the priest has a passion for Riel, and for his cause, but to hear him tell it, there was much more to Reuben Wake than we know. His subterfuge in infiltrating Dumont's expedition to Sun River would be reason enough to want the man dead, but there seems to be more to it than that."

Garnet finished his coffee. "What do you want to do?"

"Rouse Saul. Before this outfit breaks up and rides for its various postings, let's see if we can't learn more about Mr. Wake and those who held a grudge against him."

DURRANT CONSIDERED HIS options. He would need Saul in order to track down the whereabouts of Mr. Lambert. Father Lefèbvre suddenly appeared amid the baggage and crates stacked around the zareba. His dark robes nearly concealed him, and Durrant found himself reaching for his weapon for the second time.

"You have a way of appearing that will one day get you shot full of holes, Father Lefèbvre." Durrant relaxed his hand on the hilt of his Enfield.

"I am sorry. I didn't mean to startle. It's just that when I learned that Middleton is preparing to move, I feared I would not have another chance to plead the case of Mr. La Biche."

Durrant indicated a wood stump with his chin and sat down on an adjacent upturned crate. "I haven't been able to speak with Mr. La Biche for several days, as his guards have moved him."

"Where to? And why?"

"Mr. La Biche is not my prisoner."

"Are you not investigating the murder of Wake?"

"No, Father, there is no investigation. The man who is responsible for his detention sees no need for further inquiry. I am pressing him to consider other options."

"It is as I feared. La Biche is to hang for a crime he did not commit."

"Not yet, Father. I do believe there are a fair number of questions that must be answered before I can be convinced of this man's guilt *or* innocence. Questions that an impartial judge would want answered before he passed a verdict on such a case."

The priest folded his hands together in front of himself as if in prayer. "Let me pose a few more questions for your consideration." He looked around quickly, then leaned forward toward Durrant. "I do not know who to trust. Even you, sir, are unknown to me, and thus so is your allegiance. I must trust someone, and you have the look about you that tells me that, above all else, you prize the truth."

"As a member of the North West Mounted Police I prize justice, and it is my pledge to serve Queen and country in its pursuit. My allegiance is to the Dominion of Canada."

"There are those even within the field force under Middleton's charge who are members of a dark conspiracy."

"Surely not against the Queen." Durrant's posture stiffened.

"No, not against the Dominion," Lefèbvre shook his head, "but against justice; against Riel."

"Father, Louis Riel took up arms against Queen and country and for that will be tried for treason. The punishment if he is found guilty is death."

"You misunderstand me, sir. You and I will have to disagree about the justness of Riel's act of . . . resistance. I can assure you that his cause was just. The manner by which his people, and the Indians who follow him, have been treated is simply barbaric. The conspiracy of which I speak is not one to see him in irons and hanged, but rather one to ensure that he is dead long before he takes the prisoner's dock in Regina. It is a conspiracy that would see Riel silenced before he can utter a word in his own defence."

Durrant regarded the priest gravely. "Are you telling me that somehow the murder here on the battlefield of Batoche is entangled with this conspiracy?"

"I simply can't say with certainty, Sergeant. So much of what has happened here this fortnight has been shrouded in confusion and the fog of war. Reuben Wake was almost certainly involved in this trickery. Why else would he have taken it upon himself to infiltrate Dumont's Sun River expedition? I would be willing to bet, and I do not say this lightly, that if you were to search every fold in the earth in the hills around Batoche, the Métis teamster who was to accompany Dumont to Sun River would be found dead, and by Wake's hand."

"Do you have any evidence of this?"

"My faith is all the evidence I need. It was not by chance that Reuben Wake found himself in Batoche the very day that Dumont was in desperate need of a man who could manage the horses on such a long journey. It is no coincidence that the appointed teamster was nowhere to be found and has not been seen since! In fulfilling the role of aide-de-camp, Reuben Wake's aim was not to assist Dumont, but to seek a way to scuttle Riel's return."

"He failed in that effort."

"He did, and the why of this is beyond my knowledge. Terrance La Biche may have had cause to want Reuben Wake dead, but he was by no means the only one. Had he committed the crime he would be crowing from the rooftops about his deed, and, God have mercy on my soul, so might I."

"Father, where were you on the afternoon of the twelfth of May when the charge was sounded?"

"I was . . . I was in my church, praying to God for the souls of his faithful servants."

"Were there others there with you?"

"The holy spirit was with me, Sergeant Wallace."

"In the past I have found that he is unreliable in verifying a man's alibi."

"Surely you can't—"

"Father Lefèbvre, you said yourself that you would like to have seen Wake killed."

"I am a man of God."

"I have known of more than one man who could kill in the name of the Lord." The priest stood up quickly. Durrant continued, "Father, I think it wise for you to remain in Batoche until I tell you otherwise."

"I will remain in Batoche to help these people find solace in God as they rebuild their lives. And then I will follow Riel and offer what comfort I can as he faces the threat of the gallows. If you wish to stop me, Sergeant Wallace, then you will have to use the force of your arms."

Saul Armatage and Garnet Moberly stepped into view. The priest turned to regard the two men. "I must go," he said. "There is much more at stake here than meets the eye." Then, his robes pitching behind him, he disappeared into the clamour of the zareba.

"What was all that about?" asked Saul.

"That, friends, was Father Lefèbvre doing his level best to assert the innocence of one man while unwittingly impugning another."

"I assume he was here to argue for La Biche's innocence," said Saul. "Who was he implicating?"

"Himself," said Durrant.

NINE

THE HUMBOLDT TRAIL

"YOU DON'T SERIOUSLY THINK THAT Father Lefèbvre located Reuben Wake's pistol and then dispatched him with it, do you?" asked Saul.

"I don't rightly know what to think, Saul," said Durrant.

"How would he have known where Wake's pistol was?" asked Garnet.

"The same question could be asked of Terrance La Biche. It seems equally unlikely that either man could have known. Both men freely admit to their hatred for Wake, and one has confessed to conspiring to kill the man."

"I don't believe that discovering the killer's motive will lead to a conviction in the case of Mr. Wake's murder," said Garnet. "Access to the murder weapon—means—and opportunity will carry the day."

"I believe you are right, Mr. Moberly." Durrant stood. "I need to talk with the man who found the body of Reuben Wake."

HE DIDN'T HAVE to search long to find the man he was looking for. Near the stables, he was directed to where a small company of men was preparing to ride.

"Hold up there a moment, Mr. Dire." Wallace pressed hard on his cane as he crossed the muddy enclosure. Several horses stamped their feet as he approached.

Dire was a tall man, over six feet, and lean and long in the limbs. He wore the uniform of a militiaman, with a pistol holstered on his right side and a Winchester 76 fitted in a boot scabbard on the left flank of his horse. He wore heavy riding gauntlets on his hands. He looked down as Durrant approached and smiled cheerfully.

"Are you Jasper Dire?" asked Durrant.

"I am that."

"Sergeant Durrant Wallace, North West Mounted Police."

"Ah, good. I assume you've come to claim Mr. La Biche and see that he is delivered to justice."

"In a manner of speaking," said Durrant carefully. "I have a few questions for you, if you don't mind."

"I don't, but General Middleton might."

"This won't take but a moment."

"That may be so, but that's all it will take to have me cast in irons for failing to follow an order. If you wish to talk, then mount up and ride along awhile."

Durrant looked around and caught the eye of a teamster. "Can you spare a mount for half an hour?"

The teamster turned and took the reins of a tan quarter horse and walked it over to the sergeant. "Care for a leg up, sir?" the teamster asked, but Durrant simply slung himself up into the saddle and slipped his cane under the cinch straps.

"I'm just fine, thank you." Durrant turned to Dire. "Let's ride."

There were a dozen men including Dire and Durrant that set out along the Humboldt Trail, riding along the crest of the dell that dropped toward the Saskatchewan River. They took the gate of the zareba at a trot but soon put the spurs to their mounts and thundered east for a few hundred yards. When the compound was in the distance, they slowed. Dire looked over his shoulder and pulled back on the reins with gloved hands. "That ought to do it. We've got to make a show for Middleton when we take our leave, but there's no sense running these beasts ragged just to hunt down a few farmers and blacksmiths still hiding in the weeds."

The other men fanned out along the trail, several of them taking the fixings for a pipe from the folds of their coats. Durrant asked, "So, you were the one to arrest La Biche?"

"That's right. Caught the fellow pretty much red-handed."

"How did this come to pass?"

"Well, Sergeant, if you must know, there was quite the confusion that afternoon. It seems that Middleton's feint through La Jolie Prairie was a bit of a middling effort, and he returned to the zareba in something of a foul mood. He gave the go-ahead to others to try for the fortifications at the Mission Ridge and we decided to make a go of it. There was quite the ruckus as our men made for the gate and rode the Humboldt Trail for the Mission Ridge. I was among the last to catch my horse up, and as I did, I heard a shot from quite close by." Dire slowed his horse and turned it to look back toward the compound, now a mile behind them.

"I didn't think there ought to be fighting so close in on the zareba. I figured maybe one of Dumont's men had come upon our fortifications from the south and managed to climb the barricade. I feared that he might be trying something of a suicide run in our midst, so I made my way on foot as quick as I could toward the sound of the shot."

"You were alone?"

"The others in my company had already mounted."

"And you went on foot?"

"I hadn't saddled up as yet, and it seemed easier for navigating my way among the wagons. I just looped the reins of my mount and drew my pistol."

"What do you shoot with?"

"A Webley Mk IV. A .38."

"Near the same weapon as I carry."

"Likely as awkward. Tough in a pinch, I've found. Mind, I never did have to draw it in the last two months on the trail. The Winchester is a better weapon for open country."

"So, what did you find when you went to search?"

"Nothing at first. But I did see a man who looked to be Métis making his way through the wagons and so I followed. He led me right back to the cookery. It was Mr. La Biche. I ordered him to stand pat and he did, and when I searched him I found that Colt revolver in his pocket. Barrel was still hot to the touch. Not much question that it had been fired recently. I gathered up a few fellows and we all went together to the paddock for a search. That's when we spotted Wake just lying there in the mud."

"How did he look when you found him?"

"He had a hole shot in the side of his head as big as a silver dollar. There wasn't much in the way of blood, just a big dark hole."

"He had been shot more than once?"

"Not that I could see. I didn't handle him. The Red Coats took over then. I haven't laid eyes on the cadaver since."

"Have you ever seen a man shot before?"

Dire shook his head. "Back in Regina, I work in a warehouse. I go to church on Sunday. I live a pretty quiet life, Sergeant Wallace. I've never seen a man shot before this."

"Not even in the four days of fighting at Batoche?"

"I think I saw one of the Métis in a rifle pit hit, but it had to be three hundred yards away. Not like this."

"After you'd found Mr. Wake, what happened next?"

"We threw the man in chains. One of the Mounted Police marched him right over to a wagon where he was keeping a few other prisoners and chained him there. Later on a man named Dickenson came back from the fighting and asked me for the revolver, which I handed over. Said it was evidence. That was fine with me. I didn't want it. That was the end of it. He sent me on my way."

"Did any other members of the Mounted Police come to ask you questions?"

"Not till you." They had turned and were riding again, several hundred yards back from the others.

"What do you expect will happen to Mr. La Biche?" asked Dire.

"If he's guilty, then he will hang."

"He's guilty, I believe. I don't see any question about it. He had

Wake's own pistol. Said that he knew what Wake was up to, and that he had to be stopped for the good of the resistance."

"Say that again?"

"Said that Wake had to be stopped for the good of the resistance."

"Did he confess to you or Dickenson?"

"As near as."

"But did he say, 'I killed that man because . . .'"

"I can't remember if he said those exact words."

Durrant was silent for a long moment. "Mr. Dire, I expect that you're going to be called on to testify at Mr. La Biche's trial. I would hope that you will remember to tell this story just as you've told me here today."

"I hope this whole business with Riel is over so that we can get on with life. It's been a terrible distraction," said Dire.

Durrant thanked Dire and turned his horse and started back to the zareba. He had two miles to ride, and it was the first peace and quiet he had found to consider the events surrounding Reuben Wake's death since arriving on the twelfth.

It seemed possible, though not likely, that Terrance La Biche had killed Reuben Wake. He had, after all, been caught with the murder weapon, supposedly, and Wake's own revolver at that. Was it the business in Sun River with Wake that motivated this Métis man to seek out Wake above all others? Or was it something in the history between the two men dating back even further?

And what of this half-hearted confession that Wake had to be stopped? Stopped from doing what? If Durrant could ever get close enough to La Biche again, he would have to ask.

Durrant was a mile from the zareba when the shot came. It sounded like little more than a crack in the still prairie air, but the horse didn't mistake it and reared up suddenly. Durrant grabbed the reins hard to pull the horse down, but the beast kicked and stepped and, when the second shot came, bucked hard and threw him to the Humboldt Trail. Durrant landed on his prosthetic and then his back and lay dazed on the ground a moment, staring at the sky. He heard the horse gallop off toward the compound.

Gasping to pull air into his lungs, Durrant reached for and drew his revolver and cocked the hammer, carefully rolling onto his side. He was on an open stretch of road with few bushes or trees for cover. His first assessment was that a Métis sharpshooter was lying in wait along the crest of the bank of the Saskatchewan, just a few hundred yards to his southwest. If that was the case, why not fire on the party of riders who had just passed? Better chance of hitting one of a dozen men on horseback than just a solitary rider.

His next thought was more sinister. Someone had witnessed his leaving the zareba and followed him, knowing he would return along this route. Someone who didn't want him undertaking this investigation. A person, now unseen in the vast country that surrounded him, whose sights were set squarely on Durrant Wallace.

TEN

CROSSING THE FOX

LYING FACE DOWN IN THE dirt of the Humboldt Trail, Durrant experienced the dream-like sensation of déjà vu. It had been almost five years since he had been gunned down in an ambush in the Cypress Hills while tracking moonshiners. His horse had been shot and Durrant had lost his left leg below the knee; his right hand had been deformed by frostbite while he clutched his pistol on the frozen ground. Now he lay on his side, his Enfield in his left hand, his whole body aching from being thrown. His prosthetic had been dislodged by the fall and was bent at an awkward angle. The horse was nowhere to be seen and likely halfway back to the zareba. He would need to reaffix the prosthetic if he was going to get anywhere in this open country.

Durrant scanned the surrounding landscape. The shot seemed to have come from the south, along the bluffs above the river. There was a dense tangle of tall willows there. He immediately considered that there might be more than one man lying in wait, so he turned and scanned the country to the north. The nearest cover was nearly five hundred yards off, a low cluster of willows and a few aspens that might conceal a man. His quick visual reconnaissance complete, Durrant had to decide what action to take next. Exasperating this effort, however, was a wave of self-loathing at being thrown into the dirt, without cover and poorly armed at that.

How could he have let this happen again? He should have insisted on interviewing Jasper Dire in the safety of the zareba. He knew he had little right to give orders to these men; his investigation was not official. Dire had led him here, even turned and sat his horse in the road as they spoke, and allowed some distance to be put between him and his fellow scouts. It suddenly occurred to Durrant that Jasper Dire himself may have doubled back along the rim of the river and was fixing the sights of his Winchester on him now.

That was just one possibility. It was just as likely that the man Durrant sought had been alerted when he left the zareba.

Durrant laid his Enfield on the road and reached down to hike up the left leg of his wool trousers. There was a thick smear of blood where the prosthetic had bit into his stump when he was thrown. He did his best to reaffix the leg using its suction socket and then rolled down the blood-wet pant leg. He picked up his pistol.

Durrant fixed his eyes on the hedgerow to his south. If he waited long enough, someone would come along the trail and find him. It was the safest course of action: when his horse returned to the zareba riderless, the teamsters would send out a party to look for him.

Jasper Dire was certainly in the best position to frame Terrance La Biche. If he was working with Sub-Inspector Dickenson, the two of them could have easily planted the pistol to prove La Biche's guilt. What connections were there between Dire, Wake, and Dickenson?

Durrant zeroed in on the association: all three men hailed from Regina. While the men fighting at Batoche and Fish Creek were from all across the Dominion, these three men called Regina home. Durrant thumbed the worn hammer of his Enfield. This postulation was not getting him any further ahead. He wouldn't just wait for some rider to come along and find him, hapless as a fish out of water, lying in the dirt of the road. Durrant forced himself to stand. He felt the uneasy sensation in his chest as he imagined the shooter zeroing in on him. Instead of walking back toward Batoche and the safety of the zareba, Durrant turned south and, with the Enfield held at his side, walked toward the verge of willows.

Travelling over the rough, muddy ground was hard for Durrant. He planted his feet carefully, measuring each step against the risk of falling. He scanned the shrub border before him, pistol pointing toward the unknown gunman. He made the willows after a few minutes of slow, careful walking and, using the Enfield, parted the bushes. Durrant looked back at the Humboldt Trail. He could see where his horse had thrown him. He could see his own path through the frost-tipped grass; it traced a dark line through the silvery dew. The frost was what allowed him to see clearly where his assailant had been. Behind the first row of willows, not twenty feet from where Durrant had entered the verge, he saw a place where a man had lain, the grass dark from the man's heat. And there, caught up in the vetch, two shell casings from a .32-calibre rifle.

Durrant picked them up and slipped them into his pocket. He peered into the darkness of the hedge, the barrel of his Enfield tracking an arc across his line of sight. A branch snapped. Durrant could see the path his shooter had taken. The world became a tunnel through which he peered toward the possible threat. Durrant heard movement in the tangle of growth, and he quietly thumbed the hammer on the pistol, the cylinder rotating as a .38-calibre cartridge was positioned beneath the firing pin. Time seemed to halt.

Something red moved in his peripheral vision. Durrant quickly swung his pistol toward the motion. Could this be a red jersey? He straightened his left arm, aiming. He drew a steadying breath.

A red fox stepped from the willows just fifteen feet from where Durrant crouched. He released a long breath and the fox, startled, bolted for cover.

THEY MET HIM after he'd walked half a mile toward the zareba. Garnet Moberly was riding at a gallop in the fore, three other men from the Survey Division following close on his heels. They had the horse tethered behind them, and it was breathing hard and sweating. "Are you all right?" Garnet dropped from his mount and scanned the country around him. He had his rifle in his hands.

"I'm fine, Garnet. No need for the cavalry." The other riders had fanned out around them and were scanning the open ground for signs of trouble, rifles held at the ready.

"What happened?"

Durrant dug into his pocket and produced the two shell casings. He held them out in his hand for Garnet to see.

Garnet took them in his hand and considered them. "You're not hit?"

"Not even close. My horse spooked pretty good and threw me. I went and looked for the shooter, but this is all I found. The gunman is long gone, and the woods there along the riverbank are a maze of animal trails. I don't think we'll find anything now."

Garnet looked down at the shell casings in his hand. "Thirty-two calibre. Same round as fired from the Winchester. Standard issue."

"Not for the Métis."

IT WAS WELL past the noon hour when Durrant rode into the zareba. He watched the faces of the men he passed with interest, hoping to detect some glance, some sign, that might give away the identity of his attacker. But he could see none.

He rode straight to the stables and dismounted, leaving the horse with a young stable hand. He took his cane from the cinch strap of the saddle and headed off to meet Saul Armatage. Passing a buckboard wagon, he overheard a heated argument between Sub-Inspector Dickenson and a well-dressed, elegant-looking man who wore a beaver-felt hat and a long, dark heavy coat. Durrant stepped back behind the wagon but could not make out what they were saying. He decided on a more direct approach and simply turned the corner once more and kept on walking.

"Good afternoon, Sub-Inspector," he said as he walked past the men, trying not to betray the ache in his leg and back from his fall.

"Wallace," said Dickenson by way of greeting, his closely set eyes regarding Durrant contemptuously. The man in the beaver-felt hat turned to consider the one-legged man.

"Who is your companion, Sub-Inspector?"

The well-dressed man scowled. "I am Stanley Block. And who might you be?"

"Sergeant Durrant Wallace, North West Mounted Police." Durrant extended his left hand.

"Mr. Block owns *The Regina Examiner*."

"Always a pleasure to meet an esteemed member of the fourth estate. What brings you to Batoche?"

"I am here to cover this great expedition of General Middleton's army."

"I see. It *has* been something of a grand adventure," responded Durrant.

"Have you been involved in the fighting?"

"No, sir, I just arrived at Batoche four nights ago. The first shots I heard were just this morning on the Humboldt Trail!" Durrant let his gaze slip from Block to Dickenson.

"Do tell, Sergeant," said Block.

"Not much to tell." Durrant watched for a reaction. "Likely just someone out hunting for his supper."

"Mr. Block"—Dickenson shifted his weight from his left to his right foot—"I must attend to my prisoners."

"Have you been out hunting today?" Durrant asked Dickenson.

Dickenson's face seemed to curl at the edges. Durrant could see the tips of several teeth, like bared fangs, press against his lower lip. "If I had been, I would have certainly bagged my prey."

Block turned back to Dickenson. "Sub-Inspector, I suppose that we will have to settle the matter some other time."

Durrant watched Dickenson stalk away, then turned to Block. "Sounded like the two of you were having words, if you don't mind my saying."

"Nothing of consequence. A newspaperman has got to do his digging, is all. I had wanted a word with the murderer of Reuben Wake. He was a well-known member of the community in Regina and his killing will cause a stir."

"Dickenson would not permit it?"

Block shrugged. "There's always another way, Sergeant."

"Indeed there is. What is the story you have to tell about what happened here at Batoche, Mr. Block?"

"There are many stories to tell in a campaign such as this. The battle itself is just one. It is the human element that enthralls readers and makes them wish to turn the page and buy the paper again the next morning."

"And that is what it is all about, is it not, Mr. Block?"

"What's that, Sergeant?"

"Selling papers."

"I take offence to that, sir."

"Take it if you wish, Mr. Block, but I am only speaking the truth of the matter. You are in Batoche to print stories and sell your papers?"

"You make it sound tawdry. There is nothing wrong with a businessman wishing to sell his wares."

"I agree insomuch that the manufacture of those wares comes at such a cost—"

"There is no basis for such an accusation. Riel has been spoiling for a fight since '74. He should have been hanged then for the death of Thomas Scott. Instead Macdonald let him evade capture and seek his asylum in the United States of America. If Riel had been a Protestant and a Liberal that would never have happened. I am only reporting on the goings-on. The press has had no hand in creating this conflict whatsoever."

"Every word you have penned has been fuel for the fire of this rebellion."

Block shook his head. "The press is an important part of our democracy in this young nation, Sergeant. We hold the elected representatives in Ottawa to account. We press the case of these backwoods locales with the elected officials. Someone must be made to answer for what has happened here."

"Is that so? I take it then, sir, that you are not a member of the Conservative press?"

"If I must take a side, I would say that I am a Liberal, but that doesn't matter. What matters is presenting the truth of the story."

"Truth is a matter of perspective. I'm not certain that the truth of what has happened here, and at Fish Creek, Duck Lake, and Cut Knife Hill, will ever really be known."

"You are too young a man to be a cynic, Sergeant. I suspect you have come by your scars honestly, and that has sullied your perspective on mankind."

Durrant regarded the newspaperman a moment. "You say that Mr. Wake was a prominent member of Regina society."

"I said he was well known, not prominent. He owned a livery stable and so enjoyed a station in society on par with other businessmen of a certain class. He was known to be a member of several clubs in our fair city."

"Was he well thought of?"

"I cannot say, Sergeant. I believe he has had his share of ups and downs in business, and as such may have made some enemies."

"Might any of those have followed him here?"

"I can't see how they would. Look around you, sir. Do you see many men among these ruffians who might fall into the class of the business elite?"

"Present company excluded, Mr. Block?"

"I take offence to that!"

"In my experience, it is usually a sign that the arrow has found its mark."

"Sergeant, what exactly is your purpose in levelling such accusations at me? I am here to report to the readers of my paper a first-hand account of the battle and subsequent apprehension of the criminals Dumont and Riel. Nothing more."

"Mr. Block, you could have sent a mere scribe. I find your presence here among these . . ."—Durrant looked around him at the soldiers—"how did you put it? Ruffians? I find your presence here and interest in Mr. Wake and his alleged attacker Mr. La Biche curious to say the least."

"Sir, you are out of line. Assistant Commissioner Crozier will hear my complaint about your accusations."

"I report to Superintendant Steele. He's presently engaged hunting down the Willow Cree. I'm sure he will entertain your concerns when he returns from the wilderness. In the meantime, Mr. Block, know that I have my eye on you."

Block puffed up his chest and made to adjust his perfect scarf before he strode off. Durrant watched him go, thinking that for the second time that day he had met a fox.

SAUL ARMATAGE AND Garnet Moberly were waiting for Durrant. Saul offered him coffee. "How is the leg?"

"It's all right. Blasted thing came out of its socket when I was thrown."

"Durrant, you're bleeding right through your trousers. For Christ's sake, let me look. I'm going to need to attend to this. You'll need stitches and I'll have to re-bandage the leg. You need to—"

Durrant cut him off. "Don't tell me to stay off of it, Saul. I won't. It's taken me five years to get back on a horse and earn the respect of Steele and the others. I won't play lame while there is important police work to be done."

Saul set to work on the leg, taking what he needed from his haversack. "Tell us what you have learned."

Durrant sat on a stump and drank his coffee and then accepted a plate of pork and beans while Saul cleaned and then stitched his leg. Durrant flinched only once and told them of the events of his conversation with Jasper Dire up to his confrontation with Stanley Block. "And what about you gentlemen?" Durrant asked. "What have you learned?"

Garnet spoke first. "I spent the best part of the morning inquiring after our gravediggers. None will attest to burying Reuben Wake or admit to knowing the whereabouts of his corpse. It seems as if he has been spirited from these parts. We shall have to turn our eyes farther afield, I fear."

"If you wished to dispose of a body in these parts, Saul, as a medical doctor, where would you do it?" asked Durrant.

"I suppose the best way to take leave of such a thing would be to consign it to the Saskatchewan and let it drift downstream."

"He could be halfway to Prince Albert by now, Durrant," added Garnet.

"Speaking of the river," said Saul, "upon making my rounds this morning I had a moment to speak with Jacques Lambert. At first the scouts who discovered this man felt that he, as others had, might have been trying to reach the zareba. Upon closer inspection they discovered that he was armed only with a knife, and that he had made cuts to his own wrists. The men quickly bandaged them and, with Lambert protesting, brought him to Middleton's doctor for care.

"Lambert tells me that he was recruited to fight for Dumont; he left his farm in the care of his wife and two teenaged children. A boy not more than eleven, the girl just fourteen. Word travelled to Lambert's ears that the farm lay in the path of the advancing army of Middleton, and that some of the men had taken to looting. He discovered on the first day of the battle that several men had looted his wares and burned his farm to the ground. And, as you have heard, his daughter was raped."

"Blue Jesus," said Durrant. "I don't suppose this Lambert heard the name of the lout who committed this foul deed."

"I'm afraid he did. He knew that the man who committed these atrocities was Reuben Wake."

ELEVEN

THE MISSION RIDGE

JACQUES LAMBERT LAY WITH ANOTHER man in the back of a wagon, a thin wool blanket pulled up around his chin. His face carried the countenance of the defeated. Durrant watched him from a distance. "Can he be moved?" he asked Saul.

"There's really very little wrong with him. His wounds are healing well. He's only spoken to *me* since arriving, and just those few words at that. I fear that maybe the mental trauma he has suffered has robbed him of his faculties."

"What say we take him to the church and provide him the comfort he needs to tell his tale?"

"Very well, we can ask." Saul led Durrant to the wagon and introduced him to the infirm man. "This man is Durrant Wallace," said the doctor. "He's a Mounted Police officer, and has been asked to investigate what happened on your farm." Saul saw Durrant look at him and then back at Lambert. "He would like to talk with you. What do you say we take a little walk over to the rectory and you can tell him what you told me?" Saul helped Lambert stand. "Let me give you a hand."

Lambert hadn't walked in four days, so they started slowly. Saul gave him one of the cook's biscuits and a cup of tea, which revitalized him. "You're looking into the trouble at my farm?" asked Lambert.

"We're looking into it. We're going to do what we can."

"If you don't have an objection, I will tell it from the start. The context is important to what I've got to tell." Lambert spoke in easy English, and Durrant detected the diction of a man who had been schooled in Ontario as Durrant himself had. "After the fighting at Fish Creek, General Dumont pulled his men back to

Batoche. We thought for sure that Middleton would push through, but instead he camped out for two weeks. It gave us a lot of time to get the town ready. We knew that Middleton would come up the Humboldt Trail, and attack us here, along the Mission Ridge." Lambert pointed a finger toward where the land dropped down to the town of Batoche. "Dumont didn't want Middleton to gain the height of land above the town, so we aimed to make our stand here. We'd seen the four field guns that he had with him when we clashed at Fish Creek and we didn't want to give him a clear shot, so we dug in. We had rifle pits throughout the woods around the church and to where the St. Laurent Road crosses La Jolie Prairie. And there, along the cemetery." Lambert pointed and started to walk in that direction. Durrant and Saul followed.

"That's where I was, the cemetery. We waited for two weeks. We knew that Middleton was taking his time. We had our scouts out along the Humboldt Trail and that's how it came to pass that I learned about my farm.

"On the morning of the ninth of May, around seven o'clock, we got word that the field force was sending a steamer up the river."

"That would be the *Northcote*," said Durrant.

"The steamer was supposed to pass by Batoche at the same moment that Middleton's ground forces came upon us from the east. The men were late in arriving, but eventually his mounted soldiers and riflemen were able to fight their way past the church and the rectory. Our lads scrambled back to their rifle pits in time to keep them from taking the Mission Ridge."

The three men reached the cemetery. "We got back in time to put up quite the fight," Lambert continued. "It was at times close quarters. We were just fifty yards from one another. They even managed to get their field guns up to the crest of the ridge and fire down onto the town. We had the advantage of cover, while they were mostly lined up in the open. That's the way it went for several hours. Middleton would press any advantage he could find, and we'd fend off his advances.

"Around three o'clock, General Dumont decided to try and circle around the soldiers on the north flank. They had that Gatling gun on loan from the Yanks, and put it to good use. Dumont ordered that a brush fire be set and we would advance on their border through the smoke. It would have worked. We might have surrounded them, had they not turned that gun on us. It held us at bay.

"This whole time I was in this rifle pit." Lambert carefully stepped down into the pit and leaned against the logs that had been stacked on its north wall to provide cover and a slit through which the Métis man could fire his weapon. "I was armed with an old single-shot Sharps Silhouette. It was my buffalo gun. I don't think you whites understand. We are starving. Our crops have failed, the buffalo are gone, and the food that Macdonald promised is being lorded over us by the Indian Agents. We have become beggars. It was the last straw of many, many insults. That's why Dumont told us to fight. That's why Riel returned. I sat in this pit and shot at Middleton's soldiers."

"Did you shoot anybody?" asked Durrant.

"There was but one man dead from Middleton's forces that day, and it was out yonder, on the Mission Ridge. Fellow named Phillips gunned down when they tried to take the ridge early in the afternoon. We suffered our losses too. I might have zipped a few fellows, but I didn't kill a man."

"Tell us about Rueben Wake," Durrant said.

"I told you about our scouts and spies. We watched Middleton's advance up the Humboldt Trail. It turns out that those bastards took to looting as they went. I had left my family at my farm, believing that if this was to be a fair fight, they would be safe there. That was a mistake. Just about the time that the *Northcote* was steaming up toward Batoche, mon ami arrived to tell me the news. My friend told me that the night before, men had gone to my farm, just a mile off the road, and there found my wife and children.

My friend, he watched much of this from the hill above my farm, but he was alone, and there were a dozen men. He said that they were the men who cared for the horses, coming along behind Middleton's forces. They took my family out of the house and took all of our stores and put them in a wagon. They torched the house and watched as it burned to the ground. Mon petit garçon—he is but eleven—he tried to stop him and they beat him. One of the men took my little girl away to the barn."

"Did your friend see what happened next?"

Lambert pushed tears away from his face. "No, he did not. But what is a man to believe?"

"How do you know it was the man Reuben Wake?"

"My friend had seen this man before in Batoche. He had come often, with his horses and wagons, bringing supplies, trading. He had been here when Dumont went to bring our father Riel back."

"You were told, just before the fighting, that your farm had been burned, and that your daughter may well have been hurt by the man Wake. What did you do?"

"What could I do? The fighting had started! When Middleton retreated to his compound that night, he posted men all along the bluffs and the river, and try as I might, I could not get past them. I slept that night just two hundred yards from your encampment. In the morning, I decided that for the honour of my family I must kill this man Reuben Wake."

"Did you?" asked Durrant.

Lambert was sobbing now. "How could I? I could not get to him! I heard that on the second day he did not leave the enemy camp. On the third, he went with Middleton to La Jolie Prairie, and there he received a wound and once again hid in the compound. I broke ranks that day! God forgive me, but I saw how things might go for Dumont. We had nothing left. We were out of bullets. We were melting down lead balls pried from trees to make something to shoot. I went again to the compound to try and find Wake but could not, as there were too many soldiers, and in the afternoon there was a great charge, and the town fell. Dumont fled, and Riel hid, and the resistance came to an end."

"You were found on the riverbank, near suppertime. Doctor Armatage tells me you tried to cut your wrists."

"I had fired my last round. What could I do? If I had a single cartridge left, I would have taken my life with it, but all I had was my knife. I cut my wrists and waited to face the punishment of God for my sin. But instead—"

"Instead the soldiers found you and took you to the zareba."

"That's where I saw Reuben Wake, already dead."

"You saw him?" asked Durrant, his voice betraying his astonishment.

"I was put down on the ground to await the doctor just a few feet from where this devil lay!"

"How did you recognize him?" asked Durrant.

"I saw him when he was in our midst, under the guise of a friend. I will never forget him."

"Did you see what happened to his body?"

"What do you mean?" asked Lambert.

"His body is missing. We can't find it."

Lambert spat into the dirt at his feet. "That band of crows has come to peck out his eyes! Before I was taken to have my wounds dressed, I saw two men come and take the body away. I suppose they were to bury it. I wish that I had thrown the first shovel."

"Mr. Lambert, I know you have suffered a terrible blow, but I must ask you a question. Did you find a way into the zareba, make your way to Wake, use his pistol, kill him, return to the river, and cut your own wrists?"

Lambert looked at Durrant. "If I had killed him, I would have gone to my family and told them immediately. If I had been able to dispatch this beast, I would have gladly declared it to the world. My only crime is not having avenged my family's disgrace."

Durrant stood up, pressing hard on the cane as he did. Now there were three men who would have gladly killed Reuben Wake, all proclaiming their regret for not having been able to do it.

WHEN THEY RETURNED to the zareba, Durrant and Saul returned Mr. Lambert to the infirmary and instructed a member of the North West Field Force that he was not to be allowed to leave without Durrant's consent. They quickly went in search of Garnet Moberly and found him with other members of the Surveyors Intelligence Corps, preparing for the evening meal. "Ah, Durrant, and the good Doctor Armatage, you must both join us for supper." About thirty men sat around a roaring blaze. They wore no uniforms but instead bore the dress of men accustomed to living and working in rugged country: sturdy boots and heavy coats. Each had a rifle leaning on a leg or close at hand, and several had pistols tucked into their belts.

Garnet stood on a crate of tinned meat and introduced, with some rhetorical flourish, the company's two guests. The surveyors clapped and hurrahed and then tin plates were passed to the men. Durrant tucked in and looked at Garnet. "This is not the bully beef we've grown accustomed to. This isn't from the main cook tent, is it?"

"No, sir! My Mr. Jimmy has been serving as company cook and steward since we assembled with Wheeler this last month."

"Luckiest company of soldiers in the field force." Saul ate appreciatively.

"Let us tell you what we have learned," said Durrant.

"Excellent," said Garnet, "and I have news for you, but I'm afraid it complicates matters further."

"I should expect nothing less," said Durrant. He shared his information with Garnet.

"That sounds eerily like the confession of Terrance La Biche," said Garnet. "It would seem that few who knew this man Wake did not wish him dead."

Durrant continued. "It turns out that after Mr. Lambert was confined to the infirmary for his self-inflicted wounds, he actually laid eyes on the deceased man, only to witness two men carting him off, supposedly for burial."

"Might he identify these men?"

"He may. We've posted a watch and will continue our conversation with the man in the coming days. Now, what news do you bring?"

"These good fellows have been charged with being my eyes and ears about the camp and through the surrounding country. I trust them and they are careful observers," said Garnet, regarding the surveyors. "Word has come to my ears this afternoon that there is a small encampment of Dakota Indians on the western bank of the river. These were men cajoled into fighting in Dumont's army after he hazed off their livestock and browbeat them to take up arms. They did little in the way of actual fighting, and most fled when the going got hot, but I have learned that there is one man who also had a history with Reuben Wake."

"Good Lord Almighty, is there no man in the North West Territories that Wake did not cross?"

"It seems that Wake was an Indian Agent some four years ago, and at the time committed some grievous wrongs against the Dakota, including one of the warriors in this particular band. That man is still in the camp."

Durrant put down his plate. "I suppose come first light we shall have to inquire about a ferry."

TWELVE
ACROSS THE SASKATCHEWAN

MAY 17, 1885.

Durrant woke to the sound of birdsong. He rose, affixed his prosthetic, and gathered his greatcoat about him as he went in search of coffee and something that might pass as breakfast. The zareba was noticeably quieter. Nearly one third of the twelve hundred men had marched west the previous day. Within an hour, he, Garnet Moberly, and Saul Armatage were warming their hands by a small fire.

"I think it best if just we three visit the Dakota camp," said Garnet. "The lads from the survey corps would gladly come along, but I don't think it would serve our cause."

"I aim to make our presence there about more than just this inquiry." The doctor finished his coffee and tapped his cup out on a rock next to the fire. "I'll be bringing some medicine and will ensure that those who are willing are doctored."

"It's a good idea, Saul," said Durrant. "Maybe Garnet and I might see if we can liberate any of the cook's biscuits and beans and offer them as a means of easing hunger and suspicion. I'll ask Tommy Provost to help secure some of these supplies. He has an air of authority about him."

Garnet smirked. "I'm not certain that those biscuits would be considered a peace offering. More like a declaration of war."

Durrant found Provost and by nine o'clock the four men, along with a fifth horse loaded with supplies, were riding out of the zareba. They rode through the town and were greeted with suspicion and contempt by the Métis, who were hard at work repairing holes in roofs and walls.

"Jacques Lambert told us yesterday of the starvation among the Métis, Cree, and Dakota," said Durrant.

"The Queen, upon signing the treaties with these people, promised them relief from famine. In the direst of circumstances, it was promised that stores would be brought in from the east," said Saul, "but still these people starve. The bison were hunted to extinction, and the agents who were to provide lessons in farming have failed to do so. They are more interested in keeping what they can for themselves."

Provost seemed uncomfortable with the subject matter. He stood stiffly next to his mount and looked down at this boots.

"You told us yesterday that Reuben Wake was an Indian Agent," said Durrant to Saul.

"He was. I can well imagine how he must have meted out both his knowledge and the stores to which he was entrusted."

Provost cleared his throat. "These agents were to serve the Indians, not make their lives miserable."

"I'm afraid that human nature breeds its share of malfeasance," said Saul.

The ferry was nearing the eastern shore of the Saskatchewan, and the four stepped up their mounts. When the rig was ashore, they pressed the animals forward. Garnet spoke to the ferryman in French and they began to cross.

"You constantly astound me." Durrant regarded his friend.

"How so, Sergeant Wallace?"

"You speak French?"

"Of course. After the trouble with the Zulu"—he put a gloved finger to the scar that ran down his face, dissecting his left eye—"I was asked to serve Her Majesty for two years as an assistant to the attaché in Côte d'Ivoire. I suppose I was a sort of bodyguard. Needless to say, French was a necessity."

The men rode away from the river. In five minutes they were at the Dakota camp, where a dozen tipis were set back from the trail and surrounded by a grove of what would be gentle poplars later in the spring but were now the skeletal remains of winter. The four men slowed their approach. Several mange-stricken dogs advanced from the camp.

A pair of men emerged from the nearest tipi to greet them, pulling heavy buffalo robes around their shoulders. They were cradling rifles in their arms as they approached the riders, who all swung down from their mounts. When the two Dakota men were before them, Garnet stepped forward and offered his hand.

"Do you speak English?"

"A little bit." The first man offered his hand from under the robe. The naked arm looked thin, even emaciated, to the men. Saul's face grew sombre.

"We come with food and medicine," said Garnet.

"My English name is Iron Crow—*Kangi Maza* in our own words. This is my brother-in-law, Stands-his-Ground. We are Dakota. Dumont and his Métis forced us to fight. Our cattle were run off. Now we have nothing."

"We can help." Durrant spoke in Sioux.

"You speak our language?" asked Iron Crow. Durrant noticed for the first time that Iron Crow had lost several of his teeth.

"I speak Lakota, in the Sioux tongue. I was stationed at Fort Walsh for many years. Although the dialects are different, we may understand one another a little bit. I am here to ask questions, because among you there is one who may help me understand a murder that I am . . . interested in. What we have brought with us we will leave whether or not there are answers. My friend, the doctor, would be happy to help anybody who might be ill."

Iron Crow turned and looked at Stands-his-Ground. He spoke again in English. "As for the ill, that would be nearly all. As for your questions, ask what you like. I am the one who can tell you what you want to know. I will sit with you now."

DURRANT WAS WELCOMED into Iron Crow's tipi. There in the darkness were half a dozen other people. The space was warm and

91

smelled faintly of leather. Heavy buffalo hides had been stretched out to create a comfortable floor. Iron Crow spoke in Dakota to the others in the tipi and asked them to leave.

Durrant spoke in the Lakota dialect of Souix as they gathered their robes about them and made for the door. "They can stay."

"It is best. Some things should only be spoken between men."

Durrant realized that there were only women in the tent, and wondered how many men were left in the encampment.

"Let us speak in English, so we might understand one another better. Please, sit," said Iron Crow, and Durrant awkwardly lowered himself to the floor. "You are the one-legged Red Coat. I've heard your story. Did you catch the men who did this to you?"

"Not yet. But I haven't stopped looking."

"That's the thing about you whites. You never stop looking. Our leader, White Cloud, fled when the soldiers stormed Batoche. I am an old man and did not do any real fighting. I just scouted. But I fear that the whites will not stop looking for someone to take their anger out on."

"I can't promise you that Middleton's soldiers won't."

"Most other whites would try to tell me a lie. They would say that nobody would harm my family if only I would tell them what they want to know."

"I learned to parley with the Lakota in the Cypress Hills when they fled the Dakota Territory after Wounded Knee. Sam Steele told me never to lie. Never. I won't lie to you. Do you know who the man was who was murdered inside our camp?"

"He was the white man called Reuben Wake. Some years ago, when my people came to the Saskatchewan Territory, Mr. Wake was an Indian Agent in the Willow Valley, to the east of the Cypress Hills. We settled awhile there. We hoped to hunt but were told that we had to farm instead. Since the start of time, my people have been hunters moving with the seasons to follow the animals. Mr. Wake, and others, told us that we had to live in sod huts and grow crops. He told us that Macdonald would take care of us if we did. Some of us tried. When things didn't work, we decided that we had to move north to find game. Mr. Wake told us that we could not.

"He told us the good country in the Qu'Appelle Valley and along the Saskatchewan River was for the whites, and that the Métis had already been driven off. I was a younger man then, and stronger. When Wake told us this, we quarrelled. He told me that if my people didn't remain where we were, he would kill my family." The fire popped and a cluster of sparks rose and circled toward the opening in the ceiling. "What could I do? I knew for him it was about money. He was stealing the money that he was supposed to use to buy food and blankets. We Sioux had fought for and lost our homes in America. Now we were going to lose our homes again? We had a council, and it was decided that we would wait for our own chance to live once again as we always have."

"How did Wake take this news?"

"He put a knife to my throat and told me that if I rode to town he would kill my wife and my children. I could have killed him, but there were other whites in that place who believed we were savages. I waited. It seemed as if the waiting was the right thing to do, because the following year Wake left. It was only later I heard that he was filled with more evil than I could have known."

"What do you mean?"

"Several of the young women in our camp had been . . . hurt by this man. I wish now that I had killed him when I had the chance."

"So six years pass, and you find yourself in Batoche?"

"When Wake left, a new agent arrived and we were allowed to leave and come here. We have been hunting in these woods and plains ever since. There are no buffalo, but there are deer and bear. We have some cattle. We have made peace with our half-blood brothers and with the Cree."

"But then the Métis rebelled."

"We wanted no part of it, but Dumont told us we had to fight or we would be sent back to America and hung. He ran off our cattle and told us the only way we would be given food was if we killed the soldiers. Several of the young men took up with White Cloud to fight."

"And then Reuben Wake appeared."

"I recognized him at once. It was on the second day of the fighting. My brother-in-law and I had hid for much of the first day. The second day was quiet and Dumont sent us to scout the enemy camp. We snuck past your soldiers and got inside the camp."

"How?"

"It was easy. We climbed over your crates and crawled past sleeping soldiers. Wake was with the horses. He was laughing. My brother stopped me from killing him. There were too many other men with him. We came back to report to Dumont."

"Did you return to kill Wake?" asked Durrant. Iron Crow shook his head. "You didn't come back to the camp on the last day of fighting to finish what you should have all those years ago?"

"No, I did not. You see, Sergeant, I am sick. I lost my will, seeing Wake tending to the horses and laughing at a man's joke. The fighting on the third and fourth day threatened to overrun Batoche, and our camp. I stayed behind to protect my family."

"You didn't leave the camp at all during the last two days of the battle?"

Iron Crow was quiet for a moment. Durrant watched the play of light on his face. "On the final day, I went down along the river to see if I could find once more a chance to exact my revenge on Wake. But I could not. There were too many soldiers."

"How far along the river did you get?"

"To a place just below the soldiers' camp."

"Can you recall what time of day?"

"It was in the afternoon, as the soldiers were coming into Batoche."

"Did you see anybody else there along the river?"

"There was nobody else there."

"If you had gotten into the camp, how would you have killed Wake?"

Iron Crow watched Durrant for a long time. "I would have used my tomahawk. It would have been most painful."

THIRTEEN

SEVEN SUSPECTS

IT WAS LATE IN THE afternoon when the four men made the return trip. "I think we had best keep our suspicions to ourselves," concluded Durrant, "for the sake of peace and for the safety of those people."

"You believe that Iron Crow might be involved in Wake's death?" asked Garnet.

"He's not above suspicion, but he is not my prime suspect. It seems as if men are tripping over themselves to confess their hatred for Wake. The range of motives is astonishing.

"Terrance La Biche certainly had means, motive, and opportunity," said Durrant. "He had Wake's pistol, but we shall need to spend more time with Mr. La Biche, if we can get close enough. He has motive for certain. He was on the verge of revealing it when Sub-Inspector Dickenson spirited him away."

"You think it's possible La Biche might have found enough time to rummage around Wake's wagon for a murder weapon?" asked Saul.

"It might have been pure luck that led him there. Maybe he had the meat hatchet and was searching for Wake when he found the pistol and decided to use it instead."

"What motivates a killer is likely to influence their choice of weapon," explained Saul. "I've been participating in a conversation, held entirely through correspondence, with some of my learned colleagues on this matter. A man motivated by hatred that is personal chooses a means that brings him into contact with his victim. He wants the satisfaction of feeling the man beneath his weapon. Strangulation is the most intimate of killing methods, and stabbing or butchering comes close behind it. Poisoning is the most remote. Shooting a man, even at point-blank range, is a little more detached."

Durrant considered this for a moment. His recent conversation with Iron Crow came to mind: the Dakota Sioux man had said he would have killed Wake with his tomahawk. "So a man whose hatred is political, say, or even ideological, might not feel the same vehemence and choose a more distant method of killing?"

"That's why political assassinations are often done by poison or with a pistol," said Saul.

They rode a moment in silent contemplation of the doctor's revelations. "Terrance La Biche isn't the only man who has confessed his ill will." Durrant indicated the silent rectory as they rode past its bullet-riddled eastern wall. "Even the good Father Lefèbvre has confessed to an unnatural hatred for this man Wake."

"Any man is capable of murder. A dedication to God has not kept men from massacring one another over the long arc of history," Garnet stated.

"Father Lefèbvre could come and go in the zareba as he saw fit," said Durrant. "And if he had gotten to know him over the time that Wake was here in Batoche, it is possible that he may have known where this man kept his pistol. I would say that the priest is not above any of this.

"I suppose, given that there are Métis loyal to the Dominion in the service of General Middleton, it is conceivable that Mr. Lambert could have made his way into the zareba with only nominal disguise—"

"Yes, say as a tradesman or even acting as a teamster—" Saul interjected.

"—and therefore found his opportunity. Then, wishing to atone for his sins, he compounded them by attempting to take his own life." The zareba had come into view as the four rode and talked. Durrant pulled up on the reins and they stopped in the road. "Iron Crow has told me that on the twelfth of May, as the town was being overrun, he returned to the zareba. He claims not to have been able to get past the sentries."

"How is it that he was able to infiltrate our compound just days before, but not on the final day, when most of the soldiers were rushing the field?" asked Tommy Provost, breaking his silence.

"It's a good question, Staff Sergeant. What I also found interesting was that he made no mention of seeing Mr. Lambert on the banks of the river. He says that this was his path, but Lambert was nowhere to be seen."

"It's possible that Lambert was farther along the bank from where the Sioux traversed," suggested Saul.

"It's possible that while Iron Crow was entangled in our pickets, Mr. Lambert was dispatching Mr. Wake. That's why he didn't see him," added Durrant.

"Among those we have discussed here, the Sioux man seems the least likely to have committed the murder," said Garnet.

"And why is that?" asked Durrant.

"I simply don't think the man physically capable."

"Just because he is of diminished physical stature," said Saul, "doesn't mean he could not have taken Wake by surprise."

"He did admit an ability to steal into the zareba unseen," said Durrant. "But he told me that he would have used his tomahawk on Wake, and I believed him."

"What about Dickenson?" asked Garnet.

"I should dearly love to find him responsible for this crime, but I simply can't see it," Durrant confessed. "He is involved in this debacle somehow, but I don't think he killed Wake. He didn't have the opportunity. Sub-Inspector Dickenson was indeed on the charge down the Mission Ridge at the moment Reuben Wake was dispatched. He was back in time to take charge once La Biche was in irons."

"He could have killed the man before he rode from the compound," said Saul. "It was chaos, and he might have had time, given that Wake was killed so close to the stables."

"I won't discount your theory," Durrant said. "What might have been his motivation?"

"I have no idea, Durrant. I'm a doctor; I'll leave the matter of motive to the lot of you."

"So there you have it," Garnet summarized. "La Biche, Lefèbvre, Lambert, Iron Crow, and possibly Sub-Inspector Dickenson. Five men who could have killed Reuben Wake."

"Not so fast, Garnet," said Durrant. He had his left hand resting gently on the pommel. "Five is a good beginning, but one thing I have learned is not to discount the obvious. There is another man who seems to be entangled in this that we cannot overlook: the newspaperman, Block. Mr. Block has a long relationship with Wake. I need to learn more of this. He came and went throughout the camp freely, so there was every opportunity."

"Is there anyone else you suspect?" asked Saul.

"Jasper Dire," Durrant replied.

"He arrested La Biche. He found the weapon," Saul protested.

"Who better to surreptitiously plant the same?" asked Durrant.

"None, I suppose," admitted Saul.

"Why not simply arrest the whole field force?" asked Garnet.

"It may come to that. The trouble, dear friends, is that as yet there is no investigation, and I have no authority."

"When have you ever let a simple matter of authority stand between you and an inquiry, Durrant?" asked Provost.

"Not often, I will confess."

"And so how do we proceed?" asked Garnet.

Tommy Provost let out a short grunt at this question. "Remember, gentleman, as Durrant said, you have no authority to investigate anything here. I fear that you may be treading on ground you are not welcome on."

"A man's life is at stake, and another man is dead, and as a Mounted Police officer I have an obligation, regardless of the circumstances, to investigate." Durrant looked toward the zareba.

"I suggest we proceed carefully. I shall take it upon myself to ascertain the whereabouts of the murder weapon itself. Something might be gained through its examination. Both Dickenson and Dire have told me that the weapon had been discharged twice." Durrant turned to the doctor. "You examined the body of Reuben Wake. How many times was he shot?"

"Once that I saw, but my examination could not be taken for a post-mortem assessment."

"Unless the killer missed on his first shot, or deliberately wounded Wake first, say with a bullet to the knee, then where did the second round go? Did the killer miss at point-blank range?"

Garnet held up a hand. "He didn't miss. He misfired!"

"That is a fair likelihood," agreed Durrant, "and another reason to examine the Colt."

"And what of the body?" asked the doctor.

"If it's been committed to the river, as we suspect, then we may never have the chance to learn its secrets."

FOURTEEN

PHYSICAL EVIDENCE

THEIR ARRIVAL BACK AT THE zareba did not go unnoticed. Sub-Inspector Dickenson met them at the stables. He had three other men with him, all in the plain dress of the militia that had been assembled out of Regina. Tommy Provost had already gone, leaving Saul, Garnet, and Durrant to face Dickenson alone. Durrant was unsaddling his horse when Dickenson stepped before him. "I'll have a word with you, Wallace."

"You'll have a mouth full of saddle if you don't stand down, sir. I'm not as steady on my feet as I once was."

"I've learned that you and your fellows here have raided our stores to give comfort to the enemy. My scouts have followed your actions. I'll have you in shackles for that."

As Durrant swung the saddle up onto the sideboard of a buckboard wagon to dry, he missed Dickenson's head by a few inches. The officer took a step backwards. "Sub-Inspector, the food, medicine, and blankets were drawn with the permission of General Middleton himself and taken from the surplus that arrived in the care of the Surveyors Intelligence Corps, with whom Mr. Moberly is lieutenant. The medicine was drawn from Doctor Armatage's stores, which he purchased with his own resources before leaving Regina."

"You have given comfort to those who wished to harm and kill members of the field force."

Durrant leaned against the wagon and regarded Dickenson coolly. The man was red in the face. Behind him, the three militia-men stood with arms crossed. Several wore pistols in their belts. Durrant was aware of Garnet's careful positioning, his back to a wagon. A fight with these men in such close quarters had to be avoided, for their own sake.

"White Cloud, who took up arms, is on the run, and I have no doubt he'll be hunted down and put to trial," said Dickenson.

"Your time on the force may be too short to know this, Sub-Inspector, but those of us who made the March West were ordered to make peace, not war, with the Sioux, the Assiniboine, the Cree, and the Blackfoot. That's what we did. This is the Dominion of Canada. Need I remind you of that?" The words felt strange coming out of Durrant Wallace's mouth; he had been reminded of this very fact while settling scores with his fists or pistol many times over the course of his career. "I find your presence here very curious, Sub-Inspector," he continued. "Such strong emotions surrounding this venture, and all of it seemingly directed toward me and my questions about Reuben Wake."

"What is curious is your insistence on interfering with this matter, Wallace. It's none of your business. You have no standing."

"As a member of the North West Mounted Police, my interest is in justice. I simply wish to ensure Mr. Wake's demise is given the full benefit of our policing powers."

"And so it has. A man is in shackles. The matter is closed. He shall stand trial, and hang, and that will be the end of it."

Durrant could feel Garnet Moberly standing completely still and alert a few feet from his side. Saul Armatage shuffled uncomfortably. "Tell me, Dickenson"—Durrant dropped the respectful title of the man's rank—"what is it that you are hiding? What are you trying to mask with this façade of confidence about Terrance La Biche's guilt in this killing?"

"Not a goddamned thing, Wallace! You keep your nose out of this matter. You poke around in this, and you'll likely as not end up like Wake himself."

At that, two of the men behind Dickenson took a step forward, and as fast as lightning Garnet drew his twin Webley revolvers and set their hammers at full cock. He aimed the pistols into the cluster of men behind Dickenson. One of the men made to reach for his revolver, but Durrant said loudly, "Stand down! All of you! Dickenson, you've threatened me for the last time. I suggest you and these ruffians take the first wagon train back to wherever you come from. You might outrank me, but I have the force of right on my side, and if you so much as lift a finger in the direction of my friends again, I'll see to it that the force throws you in leg irons."

A moment passed and then Dickenson began to laugh. "We shall see, Wallace, who it is in irons at the end of this affair." He turned and said, "Lads, we'll have our fun soon enough." All four men left the confines of the wagons, sneering and looking back over their shoulders.

Garnet deftly holstered his pistols. Durrant looked at Saul, who had broken into a sweat despite the chill.

"What do you say we find some dinner, gentlemen?" suggested Durrant.

"I'm a mite peckish." Garnet patted his stomach.

THE MUCH-NEEDED PHYSICAL evidence in the mystery surrounding Reuben Wake came the next morning on the bow of the steamer *Northcote*. The surveyors patrolling along the river could clearly see a body laid out on the bow deck of the steamer and reported the news to Garnet. Garnet alerted Saul and Durrant, and the three of them rode down to the ferry crossing. A crush of men were taking in supplies. Durrant made his way through the throng and stepped onto the deck of the boat. The captain of the *Northcote* received them.

"Captain, I'm Sergeant Durrant Wallace of the North West Mounted Police."

"Yes, Sergeant. Very good. I'm glad you're here. We found a body floating in the river, maybe twenty miles downstream. It was caught up on a log boom."

"Recently dead?"

"I'm no expert, but I believe so."

"Let's have a look, shall we, Doctor?" Durrant turned to Saul, who stepped forward. The main wheelhouse of the *Northcote* concealed them from the view of the men unloading crates from the steamer. Saul stepped to the body wrapped in tarps and squatted beside it. "I don't expect this will be a pretty sight if he's been in the river for these many days. Thank goodness it's May and not July." Saul turned to Garnet. "Here, lend a hand, will you please?" The two of them gingerly pulled back the tarp. Durrant and the captain looked on.

"Blue Jesus," muttered Durrant at the sight of the cadaver's face. The eyes of the man had been pecked out; only remnants of the gelatinous orbs remained. His hair fell in thin, tattered patches across his forehead. His face was bloated and white, but there was, very clearly, a half-inch-wide hole in the side of the head, near the temple.

"Any doubt that this is Reuben Wake?" asked Durrant.

"No," said Saul. "I would say not. I'd say by the look of him that he has been in the water since his corpse was removed from the zareba on the twelfth. You see his skin? It's developed cutis anserine."

"In English, Doctor?" said Durrant.

"Gooseflesh. Pimpling of the skin."

"Let's get this body under cover and find a place where you can do your work, Doctor."

FIFTEEN

THE CONTENTS OF THE CRANIUM

"WE'LL HAVE TO MAKE THIS quick. Before you know it, Dickenson and his thugs will set upon us and we'll have to fight just to complete an autopsy on this corpse." Durrant peered around the deck of the steamer. "Can we load him into that pushcart and make for Batoche? We'll find a place there for the doctor to do his work."

Garnet went and got the cart. With the captain, they loaded the cadaver into it. At Batoche, the doctor led them to the rear of Xavier's Store. "You've been here before, Doctor?" asked Durrant, pushing the door open and peering into the dark space. He stepped in cautiously, his hand on the hilt of his Enfield. There was nobody in the room.

"On the last day of fighting, I followed the field force down the Mission Ridge and into the town. There were many wounded. It appears as though the mercantile hadn't opened before the fighting broke out. I had a makeshift triage set up here in the back room. It will do."

Saul came inside and found a lantern hanging in the darkness. He trimmed the wick, found his matches, and lit the lamp. "Let's put him here." He motioned to a long table used for butchering meat. It was solidly constructed and had gutters to drain blood. The men were in a multi-purpose storeroom. It had a door that opened to the front of the shop, and a set of stairs that seemed to be an entrance to the living quarters above.

"Are you sure nobody is home, Saul?"

"Can't be certain, but most of the townsfolk fled before the fighting even started. I know some of the men have returned, but I don't know if Xavier has come back from St. Laurent."

"Okay, then, let's get on with this," said Durrant. Saul and Garnet hoisted the body onto the table. Durrant tried not to get in their way.

Saul removed the shroud. "As I knew I would be operating during this expedition, I brought along some of my more advanced tools." The doctor was digging in his bag. "I should think they will be some help to us."

Saul pulled out a scalpel and made an incision around the man's temple where the large, dark bullet hole could be observed. "I should be able to estimate both the calibre of the cartridge and the distance from which it was fired. See, look here. Already, despite the bloating, I can tell you that Mr. Wake was shot at very close range. Two feet at most, but not point blank. The flesh around the bullet hole has been burned, but there is no star-shaped tearing, indicating that the weapon was not pressed against the man's head. Now as for the calibre"—the doctor took a caliper from his bag—"we shall have to see." He leaned in close to the corpse and measured the bullet hole. He turned his head toward the ceiling and closed his eyes while he considered what the measurement meant. "I make this to be a .44 or .45 calibre."

"That's consistent with the Colt that was found in Mr. La Biche's jacket—the same that belonged to Mr. Wake," said Durrant.

"Now what I find strange, gentlemen, is that there is no exit wound. If Mr. Wake had been shot in the head from this angle"—Saul made his hand into a gun and held it two feet from the cadaver's head at a right angle—"then frankly, the exit would be the size of my fist, and we would have very little left of Mr. Wake's grey matter."

"If any existed in the first place," cracked Garnet.

Saul rolled Wake on his side, and water drained from the man's mouth and ran into a bucket on the floor. "You can see by looking here"—he pointed into the wound—"that there are plenty of brains left in his head. The only conclusion I can draw is that the cartridge is still lodged there."

"Can you retrieve it?"

"Yes, but let's look over the rest of his face first . . . Ha! Look here." The doctor pointed to the man's heavy brow. "I suspected as much." Saul pulled a pair of forceps from his bag and began pulling at something lodged in the man's face. "It's part of a cartridge casing. And look at the angle it's lodged in his brow: straight on."

"He was shot at twice," said Garnet.

"Yes, but the first time, the cartridge detonated in the pistol," said Durrant.

"Leaving Mr. Wake here a moment to turn and try to flee," added Saul.

"But not enough time to outrun his meeting with destiny," concluded Garnet.

UPON FINISHING HIS examination, Saul fitted Wake's skullcap back in place, folding the neatly cut skin back over the bone. He withdrew needle and thread from his bag and made several crude sutures to hold the skullcap firm. Then he pulled the shroud back over the body. Durrant looked toward the door. "Let's get some air and I'll tell you what I think." They stepped into the cool, bright day and each man drew a deep breath. Durrant looked around. He could hear men on the main road on the other side of the building.

"You have a theory?" asked Garnet. He had found his pipe in his pocket and was packing it with tobacco. Durrant was grateful, as the strong weed might erase the stench of death in his nostrils.

"I do. It's simple, really. Mr. Wake knew his attacker. It seems to be the only way that a man could approach him from the front and not arouse suspicion. When the killer drew his weapon and misfired, Wake tried to flee, but the gunman was too quick. He was able to fire a second round rapidly, and it took Wake's life. I think our best suspects are those who Mr. Wake either was familiar with or had no reason to fear or distrust."

"That all but rules out La Biche, Lambert, and Iron Crow. Any of these men would have aroused suspicion in Wake. He would have been on his guard," said Garnet.

"We also know that the killer would have had to be handy with a pistol," said Durrant. "The Colt is a fairly dependable weapon. A misfire is rare. That a second round could be chambered and fired under the circumstances is a comment on both Mr. Colt's hardware and the killer's familiarity with firearms. Finally, I would think that our killer would be nursing a wound. Don't you, Doctor?"

"Of course he would!" said Saul. "If the exploding cartridge left shell fragments in Mr. Wake's flesh, then surely the shooter would have received burns as well!"

"Now all we need to do is ask to see each man's hands?" asked Garnet.

"It may not be so simple," said Durrant. "With the exception, maybe, of Iron Crow, any of these men may have been wearing gauntlets when they pulled that trigger. We may never be able to tell with any certainty if a mark on leather is recent or has been there for some time."

Durrant had just finished his sentence when there was a commotion on the road in front of the building. The sound of horses being drawn up short and angry shouts caused all three men to take defensive postures. Two horsemen rounded the corner of the building and bore down on the three men. At the same time, the back door of the mercantile was kicked out from inside and several men burst from the room. Durrant's hand reached for his Enfield; Garnet already had his Webley pistols in his hands. The mounted men held Winchesters aimed at the trio. Sub-Inspector Dickenson emerged from the foul-smelling room, his face twisted and grey. "Sergeant Wallace, what in the name of God have you done to Reuben Wake?" He too held an Enfield pistol at his side.

"I was coming to find you, Sub-Inspector, to ask the same. The body that was to be in your care was found by the *Northcote* along the river twenty miles from here. It seems that the premature burial was in fact an effort to hide important evidence."

"You had no right to desecrate that man!" said Dickenson.

"Seeing that you couldn't keep track of it the first time, I decided that Mr. Wake's remains would be in better hands if I took them. I also believe, having examined the body, that the investigation into his murder would be better served if I conducted it from this point on."

"You'll lose your stripes for this, Wallace. I am giving you a direct order, Sergeant. You are to turn over that body and leave Batoche immediately. You may still walk away a free man, though your days as a non-commissioned officer are almost certainly over. Your partners in this crime may only have to serve a few days in irons." Dickenson turned to look at Garnet and Saul.

At that moment, the sound of another horse was heard, and everyone turned to see who it was. The horse was reined in just a few feet from the cluster of armed Mounted Police and militia.

"Assistant Commissioner Crozier." Durrant saluted.

"Sergeant Wallace. Sub-Inspector Dickenson. What the Blue Jesus is going on here?"

SIXTEEN

THE SECOND CONSPIRACY REVEALED

DURRANT AND SUB-INSPECTOR DICKENSON STOOD side by side in Assistant Commissioner Leif Crozier's tent. It was late in the day, and the enclosure was lit by two oil lamps that smoked and made Durrant want to trim their wicks. Before the men was a rough and ready desk fashioned from several planks of wood, which looked to have been fetched from a local barn, supported by empty crates at both ends. Crozier sat upright in his wooden camp chair, smoking a pipe while reading cables and briefing notes scrawled on letter paper. It had been half an hour, and Durrant could feel his prosthetic biting into his leg. He dared not move.

Crozier cleared his throat. The air in the room seemed to crack. "Thank you both for so hastily preparing these briefing notes for me. Middleton brought this business with Wake to my ears and asked that I determine the best way to proceed. With our Mounted Police serving under various units of the reserves and militia, he felt it best for me to decide how to investigate. I wanted to get each of your perspectives. This is most helpful."

"Sir, I wonder—" Dickenson leaned forward to press his case but Crozier silenced him with a hand.

"I have what I need, Sub-Inspector. I wonder if you would be so good as to wait outside. Why don't you find yourself some supper? I will send for you when I am ready."

Dickenson looked at Wallace, then back at Crozier, bewildered. He straightened and saluted. "Yes, sir, as you wish." He skulked from the tent.

"Would you care to sit, Durrant?"

"If you don't mind, sir."

"Please." Crozier pointed to a crate. Durrant sat. "How is the leg?"

"It's fine, sir."

"It's good to have you back in the saddle, son. Not much of a Mounted Police officer if you can't sit a horse, I suppose. Now, let's discuss the matter at hand." Crozier drew on his pipe, and the smoke circled him a moment before dissipating into the darkness of the tent's ceiling. "Sergeant, I am placing you in charge of the investigation into Mr. Wake's murder."

"Thank you, sir."

"Don't thank me, son, until I've told you what I'm about to say. What I'm going to tell you is for your ears alone. I don't want this written down, and I don't want it turning up in any of the god-damned eastern press. Am I clear?"

"Yes, sir. Assistant Commissioner, I should tell you that I have something of an investigative team here in Batoche—"

"Is that so?"

"Yes, sir."

"Blue Jesus, man, that's one thing Dickenson got right—might be the only thing: you are a pain in the ass."

"Yes, sir."

"All right, who is it?"

TEN MINUTES LATER Garnet Moberly and Saul Armatage had been introduced to Crozier.

"Lieutenant, your reputation precedes you." Crozier shook Garnet's hand. "And Doctor Armatage, I suppose you expect me to thank you for saving this man's life after that trouble in the Cypress Hills."

"I can accept no blame for what has come after, sir."

"Very well, then. Please, gentlemen, take a seat. I have information that has come to my ears through the privilege of my position in the North West Mounted Police and as a member in good standing in some circles in Regina and elsewhere across the Dominion. I am asking you to investigate the murder of Reuben Wake and bring to justice his killer or killers, whoever they may be. But there is more.

"There is a conspiracy afoot. Several, in fact. There are Liberal Catholics here in the territories who judge Louis Riel a hero and the rebellion as really a resistance of eastern infringement. These men believe that Riel should go free. They elected him to Parliament three consecutive times, despite the fact that he was wanted for murder! No doubt it has already come to your ears that there is a movement afoot to free Riel—a sort of jailbreak, if you will. This has been whispered in secretive circles since the outbreak of hostilities; if Riel should be captured, there are those who would work to set him free, at any cost."

"We have spoken to some who hold with that conviction," said Durrant.

"I am sure that you have. There is a second Riel conspiracy. One that is far more dangerous, and deadly. There is a plan among some in Regina—that is what they call themselves, the Regina Group—not to free Riel but instead to kill him before he can ever stand trial. Reuben Wake was one of the leaders of these men."

SEVENTEEN

CHOICE OF WEAPONS

IT WAS DARK WHEN THE three friends left Assistant Commissioner Crozier's tent. They didn't speak as they walked but instead watched about them in the camp. The news of the dual conspiracies—one to free and one to kill Riel—had set them all on edge. Crozier's last words to the men before they left had been, "You have very little time."

Durrant knew that in the coming days much of the field force would decamp for Fort Pitt, two hundred miles west on the Saskatchewan River. There they would muster for the fight with Big Bear's Cree. Riel and the rest of the prisoners would be sent to Regina, there to await trial and what other mishaps of fate awaited them. Terrance La Biche would go, too. There was more to Crozier's warning than simple logistics.

When they were back at their fire, Durrant spoke first. "I suppose it goes without saying that Sub-Inspector Dickenson will be no help to us. We'll need to move quickly in the morning to secure the prisoner, retrieve the murder weapon, and locate the men who were charged with burying the body of Mr. Wake. There are a few men in the camp from my time at Fort Walsh, including Tommy Provost. I will recruit them to serve as guards for La Biche. I trust them and know I can count on them."

"I will take it upon myself to locate the murder weapon," said Garnet.

"I suppose that leaves with me the task of discussing the foul deed of the disposal of Mr. Wake," Saul concluded.

"I shall aid you in your discussions, Saul," said Durrant. "I don't expect that the ruffians who committed this undertaking will be forthcoming about it. Some persuasion may be needed. We had all best watch our backs. No doubt the conspirators who have it in for Riel will be aware of our investigation. They may move to put a stop to it."

The three men lay curled inside blankets on the bare ground, looking at the fire. Durrant watched as his comrades drifted off to sleep. It felt good to have these men at his side. There was no way to tell what the path ahead would hold for them, but at that moment Durrant Wallace felt that together they could bear any weight and weather any storm.

ON THE MORNING of May 18, Durrant located Terrance La Biche and approached the young man who was guarding him. "These men will be taking over the security of Mr. La Biche." Behind Durrant stood Tommy Provost and two colleagues dressed in uniform. "You're relieved of your duty, son. Go find yourself some breakfast."

When the militiaman had left, Durrant climbed into the wagon. La Biche was shivering under his blanket. Durrant had one of the constables retrieve another blanket and gather wood for a fire. He sat down next to the prisoner and said, "I've been placed in charge of the investigation into the death of Reuben Wake, Mr. La Biche." The Métis man just stared at him. "I would like to ask you some questions."

The constable returned with a heavy Hudson's Bay blanket. "I'll have a fire going in a moment, Sergeant."

Durrant continued. "When we spoke on the thirteenth of May, you were beginning to tell me more of the circumstances that led to your arrest. I want you to tell me about the conspiracy to free Louis Riel."

When the fire had been kindled, Durrant helped La Biche out of the wagon and they huddled together in the morning chill. One of the Mounted Police brought the man a breakfast of porridge and coffee. "I don't know much of the details. It's just guessing." La Biche spoke between bites. "I believe this is about Sun River, where

Riel taught school. In the Montana territory. It's because of what happened there. Wake travelled there with Dumont. He signed on to care for the horses. Remember, Dumont had selected a young man from St. Laurent to tend to the horses, but when the time came to depart, the lad could not be found, so Dumont was in a bit of a bad way. Reuben Wake had been coming to Batoche for several years at that point, ferrying supplies and stock. He had made like a friend. He happened to be in the town that very morning, and presented himself to Dumont. In the confusion to get on the trail, Dumont agreed."

"Wake went to Sun River to try and scuttle the effort, to undermine it," confirmed Durrant.

"I can't believe that," said Provost.

"It's true." La Biche finished his breakfast and wiped his mouth with his sleeve.

"What happened in Sun River that turned the tide of events against Reuben Wake?"

"The only thing I'm sure of is that when Dumont returned with Riel, Wake wasn't with them. We hoped that he was dead, but then he turned up at Fish Creek. That's when I saw him. I simply couldn't believe my own eyes!"

"Had Dumont or one of the other men made it clear what Wake's intent had been?"

"By the time Dumont returned with Riel, the story of Wake's treason had become well known, but nobody spoke of what became of him. We took it to mean that what was done was done. But it wasn't—not for Wake. And not for me. The man deceived us and betrayed Riel, and it was my aim to make the man pay. But he was shot. I didn't have access to the man's Colt. I was going to use the butcher's hatchet I had pilfered."

"While I am inclined to believe you, I'm afraid I'm not the final arbitrator of this matter. The news of Mr. Wake's death has reached the ears of my superiors in the North West Mounted Police, and they will not release you until such time as we have another man in irons. There is the matter of your disappearance from the scullery at the very time when Wake was killed. I would like to know where you were."

"I told you, I was in the lavatory."

"What more do you know of this conspiracy to free Riel?"

"Believe me or not, Sergeant, but I am in fact just a simple farmer. I don't travel in circles that would allow me to plan a jail-break. I don't have the thinking for such a thing."

"Who does?"

"You're asking me? I have no idea. I suppose if you were to spirit a man like Riel out of the country, you'd need two things: money and influence. I'd start looking for someone who has both. Someone who can convince a lot of people to work together, and do it in secret."

Two such men immediately came to Durrant's mind. "I've asked Staff Sergeant Provost here to be in charge of your security," he told La Biche, and Provost smiled and nodded. "I trust this man. He'll see to it that you are safe until we settle this matter. In the meantime, I want you to think about what I've asked you. If there is anything else you know, tell Mr. Provost and he'll fetch me, and we'll talk again."

Durrant started to push himself up but La Biche put a hand on his arm. For a moment Durrant tensed, but when he saw the man's eyes, he relaxed. "What is it?" he asked.

"Well, it's just that by all accounts Reuben Wake was a terrible man. He deserved to die. I suppose what I'm wondering is, why are you so eager to find his killer?"

Durrant looked at Provost and the two other constables standing before him. He and his friends had considered that question a great deal over the course of the last week. "I have a job to do, Mr. La Biche. It doesn't matter to me if Wake was a good man or a bad one. He was murdered. Maintaining the rule of law is the responsibility of every Mounted Police officer in this force. I aim to uphold it."

Durrant stood up and Provost pulled him aside. "Nice speech. Do you really believe all of that?"

"For the most part, Tommy. Don't you?"

"Sure I do. Sometimes things get complicated. It ain't like it was in '74 when we rode west. Everything is so political now."

"Regardless, we have a job to do. There is justice to be delivered."

SAUL ARMATAGE AND Durrant Wallace sat with their backs to the zareba wall. Jacques Lambert was huddled between them, a buffalo skin pulled around his shoulders. On the far side of a cluster of wagons and horses they could plainly see a group of militiamen preparing their kits to march to Fort Pitt.

"Do you recognize any of those men?" asked Durrant.

Lambert shook his head. "They all look alike in their uniforms."

"What about those men there?" Saul pointed to a cluster of men standing by a fire. Again the Métis man shook his head. "Try to remember the morning when you saw Reuben Wake taken away."

"They wore beards, I recall, but then, many do." Lambert looked at Durrant, who had a closely trimmed beard, then at Saul, who had recently shaved off his rough whiskers but left a long pencil moustache. "There," he said after another moment. "He was one of them."

"Which one?" asked Durrant.

"The man with the rifle slung over his shoulder. That's one of them for sure."

"He was one of the men who was with Dickenson yesterday," said Durrant. He instructed Saul to take Lambert back to the infirmary, where he would continue to be watched over.

"Where are you going?" the doctor asked.

"To see if I can't press this lad for some information."

"Be careful," implored Saul.

"When am I not?" Durrant tracked the man Lambert had identified through the camp, watching to see that he himself was not being followed. When the man entered one of the crudely fashioned outhouses, Durrant positioned himself by the door. He found a long pole, one that had likely been cut to use for a tent, and wedged it under the knotted handle of the privy. "I've locked you in, Private."

"Who's there?"

"It's Sergeant Durrant Wallace. I'm in charge of the investigation into the death of Reuben Wake. We met the other day at Xavier's Store."

"Open the goddamned door."

"I have a couple of questions for you. Answer and I'll let you out."

"I'll blow a hole in the door before I answer you."

"Your Winchester is too long. You don't have enough room to get a clear shot. I noticed you don't have your Enfield with you."

"You're a son of a bitch, Wallace."

"Be careful how you speak of my mother, Private. It would be embarrassing to have to call for help in your position. Who ordered you to throw Reuben Wake into the Saskatchewan River?"

"Dickenson. Who the hell do you think?"

"Why?"

"Maybe we was just too lazy to bury the man. I don't know."

"That would not surprise me, Private, but I think there's more to it than indolence."

"Well, then, you tell me if you're so goddamned smart."

"I think you were hiding something. Maybe whoever killed Wake didn't want his body to be examined."

"That half-blood La Biche killed him. He had the weapon on him."

"Did Dickenson order the body thrown in the river so nobody would see that the first shot was a misfire?"

"I don't know what you're talking about. Wasn't no misfire. That half-breed shot him in the temple, plain and simple."

Durrant wasn't learning anything he didn't already know. He changed direction in his questioning. "Where's the Colt?" There was no sound from the privy. "You know, it's possible that a man could die of asphyxiation breathing in the methane produced by one of these lavatories."

"Dickenson has it."

"And where is he?"

"He's long gone," said the man, with a laugh.

Durrant put his face to the planks. "Where did he go?"

"To hell, just like you, Wallace."

"We'll see. Which way did he go?"

"He went to Fort Pitt. He's scouting for Major Boulton."

"If I let you out, are you going to be polite?" The man in the privy didn't say anything. "Well, I suppose you'll have to wait for the next man to come to drop his drawers."

"Blue Jesus, Wallace, I can't breathe in here!"

Durrant knocked the stick from the door. The man burst out of the privy, his Winchester in hand, looking about him wildly for a sign of his foe. Durrant had his Enfield out and pressed to the man's temple before he could turn. "I bid you remember, sir, that we are all on the same side."

"You don't have the faintest notion of who is on what side."

"You walk away. If I ever see you or your friends again, I'll arrest you on the spot. You so much as raise a weapon in the direction of me or any of my friends, I'll cut you down. Are we clear?"

The man laughed. "You had better not find yourself in Regina, Wallace."

"Given that remark, I would say you can count on it. Now shoulder that weapon, report to your company, and follow your orders." Durrant lowered his pistol. He became aware that there were others now observing the interaction.

"You're a dead man, Wallace."

"Won't be the first time."

DURRANT WALKED BACK toward the spot where Saul and Garnet had agreed to rendezvous at lunchtime. Durrant told them about Dickenson's flight for Fort Pitt. "You think he's marching on Middleton's orders?" asked Garnet.

"Maybe he is, maybe he isn't. But if we want that pistol, we'll need to catch up to him."

"Most of the camp will be struck by nightfall, and we'll be making for Pitt in the morning," said Saul.

"I'll have to ride ahead and see what can be done to catch up with this man." Durrant turned to Garnet. "What did you learn this morning?"

"I've spoken with several of my fellows in the Surveyors Intelligence Corps. Much of the citizenry has been split on the issue of Riel. Free him or hang him. There are those among them who believe that should Riel go to trial, it will provide some political gain for the Liberals."

"Political gain?" Wallace repeated.

"War is always about politics, and here the gain will be made to expose how Macdonald has once again offended the French. This, of course, can be used by his political rivals when Edward Blake seeks the office of prime minister."

"Are you telling us, Garnet, that you think Riel's enemies will try to kill him before he can take the stand and make his speeches simply to silence him?" asked Durrant.

"Nothing about Canada will ever be simple, Sergeant Wallace. A nation forged from the ashes of the greatest conflict the globe has ever seen cannot help but relive these age-old rivalries again and again. The struggle between the French and the English, between the Catholics and the Protestants, between Upper and Lower Canada, will play out over and over again across this nation. In the West, the struggle has been compounded. Here the people are so far from the centre of power that they vie to have their voices heard and opinions included while at the same time insisting that they should go about their business as they please. This business with Riel is only the beginning."

"We'll need to be on the move in advance of them," Durrant said. "Gentlemen, let's make haste with our inquires this afternoon so the moment will not be lost. At the supper hour, we will determine who is to ride for Regina and who will make for Fort Pitt."

EIGHTEEN

LA JOLIE PRAIRIE

STANLEY BLOCK WAS THE SORT of man who was more comfortable in a gentlemen's club in Winnipeg or Montreal than on a mud-soaked prairie battlefield. When Durrant Wallace went to locate him after lunch, it came as no surprise that he was found sitting in the back of a well-appointed wagon, smoking a rich cigar and scribbling in his notebook. "Sir, I wonder if I might have a moment of your time?"

"When last we spoke you levelled some unflattering allegations at my person, Sergeant. Is this to be another smear against my character and my choice of vocation?"

"Mr. Block, you may have heard that I am now in charge of the investigation into Reuben Wake's death."

"This news has come to my ears."

"I'd like more information on the events of the days leading up to Wake's demise. I hoped that you, as a newspaper man, might have some insight."

"Seems like you have changed your opinion of my profession."

Durrant dismissed this. "Why don't we take a walk?"

Block looked out of the wagon as if considering the weather. He lowered himself carefully to the ground and donned his hat and gloves.

"I was thinking that I'd like to see the scene of some of the fighting to the north. I understand that you were with Middleton there on the third day. I was hoping you might indulge me and show me where the action was?"

"It's a fair stride. Are you certain you're up for it?" asked Block, looking at Durrant's cane.

"I'll manage." The two men walked across the zareba and followed a cowpath north and west toward a heavy grove of aspens and alders. "Tell me about what happened on La Jolie Prairie, Mr. Block."

"I've interviewed General Middleton for the paper on this matter, and he is cagey to say the least," Block began. "As I can surmise, the general felt a frontal attack on the Mission Ridge and the town beyond would not succeed unless he could draw out some of the Métis forces from their rifle pits around the church. On the eleventh of May he took his mounted infantry north to reconnoitre the sweep of grassland and poplar forests that the Métis use to graze their cattle. Around eleven o'clock he arrived near where the Carton Trail crosses the road to St. Laurent. He had his scouts probe the woods and soon found his foe."

"There was an exchange of fire?"

"For some minutes, Boulton opened up with the Gatling gun, and that seemed to quiet the half-breeds. They kept their heads down after that."

They came to a broad clearing. Wallace tried to imagine the scene: Boulton probing for a weakness in the enemy's defences, and the Métis scrambling to fill any holes. "Were there casualties on the third day?"

"A few, but nothing serious."

"I understand Reuben Wake was shot that day."

Block looked sternly at him. "Is that what this is all about?"

"Mr. Block, I am investigating a murder. I have to understand how these events unfolded and what relevance they might have had with his final undoing."

Block huffed. "How could a battlefield wound be in any way related?"

"Maybe you could tell me what you know."

"Wake was a teamster. When some of the field force dismounted to probe the enemy's defences, Wake was given charge over their mounts. He and his fellows were back in those trees." Block pointed to the east of where the fighting had occurred.

Durrant estimated that the distance between the skirmish line and the woods was several hundred yards. "And where were you?"

"I was positioned just here." Block indicated a berm along the side of the road that might provide a man some cover during a firefight.

"From where you were, how well could you see Mr. Wake and his horses?"

"I could see the horses just fine. They might have been a few dozen yards back in the woods. I would not have known Mr. Wake."

"Did you see him shot?"

"No. I was too concerned with Middleton's feint. I wanted to see for myself if his reconnaissance would lead to anything. If so, I might have been able to get a story on the wire to my paper."

"The marvels of modern technology are amazing, are they not?"

"How do you mean, Sergeant?"

"Well, that you can be here in the middle of the frontier, while a battle rages around you, and with the assistance of the telegraph wire have a story in print the very next day."

"Yes, yes, it is fascinating. Now, Sergeant, I should dare say it looks like rain, so shall we—"

"We're almost through, Mr. Block. Walk with me a little more, would you?" Durrant led Block toward the grove of trees where Wake had tethered the soldiers' horses. They made the distance in a few minutes. Durrant turned and looked back toward La Jolie Prairie. The woods were dark and dense, and though their leaves had not yet opened, the aspens were close enough to provide a good deal of shelter. Durrant began to examine the terrain. "I can see this is where most of the beasts were tethered." He indicated a well-trampled area that was covered in horse dung.

"Do you notice anything odd, Mr. Block?"

"They are trees, sir. Nothing odd whatsoever."

"Would you characterize the Métis as crack shots with their rifles?"

"No. Not in the least. Had they been, this would have been a much longer battle. By day three many of them were shooting with nails packed into their weapons."

"Don't you think it odd that with the nearest Métis rifle pit at least two hundred yards away, and with this dense stand of trees between himself and the skirmish line, Mr. Wake could have been shot?"

"I suppose it might have been a lucky shot."

"Let me see your hands, Mr. Block."

Block held out his hands. He wore leather gloves.

"Please take off your gauntlets, sir."

Block pulled off his gloves. He stared at Wallace with malice.

Durrant held his cane under his arm and took Block's hands in his own. His right hand appeared very misshapen compared to the newspaperman's delicate fingers. "What happened here?" asked Durrant, indicating where Block's right forefinger and thumb were burned.

"I burned myself tending to my fire."

"Did you now?"

"Yes, Sergeant, in fact I did. It may come as a surprise to you, but in Regina we have proper stoves to cook on. It's been some years since I had to make my morning breakfast on an open fire."

Durrant looked again at the man's hands. It was hard to tell if Block was telling the truth about the origin of the burns. They could well be powder burns. He released the man's hands, and Block immediately pulled on his gloves.

"Do you carry a firearm, Mr. Block?"

The newspaperman looked flustered. "Well, yes, I suppose I do. What of it? Only a fool would set off on such an adventure without something with which to defend his person."

"Do you carry it now?"

"Yes, of course. There are still half-breeds lurking in these woods, Sergeant. Is there some law—"

"Let me see it."

"I shall do no such thing."

"Mr. Block, you can hand me your pistol or I will take it from you. The former will be far more dignified." Something about the way Durrant shifted his weight signalled to Block that Durrant was not bluffing. "Slowly please, sir. One would not want to alarm at this moment."

Block reached inside his coat and produced the weapon.

"You brought an Elliot Derringer to defend yourself with?"

"It's fine in a pinch. At close range, I assure you it's quite an effective sidearm."

Durrant cracked open the breech of the weapon. The pistol had four barrels, two across and two down, each just a little over three inches long. There were four .32-calibre cartridges loaded in the pistol. Durrant took the cartridges out one at a time and examined each barrel.

"Has it ever been fired?"

"I assure you it has, though only at targets."

Durrant flipped the breech shut, spun the weapon around in his palm, and handed it back to Block. Block fumbled it back into his coat pocket.

"Mind you don't zip yourself with that, Mr. Block."

Block looked up at Durrant with malevolence. "Once again, sir, I demand to know what you are driving at with these questions, accusations, and innuendoes."

"Only this: I don't think Reuben Wake's shooting on the twelfth of May was the first time someone tried to murder the man. I believe that on May 11 someone who had knowledge of his whereabouts, and easy access to him here in these trees, tried to use the cover of battle to dispatch him. And having failed, tried again on the twelfth and met with success."

"I think that is preposterous. There was a battle. A man was shot, and that was all there was to it."

"Well, I suppose we might learn more from examining the slug dug from the man's arm, should it still be available. Failing that, I doubt very much that even a lucky or wild shot could find its way through all of these trees. And see here." Durrant walked from tree to tree. "None other has been zinged. I'd say the shot that wounded Mr. Wake came from much closer, but in the heat of the moment he mistook it for a wild shot from the enemy rather than a deliberate attempt on his life."

"You are not suggesting that it was I who shot Mr. Wake here on the field of battle?"

"I'm not suggesting anything. My job is to investigate, and so I am. Your possession of a firearm would provide you with the means."

"Even I can see, Sergeant, that this weapon has not been fired—"

"That's by no means conclusive. A man such as yourself, with your attention to detail, would no doubt keep a weapon such as that spotless. I have no way to test for gunpowder residue here in the wilderness."

"What motivation would I have? As you've so crassly stated before, I am here to *shill* papers, not commit the crime of murder."

"I believe you knew Mr. Wake, and that you shared a sensibility that should Mr. Riel survive the ordeal at Batoche and be allowed to stand trial for treason, your cause would suffer."

"What sort of preposterous lie have you conjured now!"

"Were you not both of the mind that if Riel were allowed the forum of a fair and open trial he would incite further sympathy for his cause among the eastern elite? And that if this happened, he might turn the sentiment of Lower Canada against Macdonald's Conservatives?"

"I tell you this, Sergeant: I had never before laid eyes on Mr. Wake before our expedition. You can say what you like about my business interests, but you know nothing of my politics. I simply will not tolerate such accusations."

Durrant closed the distance between himself and Block, using his cane to bar the man's escape. "Something happened between you and Wake. I suspect very strongly that this is what you and my colleague, Sub-Inspector Dickenson, were quarrelling about when I interrupted you."

"Stand down, Sergeant—" Block pushed Durrant's cane aside and made to stride off through the woods. Durrant used the handle of the cane to grab Block's arm and spin him in his tracks. The newspaperman's hat flew off, and his mouth dropped open. "How dare you!"

"Yes, I dare. You see, Mr. Block, you no longer have the cover of your patsy Dickenson to shield you and your fellow conspirators from plain view. The Queen considers the planning of a murder and the actual killing to be worthy of much the same punishment. One might not hang for planning on killing a man, but you can look forward to twenty years' hard labour for the consideration."

"Leif Crozier will hear of this."

"I report to Sam Steele, and both he and Assistant Commissioner Crozier have sanctioned my investigation." Durrant let his cane fall to his side.

"You are in far over your head, Sergeant Wallace. I suggest you settle for what you have: a man in irons, and a half-breed at that. Surely the Crown will be satisfied with La Biche's neck in a noose for this death."

"You may have heard the story told that the Mounted Police always get their man. It is not always so, but one thing you can count on from us Red Coats is that we never stop until we have carried the day, or are in the dust from trying."

"It very well may be the dust for you, Sergeant Wallace." Block picked up his hat and perched it on his head. Durrant watched the man walk away under the threatening sky.

NINETEEN
CONFESSION

FATHER LEFÈBVRE WAS WAITING FOR Durrant when he
returned from La Jolie Prairie. The priest appeared like a black-
winged bird as his robes beat in the gusts of wind. As Durrant
walked toward him, he could see that Lefèbvre was watching
the road.

"Good afternoon, Father." Durrant stopped, feeling his leg
pulsing. If Charlene had been here, he would have caught hell
from her for overdoing it.

"Good afternoon, Sergeant."

"Just out enjoying the weather?"

"I was awaiting your return."

They stepped into the church, and Durrant felt the warmth of
the fire in the woodstove that graced its centre. Since the sergeant
had been in the sanctuary on the thirteenth of May, Lefèbvre had
restored some order to the space. "What is it that you were so
anxious to tell me?" asked Durrant.

"I understand that you are to move Mr. La Biche to Regina in
the morning."

"News travels fast in Batoche."

"Even a priest is not without recourse to the news of the day."

"Do you have some new information to share?" The priest sat
down and pressed his eyes shut. "Father, you understand that it is
I who is now in charge of this investigation. It is your duty to tell
me what you know."

"La Biche could not have killed Reuben Wake." The priest
looked up, his face stern. "It was not his orders." Durrant remained
silent as Lefèbvre looked down again. "He was not to kill him,
despite how much he and many others wanted to. That would be

a crime against God. He was to watch him, and if Wake got close to . . . to undertaking his own foul mission, then he was to intervene, but no one was to be killed."

The silence of the sanctuary was disturbed only by the howl of the wind. "Father, you're going to have to explain a little further."

The priest stood and walked a few feet, then turned to face Durrant. A momentary feeling of uneasiness came over him, as if he'd underestimated the man because of his faith. "There are those here in Batoche, and elsewhere across the Saskatchewan Territory, who believe that Louis Riel cannot be allowed to stand trial and be hanged for what has happened here. Not just Métis, but whites too. They have a plan to free him."

"I have heard of this conspiracy, Father. I assure you, Mr. Riel is well guarded. His route to Regina is a closely held secret. Even I do not know it."

"That may be so, but you do not understand the passion with which these people regard him. He is not just a leader to them, he is a prophet. To allow him to hang for returning to Batoche would be a sin. So they . . . so *we* have planned from the start that if he was to be captured, we would move to free him.

"But just as there is always a light in this world, there is darkness. And while Mr. La Biche, and others . . . myself . . . are that light, Reuben Wake and his lot are the very darkness at midnight. Wake's colleagues still plan to kill Riel. When it was discovered that Wake and this Regina Group were to be among the soldiers at Fish Creek and then here at Batoche, we had to get close. Mr. La Biche volunteered to infiltrate the enemy camp to keep watch over Wake and the others. Should things go poorly for the Métis and Riel be captured, only then was he to intervene. He was not to commit a sin against God. There was to be no murder, no matter how vile the foe was."

Durrant watched as the priest paced back and forth, his hands clasped so tightly that his fingers showed white.

"What would he have done if Wake had made a move against Riel?"

"If it had come to that, he would have alerted the guards, or even Middleton himself. If he had to, he would have detained Wake. In the worst case, he would have shielded Riel with his own body."

"To me that seems like a gambit. La Biche would never have gotten near General Middleton. For all you know, there are those within the field force who are sympathetic to the Regina Group. How could La Biche have known that the guard he protested to would not have been one of Wake's confederates?"

"He could not, but it was something we had to prepare for and try to prevent."

"To me it seems far more likely that La Biche decided to eliminate the most obvious threat."

"What good would killing just one man do, Sergeant, when there are so many other members of the Regina Group in your very midst? They wear all manner of disguises, and La Biche could not hope to eliminate them all. No, he was to watch and sound the alarm, and that is all."

"He has admitted to me, and others, that his aim was to kill Wake. He stashed a weapon with which to do so." Durrant stood and walked to the front of the church. Lefèbvre followed him.

"I implore you, sir, do not send this man to the gallows for a crime he did not commit. Someone else had it in for Reuben Wake, and for reasons I cannot even begin to speculate on. If La Biche is to hang, and Riel is left to the mercy of the Regina Group, then there shall be no justice at all from this sorrowful endeavour."

"Father"—Durrant turned to consider the man—"I assure you that very little good shall come of this conflagration. When the first shots were fired in this conflict, the reasons for them were lost in the din. All that history will remember of this day is that Métis and Indians fought and lost, and the reasons why will fade into the dust."

"I fear that you are correct, Sergeant, but must we compound that disaster with even more sorrow?"

"My aim to ensure that justice is carried out, Father Lefèbvre. The power of people's hatred for this man Wake is shocking, even to me. You yourself have called him the devil, a curse that I suspect has no equal in your vocabulary."

"But that does not make me a killer."

"It does not, but it gives you clear cause. And in my business, motive is often the best evidence."

The priest turned a moment in the aisle. "This is a house of God, Sergeant. And I am his servant. Surely you could not be suggesting that I was somehow entangled in the death of this man, no matter how heinous his life was?"

Durrant did not answer the question. "You had free rein to come and go during the events of those four days, did you not?"

"I did. As a man of the cloth I was permitted to provide last rites."

"Tell me, Father, on the third day of the battle, when Boulton took his mounted infantry to La Jolie Prairie, did you happen to accompany either of the forces?"

"I did not."

"You're lying to me, Father."

The priest turned on him. "How dare you accuse me of lying, and here, in God's house!"

"I believe that you went to La Jolie Prairie on the third day of fighting. You went there to see for yourself what Reuben Wake and his compatriots were doing." The priest sat down in a pew. "Father, do you possess a pistol?" The priest held his head in his hands now. "Do you own a firearm?"

"I don't."

"Did you procure a firearm and on May 11 travel with the soldiers to La Jolie Prairie and there, upon seeing Reuben Wake alone with the horses, attempt to kill him?"

"No."

"Father, please look at me." Durrant stepped before the priest. Lefèbvre looked up; his face was red, his eyes clouded with tears. "Did you shoot Reuben Wake?"

"No, Sergeant."

"Did you see who did? The bullet that sidelined this man was not fired from the Métis skirmish line. Someone tried to kill him on that day, and failed. Perhaps this same man was successful on the following afternoon."

"I saw none of this. I merely watched the conflict and prayed to God for peace."

"Be that as it may, you must have seen something of Mr. Wake."

"I was there to observe not only Mr. Wake."

"Who else caught your attention that morning?"

"As I have told you, Sergeant, there are many within the field force who hold the beliefs of the Regina Group. Who controls the story of this event will control how history remembers it."

"And who controls the story, Father?"

"Stanley Block does. He is first and foremost among those who would see Riel dead before he goes to trial."

TWENTY

FLUSHING A COVEY

IT WAS LATE IN THE afternoon when Durrant walked the Humboldt Trail back toward the zareba. After his conversations with Stanley Block and Father Lefèbvre, he felt as if he needed the evening to consider the interwoven conspiracies, and the motives they created, around the murder of Reuben Wake. He would not have such a luxury.

As he approached the camp he heard horses on the road. A dozen riders from General Middleton's mounted infantry thundered by him; the last rider to pass wheeled his horse in the road, and Durrant recognized Jasper Dire. "Sergeant, I would think, given the danger your life was in just a few days ago, you would be sticking closer to the safety of the zareba."

"You would be wrong, Mr. Dire."

Dire swung down from his mount and patted the horse on its flank. Its hindquarters shivered. Durrant was once again startled by the contrast of the man's jet-black hair and his clear blue eyes. "Is it true that you were once shot and left for dead—"

"Yes," interrupted Durrant. "And the men who did it are still at large after these five years."

"That must burn."

"Like glowing embers, Mr. Dire. But I do not let it consume me," Durrant lied. A day hadn't passed since leaving Calgary that he didn't think about Jeb Ensley, his brother Bud, and the prospect of bringing them to justice for their crimes high in the Cypress Hills.

"Would you like to walk with me back to the camp?" asked Dire.

"Certainly. Are you for Fort Pitt in the morrow?" asked Durrant.

"I am, along with the rest of the company, of course. I only wish that we had ridden as soon as the conflict was finished here, so that we could be of some aid in tracking down Big Bear and his Cree. I should like to get in on that fight."

"There may still be a fight to join. Steele hasn't tracked Big Bear to the end of the trail yet."

"There is simply too much country to cover. I will go with my company, but I fear we will miss the fun."

"You seem to have changed your tune."

"Have I?"

"When we spoke just a few days ago, you pined to return to Regina; now you seem disappointed that you will soon have to."

"I suppose. The din of the cannon was still in my ears then. A few days of idleness has returned my zeal. It's more the hunt that is exciting."

"You are a sportsman?"

"I've been known to take some game from time to time. I grew up south of Regina, close to the Montana line. We hunted the coulees along the Missouri breaks and up into the Cypress Hills. It's only recently that I've moved to Regina."

"Why leave the country?"

"Opportunity, I suppose. So tomorrow," said Dire quickly, "I will ride for Fort Pitt. And you, Sergeant? I should think that your work here must be done."

"Only starting, in fact, Mr. Dire."

"You are not satisfied that La Biche is your man?" Dire asked, seeming perplexed.

"Mr. La Biche denies having the Colt in his possession when you apprehended him." Durrant stopped and looked at the man. "I've been asked to lead this investigation now. You tell me that you found that pistol in Mr. La Biche's coat. He denies it. What I can't understand is how he came by it. He even went so far as to stow a hatchet to do the job. I've found *that* weapon. La Biche has a good motive too. What he didn't have was an opportunity."

"He had every opportunity. Nobody was guarding him. You

think the cook and his peelers were going to stop him? He could have gone to visit the head and done Wake in."

"And so why not boast of the act, given the vile feelings that Mr. La Biche seemed to harbour?"

"The promise of the noose would clam any man up."

"I'm not convinced."

"Well, you should be. I found that man."

"What is it that worries you?"

"Nothing at all worries me."

"You are practised at appearing calm, but your emotions betray you, Mr. Dire. You're flushed. Your breathing has changed."

"The suggestion that I am not being forthright with you has me irked, is all."

"Is that it? Or is it something else?"

"Mr. Wallace, I wish that you would just be plain with me."

"It's Sergeant Wallace, Mr. Dire. And to be plain I will say this: the first person I suspect of being a killer is the one who finds the body."

Dire stopped in his tracks as if he'd struck a wall. He regarded Wallace with astonishment. "Well, I found Mr. La Biche. There were several of us who then went in search of the murdered man. Are you suggesting that because I was present when Wake's body was found that I am a suspect?"

Durrant watched the man stammer on the words. "I didn't say that. But your presence at the centre of this murder investigation leaves me with more questions than answers, Mr. Dire."

"I have no reason to have wanted Wake dead. I didn't even know the man."

"Did you not? Regina is a small town. Have you heard of the Regina Group?"

"No, should I have?"

"They are a secret order, a conspiracy of sorts. Their purpose is to kill Louis Riel before he can stand trial to keep him from speaking.

To protect those who would be harmed by what he has to say."

"Who?"

"Their political masters in the East. Those who sent you to march on Riel and his uprising, and who will be embarrassed by what he has to tell at trial."

"Riel could have just as easily been killed in the fighting."

"I suspect this Regina Group was taking no chances."

"I simply have no idea what you are talking about. I lead a very dull life in Regina. I do not associate with the sort of political men who would devise such a conspiracy."

"You shoot with a Webley pistol, Mr. Dire. I'd like to see it."

Wake upholstered his pistol and handed it to Wallace. Durrant took it in his left hand and flipped open the cylinder.

"Take off your gloves, Mr. Dire."

"What for?"

"I want to see your hands."

"Sergeant Wallace, this is most unusual—" Dire pulled off his riding gauntlets and pushed them into his belt. Durrant held the Webley pistol under his arm and took Dire's hands in his. The fingers on both hands were black as pitch.

"These aren't powder burns, are they?"

"I should say not, Sergeant. I'm afraid it is a hazard of my trade. Machine oil is impossible to clean from the skin. Is this to be an inquisition into the care of my skin now?"

"Do you shoot much?" asked Durrant, releasing the man's hands and taking up his pistol once more.

"No, not much. I hunt on the weekends, but not with that weapon."

"What else do you shoot?"

"At home I have a Remington shotgun. Out here we were issued the lever-action guns."

"Can you hit anything?"

"I suppose."

"Care for a wager?"

"I don't—"

"Mr. Dire, I bet you a dollar that you can't hit that aspen tree twice inside of ten seconds." Durrant pointed at a tree seventy-five yards away.

"I don't know what you are getting at." Durrant handed Dire his pistol. As soon as the man had it in hand, the Mounted Policeman wheeled in the road, his Enfield coming to hand, and fired three shots as quickly as he could thumb the hammer. The aspen tree exploded twice, bark splintering onto the grass below. As the shots rang out, a covey of quail exploded into the air. Dire's horse stamped but did not start.

"You're going to bring the camp down on us!" Dire exclaimed.

"A dollar is on the line. Hurry now!" Durrant shouted. Dire raised the weapon in his hand and fired, then thumbed the hammer and fired again. Both shots found their mark. Durrant watched him.

"That's a dollar, sir."

Durrant dug in his pocket and gave the man his coin. "Best holster that, Mr. Dire."

Dire did as he was told. "What is the meaning of all of this?"

"On the eleventh of May, did you ride out with Middleton to La Jolie Prairie?"

Dire and Durrant began to walk again, the horse trailing behind him. "Yes, as ordered."

"When you formed your skirmish line to probe the enemy for weakness, did you go on foot or mounted?"

"On foot, of course."

"Who tended to your horse?"

"One of the teamsters."

"Did you see which one?"

"It was him, wasn't it? That's what you're driving at. It was Wake that was with the horses."

"Reuben Wake was shot that day, but not by Métis. Someone

behind our lines shot him but missed their fatal mark, hitting his arm. I think the same man had better aim the following day."

"Well, I assure you, Sergeant, it wasn't me. I was on the line. You can ask Middleton himself. You can talk all you like about conspiracies, but this was a simple case of cold-blooded murder," said Dire.

There were now men coming down the road at the report of gunfire. "Why is this so important to you, Mr. Dire? What is it that you are hiding?"

"I'm not hiding anything. I just want it known that I found the man who killed Wake."

"Why?"

Dire looked at the men running toward them. Then he looked at Durrant. "Because he said I'd get my name in the paper. Mr. Block said if La Biche hung, I'd get my name in the paper."

"You may well."

Half a dozen men came to a halt before them. "Everything is fine," said Durrant. "Just a little quail hunting, is all."

"Did you get anything?" asked one of the men.

"Oh yes. I got something."

TWENTY-ONE

THE PROPHET

DURRANT MADE HIS WAY TOWARD where Jacques Lambert was being held. Men were dismantling the zareba, packing crates into wagons and readying the various convoys for departure the next morning. Several large fires had been kindled, and wood and refuse were being piled onto them. A thick, acrid smoke hung in the air.

Durrant found that most men in the infirmary had been released to regiments that would return home to Regina. He searched among the wagons for Lambert. Though Lambert's self-inflicted wounds were relatively minor, Durrant had asked that the guard be maintained until he saw fit to release the man.

After some searching, Durrant found Lambert standing next to a large fire with two other men. Lambert smiled. "You have come to release me?" he asked.

"Not yet, Mr. Lambert. May we speak in private, please?" Lambert looked at the two men. They shrugged and walked off to find another place to warm themselves. "Mr. Lambert, I see that you are feeling better."

"Yes, my arms are healing. But my heart is very sick. I want only to return to my family now."

"May I examine your wounds?"

Lambert shrugged and rolled up the sleeves of his shirt. Durrant carefully considered the lacerations across each of his wrists. They were raw and red, and the dark sutures looked like angry knots. Durrant gently turned the man's arms over and looked at his hands. "Why did you try and take your own life, Mr. Lambert?"

Lambert rolled down his sleeves and shrugged. "I was beside myself with grief that Wake would live and my family was ruined."

"Why not remain alive so you could help them?"

Lambert looked down at the ground and shuffled his feet. "Grief knows no reason. I was ashamed of what had happened, and enraged with the monster Wake, and deep in sorrow for my failure to kill him. I was confused and in despair."

"Where were you on the third day of fighting?"

"I was ordered by Dumont to leave my rifle pit near the cemetery and cross the open ground above the Mission Ridge. I joined some men in a rifle pit in the woods a few hundred yards off and waited for the attack."

"Did you shoot at all?"

"I fired a few shots, just out of boredom. Most of the shooting came a few hundred yards farther on. It didn't last. The soldiers left once they decided that our position was too well fortified."

"Did you see Mr. Wake that day?"

"How could I?"

"You didn't see him with Middleton's mounted soldiers?"

"Had I known he was there . . ." Lambert's voice filled with remorse. "He was at La Jolie Prairie?"

"Mr. Lambert, do you own a pistol?"

"I don't. I am a farmer. What use would I have for one?" Lambert looked suddenly very tired. "Sergeant Wallace, had I killed this man I would gladly confess. Now all I want is to return to my farm and help my family."

"And so you shall."

WHEN DURRANT FINALLY made his way back to the quarter of the zareba where he was camped, Saul Armatage and Garnet Moberly were waiting for him with supper. He sat down on a crate, extending his leg and gratefully accepting a plate. He ate hungrily and when he was done took a proffered cup of coffee and sipped it. "Tell us about your investigations today, Durrant," said Saul.

Durrant filled them in on his myriad conversations while Saul and Garnet asked questions for nearly an hour.

"I was able to examine the hands of all of them. Block bears the scars of a burn, and was reluctant to remove his gloves when I asked. What I cannot tell is whether these burns are from a misfire or not. Lefèbvre has rough, scored hands, and Lambert has the hands of a farmer, pocked with scars and deep lines. Dire wears his gloves all of the time. His hands are stained and dark beneath. There is no way to eliminate any of them based on their hands. La Biche has had no recent injury to his hands."

"Saul," continued Durrant, "I would like you to accompany Mr. Lambert home to his farm tomorrow. I'll assign a couple of constables to join you. I'd like you to look in on his family, and his daughter. Would you do that?"

"Of course, Durrant."

"Garnet, if you can get free of the Surveyors, would you travel with Mr. La Biche to Regina?"

"You still consider him a suspect?"

"Not a serious one. But Crozier will not let me cut him loose until we have another suspect in custody."

"We're a long way from that, I fear," said Saul.

"Not as far as you might think, Doctor."

"Will you let us in on your thinking?"

"It's not entirely clear to me yet because there is something missing. We have two conspiracies afoot: one to free Riel, and the other to kill him before he goes to trial. We can be reasonably certain that Mr. Wake was a member of this second conspiracy, the so-called Regina Group. I believe that Mr. Block is among its leaders, as is our very own Sub-Inspector Dickenson. We can feel confident that Father Lefèbvre is a leading member of the group wishing to free Riel. La Biche was sent by the good father to watch Wake and the others from inside the zareba. The priest insists that La Biche was told not to kill Wake or the others, only to sound the alarm if any of them threatened Riel should he be captured."

"This is a tangle of motivations, Durrant," said Saul.

"Maybe so," Garnet said, "but really what we have here are some men motivated by the desire to protect Riel and others who want to kill him. Why would Stanley Block, or Dickenson, be involved in Wake's murder if he was part of their little cabal?"

"The simplest of motivations," said Durrant. "Wake posed some kind of threat. Here is a man who was drawing far too much attention—looting, burning, even raping a girl. Sooner or later, even with Dickenson's protection, he would run afoul of the law, and then the entire conspiracy might be revealed. If Stanley Block killed him, or had someone do the deed for him, then we might assume the motivation was to silence a loose cannon."

"Mr. Lambert's motivation was to protect the honour of his family," Garnet joined in.

"Unless Mr. Lambert is a particularly skilled liar, I don't believe that he could have killed Wake. I have come to believe that the first attempt on Wake's life came on the eleventh of May at La Jolie Prairie. In the heat of an exchange of fire between Dumont's forces and Middleton's, Wake was shot in the arm. Doctor, you told me that the projectile was from a pistol and not one of the melted-down cartridges that the Métis had begun to fire by that time. I believe the shot didn't come from the Métis line at all, but from behind our own skirmish line. There was simply no way even the most random of shots could find its way through the tangle of trees. There were no other marks on the aspens there to indicate that a volley had so much as reached those woods."

"Where does this leave us?"

"Well, there is still one more person whose motive we haven't determined."

"Jasper Dire," said Garnet.

"Dire is a member of Colonel Boulton's mounted infantry, who were alongside General Middleton's men that day. He was at La Jolie Prairie, and he could have easily directed a shot from his Webley at Mr. Wake."

"But why?" asked Saul. "Dire appears to have no motive."

"True, Doctor, none that we can tell, but let me say that he is a crack shot. He has already admitted to having remained behind the charge on the afternoon of the twelfth. This is how he came to apprehend La Biche."

"How will you determine if he is a member of the first or the second conspiracy?"

"There are four things that must be done," Durrant replied. "Garnet, in accompanying La Biche to Regina to await trial, will serve as our eyes and ears in the city and uncover what he can about the Regina Group and the conspiracy to free Riel.

"Saul, you will seek out what information you can from the La Biche farm and report back to me. I will ride ahead of Middleton and the other regiments for Fort Pitt. Along the way, I may have a chance to learn more about which side Jasper Dire is on. Finally, I will try to catch up with Sub-Inspector Dickenson and recover the missing Colt."

"What of Iron Crow?" asked Saul.

"I shall pass through his camp in the morning and parley once more with him."

"It's to bed, then," said Saul. "Reveille will come far too early, I fear."

"You two should get your rest, but I have one more call to make before I sleep."

"What night stalking are you up to now, Durrant?"

"I have to go to the source if I hope to understand these competing conspiracies." And with that Durrant slipped off into the darkness, only the silver handle on his cane reflecting the light of the fire.

DURRANT CROSSED THE zareba in silence. The moon had emerged from behind a bank of clouds and cast a pale light. He thought about Charlene, and not for the first time that day. It had been nearly a month since he had left Calgary, and he was concerned about her. While the telegraph lines between Batoche and the outside world had been restored, they were restricted for official military use. Durrant could not justify a wire sent inquiring after her safety and hoped that if her husband should appear she would have the good sense to seek the safety of the NWMP barracks.

Durrant realized that he could use her help right now. She had a sharp mind and had proven useful—even in the guise of a mute—while they had been together in Holt City the year before.

There was more than one person in Calgary who caused Durrant to worry. Durrant hoped he might still find Bud Ensley locked up there, so that he could make some persuasive inquires about the man's errant brother.

Durrant found his way to where the prisoners were being kept. Half a dozen men in uniform stood around a fire, Winchesters cradled in their arms, pistols at their sides. Durrant could see another half-dozen spaced around the perimeter of a circle of wagons. He cleared his throat as he approached, his silver cane flashing in the light. "Who's there?" a man with a corporal's chevrons called out.

"Sergeant Durrant Wallace."

"Stand pat!" The corporal approached Durrant. "Let me see your stripes."

"I don't wear the serge. I'm Durrant Wallace. I am in charge of the investigation into the murder of Reuben Wake. I report to Sam Steele and am under orders from Assistant Commissioner Crozier."

"Do you have identification, Sergeant?"

"I have my warrant card. I'm here to talk with the prisoner."

"I'll need your sidearm, Sergeant." Durrant produced the Enfield and then dug the British Bulldog out of his pocket and handed it to the corporal. He held on to the cane. "Very well," said the corporal. "Given the lateness of the hour, you can have thirty minutes. No more."

Durrant nodded and the two of them approached the tent at the centre of the circle, close to the fire. The corporal announced himself at the entrance. "You have a visitor, come to ask you questions. Sergeant Durrant Wallace of the North West Mounted Police." Durrant stood to the side as the corporal opened the flap.

Durrant looked into the darkness. "Do you have a lamp?" he asked the corporal. The Mounted Policeman returned and lit the lamp; its light cast a pall over the tent. Durrant could see the man sitting on the side of a narrow cot. "Good evening, Mr. Riel. I have come to ask you a few questions, sir."

The tent flap closed behind him.

PART TWO

THE SUN RIVER

TWENTY-TWO

ON TO FORT PITT

MAY 18, 1885. BATOCHE.

Durrant slept little through the night. He watched the sparks from the fire drift into the dark sky and merge with the veil of stars that stretched across the firmament. He couldn't stop thinking about the words of Louis Riel—the traitor, the prophet. After two hours of conversation, Riel had said, "Life, without the dignity of an intelligent being, is not worth having."

Durrant was already awake and had his things packed and coffee made when reveille sounded at five o'clock. Garnet Moberly and Saul Armatage accepted the brew. "I shall miss Mr. Jimmy's fare," mumbled Saul.

The companions organized their kits, and Garnet went to the stables to secure their mounts. Durrant was stowing his armament when Saul approached him. "This business seems to suit you, Durrant. You seem like a new man."

Durrant looked him straight in the eye. "I won't lie, Saul. You know me too well. As you put it, there is still much to *overcome*. The distraction of these past days in Batoche has helped."

Saul noted that Durrant had his prized locket in his hand. He said, "Just so long as you know that your friends have got your back, Durrant. And I don't just mean in a tight pinch."

"I understand." Durrant carefully slipped the locket into his waistcoat.

"You still carry that thing everywhere?"

"Always will." At that moment, however, Durrant's mind wasn't on the image frozen against the march of time in the tintype in the locket, but on another woman beyond his reach. "Wire me at Fort Pitt with your findings at the La Biche farm. Take care. Don't let the two constables I've assigned you to wander too far."

Garnet appeared with their horses. They hung their bedrolls and travel bags on their mounts and then formed a sort of conference. "Garnet will wire me as soon as he reaches Regina," said Durrant. "We can confer as to when the trial will be set for Mr. La Biche. I don't expect we have much time for our various investigations—maybe five or six weeks—and there is a lot of country to cover. We must be cautious. We can't know for certain who is a part of which conspiracy, and what other shadow hangs over this business. I fear that what we are dealing with reaches far beyond these North West Territories and pulls at the very fabric of the nation."

"You're starting to sound like Garnet." Saul was strapping his medical bag onto the back of his saddle.

"Well, then, maybe our departure is just in time," snapped Durrant, but he didn't mean it. The three men shook hands. Durrant put his left leg in the stirrup and swung up onto his mount. He looked down at his two friends. "We'll see you in Regina."

"For Victoria, Queen victorious!" Garnet raised a hand in the air and saluted Durrant.

Saul and Garnet waved as Durrant rode out of the zareba ahead of the chaos of the marching field force. It would be five weeks before the three men would see one another again, and during that interlude Durrant Wallace's life would change irrevocably.

DURRANT REACHED THE far side of the Saskatchewan River and rode up out of the breaks. The aspens were starting to set fine green buds like delicate filigree. As the sun rose behind him, the hills along the Saskatchewan looked like they had been dusted with a light green powder. Durrant pushed his horse forward and rode the short distance to where the Dakota Sioux had their encampment. There were few fires burning, and the entire camp had the feel of bereavement hanging over it. It took only a moment for Durrant to determine that something was dreadfully amiss.

He dismounted and led his horse to the tipi of Iron Crow. He was stopped when the man's brother-in-law stepped out. The eastern sky was just flushing with dawn, and in that half-light Stands-his-Ground's face appeared drawn and old. "You have come too late, Red Coat. Iron Crow is dead."

Durrant's face fell, and he said in his Lakota dialect, "I am sorry."

"Men came and stole the food you gave to us. They said it wasn't yours to give. They said they were taking it back."

Durrant felt a white-hot anger rise in him. He turned away so the man would not see his rage. A moment of silence hung between them. "When was this?"

"It was two days ago. A Red Coat and other men."

"Did the Red Coat say his name?"

"No. He and some others just came with their guns and pointed them at us, at Iron Crow, and told us to give the food back."

"Did you notice if he had stripes on his uniform?"

"No stripes. He wore a braid on his shoulder." The Sioux man pointed to his own shoulder to indicate where the insignia was on the Mounted Policeman's epaulette.

"He was an officer," said Durrant. "A sub-inspector."

DURRANT WALLACE HAD tracked men across frozen ground and in complete darkness, but this trail had been used by hundreds of horses over the last two weeks. He could not determine if Sub-Inspector Dickenson and his gang of thugs had travelled this way. All he could do was hope. It would take him four or five days of hard riding to reach Fort Pitt. His deepest desire was to catch up with Dickenson before he could be reassigned to a company that was pursuing the Cree north toward Frenchman's Butte. It seemed equally likely that after pilfering the Sioux's supplies Dickenson had ridden south along the Saskatchewan and doubled back toward Regina. Durrant would wire Grant Moberly and Tommy Provost. It was a long ride, and the nights were cold. One evening he knocked on the door of a farmhouse and was offered a hot meal and a bed by a Métis family. The other nights he slept rough, with his blankets clutched about him, his pistols close by, and a warming fire burning brightly.

He had time to think. Again and again Durrant considered his parley with Riel. While Durrant was convinced that the man was no prophet, this conclusion was reached because of Durrant's predilections, not Riel's. For Durrant, there was no way to right the hourglass; its sands had slipped away. There was nothing Riel or anybody else could say to convince Durrant that even a benevolent God could exist. The loss of his wife and child twelve years earlier had put an end to that question. Yet, in speaking with Riel, he understood why people believed him to be a modern messiah.

That there were those who feared Riel's words as much as his actions came as no surprise to Durrant. The motivation of those who conspired to kill Riel rather than allow him the pulpit of his legal defence was plain to see. Riel had revealed to Durrant that there had been some business around duelling conspiracies even before he had left Montana. He confided that some trouble had occurred in Sun River and that Dumont and the others had shielded him from it. When Durrant questioned him further, the man had simply said, "Look to Sun River for your answer."

On Durrant's fourth day, the trail descended toward Fort Pitt. The weather was warmer and there were leaves on the willows and alders. He let up on his horse, which he had pushed too hard these last days trying to catch up with Dickenson and his mob. Durrant's first priority was the retrieval of the murder weapon, but he admitted to himself that the chance of finding it was slim now.

It was early evening on May 22 when he saw the fort on the bank of the Saskatchewan River. He sat his horse just below the crest of a broad hillside. He had the sun in his face and knew that only a careful observer might skylight him. There was more to be concerned about than Dickenson's mob of ruffians. On April 14, a skirmish between Big Bear's two hundred-strong Cree and the handful of poorly armed Mounted Police in the fort had left one Red Coat dead, another wounded, and a third man prisoner. The fort's commander had negotiated a truce, but it meant that he and his colleagues had to abandon civilians to Big Bear to be held as hostages while they skulked across the Saskatchewan Territory and made haste for Fort Battleford. It was not a high point for the North West Mounted Police.

Fort Pitt was now back in Dominion control, but there was little left. The Cree had burned it to the ground. Durrant could see that there were tents arranged around the charred buildings. The Union Jack flew high above the stockade's blackened walls.

Durrant rode down the hill and was soon stopped by a picket of Dominion soldiers. They let him pass when he identified himself as a member of the North West Mounted Police. He boarded his horse in the makeshift stable. A company of men from the Alberta Field Force had arrived just two days before him, but already they were at work restoring the fort to a working operation, rebuilding the palisade and stringing telegraph wire where it had been burned in the fire. He crossed what was once the parade ground to where he had been told he might find the sergeant-at-arms, and inquired after Commander Steele; he had not yet arrived. Then he asked after his quarry.

"Dickenson?" The man consulted his records. "Well, Commander Dickens fled the fort a fortnight ago—"

"Not Dickens, Dickenson."

"Let me see . . ."

Durrant knew that Dickenson had doubled back and was already on his way to Regina, where he would be waiting when Riel arrived.

DURRANT SLEPT THAT night rolled in his blankets near the stable. He was woken by a tap on his shoulder. He sat up abruptly, his hand falling to the British Bulldog. He heard a gasp in the darkness, and looked into the face of a boy not more than fourteen. "Sir, you are to come with me," the boy croaked.

"What is it?"

"There is a wire from Fort Calgary."

Durrant pulled on his prosthetic and noted the boy watching him. "Show me the way, lad."

They walked to a buckboard wagon serving as the fort's impromptu telegraph station. There was a tarp over it, and an oil lamp provided illumination. Durrant was handed the wire.

> Durrant. He is looking for me. I am in hiding. Calgary cannot conceal me. Will remain as long as able. Charlie.

Durrant lowered himself on a crate of canned fruit. Suddenly, the boy snapped to attention. Durrant, shaken from the contents of the wire, followed his gaze, then stood and saluted. "Superintendant Steele."

"Sergeant Wallace. It's very good to see you, son."

"I was told that you were hunting the Cree, sir."

"I arrived an hour ago. We're here to resupply and then will track Big Bear north once more. What's the news, Durrant?" Steele pointed to the wire clutched tightly in Durrant's hand.

Durrant looked down at the wire. "Nothing, sir, a personal matter from Fort Calgary. I was just making preparations to double back for Regina. It seems the man I am hunting has given me the slip."

"Come, Sergeant, let's see if there is a coffeepot in the cook tent. I've known you long enough to know when you are lying to me."

"BIG BEAR IS going north. Strange is a good commander, but slow, and cautious. Later today I will lead the Scouts toward Frenchman's Butte, where the Cree are believed to be holed up with their prisoners," said Steele.

"Would you like for me to accompany you, sir?"

"No, Sergeant, but thank you. I have no doubt you'd prove your worth and then some, but Crozier has given you a far more important task."

"Yes, sir."

"You disagree?"

"No, not insofar as proving the Métis man La Biche's innocence goes. I believe there are other lives at stake, too. Wake was devilish in nature. I've never seen a situation where so many were eager to kill a man, and for good reason." Durrant quickly filled Steele in on his investigation and his conversation with Riel.

"It's a harsh business. Who do you suspect?"

"There were many with powerful motivation and great passion to see the man six feet in the ground."

"It may be that these passions are blinding you, Sergeant. Sometimes it's those who display little passion for the crime that we must give consideration to. Now, about this wire."

"It's nothing."

"Let me read it, Durrant."

The sergeant reluctantly handed the wire over to Steele.

"You wire Dewalt at Fort Calgary and ask that he look in on the lady, and tell him that these are my orders," Steele instructed.

"I will."

"I doubt that will do it. After the business in Holt City last year, and what with Charlene taking up residence in Calgary, I am concerned for her safety, as I know you must be."

"She fled this man two years ago," said Durrant. "She took up her station as a mute stableboy to avoid detection. Though we've never spoken of his monstrosities, we didn't need to."

"If he has tracked her to Fort Calgary, then he *will* find her there, Durrant. It's too small a town for her to remain secreted away for long."

"Could Dewalt find and arrest him?"

"The magistrate would require a charge, and that would be difficult to fabricate. Locating the man would put Charlene at risk."

"I could send a wire and ask that she take the train to Regina to be safe with Garnet."

"No doubt Mr. Moberly would keep her safe. Durrant, if you don't mind me saying, it seems that this is your job."

"My job is to find the man who killed Reuben Wake and determine to what extent a threat still exists. That is my duty."

Steele silenced him with a hand. He drank the rest of his coffee. "You tell me that Riel says there is some secret hidden in Sun River. The trial of Terrance La Biche will not be for some time. The magistrate will be preoccupied with the appointment of a prosecutor for Riel, and the selection of a jury. I have it on some authority that the Riel trial is still at least six weeks away. You have time to ride south for Maple Creek on the CPR main line and catch a train for Calgary. Find Charlene. When she is safe, make the journey to the Sun River country and learn what you can about Riel's time there, and what secrets lay buried in that earth."

"What of Dickenson?"

"I will wire ahead to our headquarters in Regina. I know men that we can trust and can work with. I will assign them the task of keeping Riel safe."

Durrant said, "I will ask Mr. Moberly to keep watch for a traitor to the force. No doubt Garnet has spied for some king during his expansive career."

TWENTY-THREE

DESPERATE MEASURES

IT TOOK HIM SEVEN LONG days to ride from Fort Pitt to the siding of Maple Creek on the Canadian Pacific main line, and when he arrived, his horse was suffering and so was Durrant Wallace. His prosthetic had nearly rubbed off the protective bandage. The night before, he had cut out the stitches that Saul Armatage had sewn in a week and a half previous. Now his leg was raw, and a suspicious-looking fluid the colour of milk had started to ooze from his stump. Doctor Armatage would not be happy with him.

He boarded the horse and took his most important gear—the Winchester, his bedroll, and his personal kit that included the prized locket—and made his way to the station, where he inquired about westbound trains. One was to arrive at midnight.

He sat on the platform and waited. The prairie sky turned rose, then magenta, and finally faded to black. The stars came out, and he regarded them with suspicion. These were the same stars that looked down on Charlene, but there was no kindness in them: they reminded him of the vast distance between them still.

On time, the whistle of the train sounded. He was the only passenger to board, and he handed the pullman porter his ticket and made his way down the aisle to a compartment with an empty window seat in it. Durrant fell asleep somewhere on the prairie and four hours later awoke to the sound of the train approaching Calgary. What if he was too late? Charlene was a resourceful woman, and she knew that even if Sub-Inspector Dewalt disliked Durrant, she could turn to the NWMP for protection. Before the train had fully stopped, he left his compartment and lurched to the door. As the brakes billowed, he disembarked and quickly made his way down the broad wooden platform to the station's main building, where he hailed a cab. As the horse and buggy pulled up, the driver regarded Durrant's armament.

"I'm with the North West Mounted Police," he explained, giving him the address of Charlene's employer and bidding him to make haste. The driver cracked his reins, and the single quarter horse set off at a trot, the wheels of the buggy spinning on the muddy streets. It took ten minutes to navigate through the city, and during that ride Durrant could not but help recall the time twelve years previous when he had raced through the streets of Toronto to find Mary and their child locked in a battle with death. Death had won.

When finally they pulled up in front of the house, Durrant told the driver to wait for him. He hurried up the walk and knocked on the door.

A moment passed, and then he heard the lock on the front door open and Derek Lloyd was standing there in his sleeping attire. "Durrant—"

"Derek, is she here?"

"No . . . she . . . You had better step in."

Durrant looked back at his cab. The man seemed to have fallen asleep. Lloyd opened the door and Durrant stepped inside. He became aware that he must smell like the inside of a barn. It had been almost a month since he'd left Fort Calgary, and in that time he hadn't had more than a washbasin to clean up with, and in freezing temperatures at that.

"Would you like breakfast, Durrant?"

"Derek, I don't wish to be rude—"

"Sit and have something and I'll tell you what has transpired."

"Is Charlene . . . is she okay?"

"I assume so."

"You assume?"

They reached the kitchen. "Sit down, Durrant. Drink this coffee, and listen. About two weeks ago, Charlene had the children out in the afternoon, and when she came home she looked ghostly white.

She said that she saw him down along Stephen Avenue. At least, she thought she did—"

"Did *he* see *her*?"

"She didn't think so. But she got scared. She mostly stayed about the house after that. A few days later, we got this." Lloyd took a sheet of paper out of an envelope on the sideboard. He handed it to Durrant.

> I know where you live. I been watching you. You'll be coming home soon.

Durrant stood up. His twisted right hand was white from the exertion of pushing hard on his cane. "Blue Jesus," he exclaimed too loudly.

"She left that night. She packed a small bag and left. She wouldn't tell me where she was going."

"What did she take?"

"Nothing much, Durrant. Very little of her clothing."

"Let me see."

They went to the back of the house where the servants' quarters were, and Durrant stepped into Charlene's room. He could smell her soap and the detergent she used to launder her clothes. The room was simple, with a small bed, a table and chair, and a tiny stove. In the corner was a plain armoire with a mirror. Durrant opened the doors and moved a few dresses aside. He looked on the floor of the closet. What he was searching for was not present. He walked back past Derek Lloyd.

"Where are you going, Durrant?"

"I can't tell you, Derek."

"Is she safe?"

"I don't know." Durrant stopped by the door. "Derek," he said in a low voice. "Do you have a firearm?"

"Well, yes, I have an old Remington."

"Get it out. Keep it handy. If he comes to the house, shoot him between his eyes."

DURRANT WOKE THE cabbie and they set off at a hard trot. The city was coming alive and there were other carriages and horse traffic to contend with, so it took them longer than expected to cross the Bow River and reach Fort Calgary. The new buildings of the fort had been completed over the course of the last year, and the sprawling complex was much grander than the palisade-bordered buildings Durrant had arrived at more than two years before. Now the fort resembled a modern Hudson's Bay Company establishment. There was no defensive structure, just a neat quadrangle comprising barracks and housing for officers and non-commissioned men, a double stable and the quartermaster's store. Durrant told the driver where at the Fort he wanted to go and when they arrived paid him his fare.

Durrant stood in front of the stable. The pine boards had matured and no longer wept sap. He walked with his cane to the broad double doors, unlatched the main entrance, and let the day's first light fall across the dark space.

He stepped inside, his cane tapping on the wooden floorboards. He walked the long aisle of stalls that housed the fort's quarter horses, making for the tack room. He was breathing hard, and his heart beat in his throat.

"Charlene?" he said slowing as he approached the room. "Charlie? It's Durrant."

He heard nothing. He drew his Enfield and held it at his side. "It's Durrant," he said again, and stepped into the tack room. The smell of leather and brass polish hit him in the nose, and he forced his eyes to adjust to the gloom.

He heard the hammer of a shotgun click. In the darkness he saw it: under a blanket in the corner was the shape of a person.

"It's Durrant," he repeated.

The figure moved. "It's about time." Charlene Louise Mason pulled herself out from beneath the blanket. She held the familiar shotgun in her hands, the spoils of a previous conflict won on the shore of Tom Wilson's Lake Louise.

"Are you all right?" asked Durrant.

"Of course I'm all right. Haven't you eyes to see?" She was standing now, placing the shotgun against the wall. She was dressed as she was when he had first met her: like a stableboy. Her long hair was tucked up under a cap, and she wore men's trousers, shirt, and waistcoat. But there was no mistaking her eyes, blue as mountain waters.

"I was worried—"

She stepped forward and planted a kiss on his grizzled cheek.

There was a sound behind them. Durrant whirled, his pistol coming up in a sudden arc. The barrel of it came to the forehead of a man standing there. He lowered the gun.

"Hello, Durrant," said the square-shouldered man.

"Hello, Paddy."

"Met my new stable hand?"

"Yes, we've been introduced."

"This one talks. Sometimes too bloody much."

Durrant looked back at Charlene. "Let's get you ready to travel."

"Where are we going?" Her eyes lit up.

"Montana."

"I LET HIM go. There was nothing I could hold him on." Sub-Inspector Raymond Dewalt was sitting behind his desk.

"I had him on charges of horse stealing," protested Durrant.

"There wasn't any evidence. None of the witnesses would come forward. Not without—"

"Without what?"

"Sergeant, none of the men who had bought horses from Jeb Ensley would testify to that without the assurance that the Ensley brothers wouldn't come looking for them."

"And you couldn't assure them that the law in Fort Calgary would protect them?" Dewalt just stared at him. "How long ago?"

"It's been three weeks or so, I suppose."

"Hell, I hadn't even reached Batoche!"

"Mind yourself, Sergeant. You might be the favourite of Superintendant Steele, but you're under my command at Fort Calgary."

The two men glared at one another for a moment before Dewalt broke the uncomfortable silence. "And what is your next assignment?"

"You mean, in addition to recapturing Jeb Ensley?" asked Durrant as he turned and left the room.

TWENTY-FOUR

THE MEDICINE LINE

MAY 31, 1885. THE MACLEOD TRAIL.

They rode the Macleod Trail for ten days. On the fourth night they reached the trail's namesake: Fort Macleod. Upon departing Calgary, Charlene had travelled under the guise of stableboy and aide-de-camp, but she happily abandoned the masquerade when they reached the fort and it was announced there would be a dance. Durrant watched as she spun around the compound with the young constables, the flames from a giant bonfire reflecting the light in her eyes. Durrant felt a stab of envy that he could not join in the fun. And then he felt something most peculiar: jealousy.

In the morning they agreed that she could abandon the disguise for good, given that everybody in the town knew who she was after the long night of merrymaking. They rode out on the prairie once more and made for the Medicine Line. At noon on the sixth day they crossed the demarcation that indicated the border. Charlene commented on the splendour of the country: the blue line of mountains to the west, and the deep valleys where the trail plunged down and forded creeks and rivers and rose up out of the hollows and crested broad plateaus.

After ten days of riding Macleod Trail, Fort Benton appeared in the distance. Traffic on the road had increased as teams travelled north with the opening of cattle season. The broad Missouri River lay between high banks of prairie. Durrant knew that the fort at Benton had been abandoned now for some time. It had once been the pivotal trading post of the American Fur Company, and later a military outpost, but was now crumbling into ruin. Even the squatters had abandoned it to the rats. The town that surrounded it was thriving, though, and as Charlene and Durrant rode across the bridge and onto Main Street, Durrant began to scan the faces of the men on the wooden walkways and on every buckboard that passed.

They had agreed to find a hotel for the night and Durrant pressed the horses toward the far end of town where he had been told there was a reputable establishment called The Grand Union that had been built three years before. They tied their horses and stepped inside. Durrant crossed the lobby to the clerk and inquired about a room. "Two beds," said Durrant.

DURRANT WALKED ALONG the streets of Fort Benton and stopped into several saloons to ask his questions. Nobody knew where Jeb Ensley was. In the third establishment he entered, he decided on a new tack. He stepped to the bar, rested his arm on the polished wood runner, and regarded the room. Half a dozen tables were filled with men drinking and playing cards. The air was thick with smoke.

He turned to the bartender. "My name is Durrant Wallace. I'm looking for Jeb Ensley. He been around lately?"

The bartender was cleaning a glass. "What do you want him for?"

"Horses."

The bartender looked him up and down. "You don't look like no horse buyer. You look like the law."

"Is Jeb in town or not?"

"What's in it for me?"

"Long life and continued prosperity."

The bartender stopped cleaning the glass and shook his head. "Jeb hasn't been in these parts for a month. His little brother got himself in some trouble north of the line, and Jeb has cut town. He's gone farther west, into the Awahee country in Oregon. He's trading up and down through the Kootenay. That's all I know."

"What about his brother? I heard he cut loose in Fort Calgary."

"If he did, he didn't come back here."

"Any of his known associates still in this neck of the woods?"

"Hell, I'd be surprised if any of them was still alive."

"That good bunch of fellas? Who would want to cause them trouble?"

CHARLENE WAS SLEEPING when Durrant returned. She sat up when he came into the room. "Did you find what you were looking for?" He didn't light the lamp. He removed the belt that held the Enfield pistol and hung it over the post of the bed. He took the British Bulldog and laid it on the table next him and sat down, breathing a heavy sigh.

"Durrant, what is it?"

"Revenge is a curious motivation."

"Did you find the man?"

"No. He spooked. Remember I told you I arrested his little brother right before this business with Riel?"

"Yes, of course."

"Word got down here pretty quick. Must have come across the wire. Modern technology." Durrant shook his head. "A lawman can't keep ahead of the renegades. Anyway, I feel as if I'm chasing a ghost."

"Durrant, we're here to look into the business at Sun River, aren't we?"

"Yes, of course. That's my duty—"

"But you thought maybe you might find what you were really looking for here in Fort Benton?"

"Yes."

"And it's revenge you're seeking?"

"Not much of a lawman, I suppose."

"You're a *man* first, Durrant."

"I am a lawman above all else, Charlene. I've seen what revenge does to a man. It will get him hanged from the neck. Revenge is the most basic of motivations for murder." He slipped off his boots and undressed in the dark.

"You're not going to kill anybody," said Charlene.

"I don't know that."

"I know you. When the time comes, when you find the men who shot you, you'll remember that you are a North West Mounted Policeman."

SUN RIVER WAS a long day's ride from Fort Benton. The earth began to rise and fall as they travelled west toward the mountains. They rode the track up out of the Missouri River and at Great Falls started along the trail into the Sun River country.

"So this is where Louis Riel was hiding all those years?"

"Not so much hiding as just living. He was a US citizen, taught school, was married and had children."

"Remind me, what exactly are you looking for?"

To the west, the Rocky Mountains drove up like torn steel, their spiny backs rising and falling in a blue line that stretched unbroken as far as either of them could see. "I don't know," Durrant admitted. "Riel told me there were secrets buried down here. I don't know if he was being literal or just aggrandizing once again. I guess we'll just have to do what any lawman would: ask a lot of questions."

"I thought that lawmen in this territory rode in guns blazing."

"You've been reading penny paperbacks again."

"Life of a stableboy."

As the sun was sinking behind the western wall of serrated rock, the town of Sun River came into view. "Not much to show for itself," said Charlene.

"I see a church steeple, and that's a good sign. We'll start there and ask about our northern prophet." They rode the flat expanse of country that bordered the broad Sun River, its banks filled to near overflowing with spring's meltwater. "It's good country. I can see why Riel made this home." They reached the church and gratefully dismounted. Looping their reins over the hitching post, they stood and regarded the tiny village and the vast country around them.

Durrant watched cattle on the ridge above the river they had just traversed disperse as an oncoming rider appeared. He watched the horseman drop into the willows along the river. A voice interrupted him.

"Evening."

Durrant turned to see a man in black robes on the steps of the church. "Good evening," said Durrant.

"Help you?"

"I hope so. We're looking for a place to bed down for the night. My name is Durrant Wallace. I'm with the North West Mounted Police. This is my . . . friend, Charlene Mason."

"A little out of your jurisdiction," said the priest.

Durrant noted that the man was a Jesuit. "Yes, Father, I am. I'm here to ask about Louis Riel."

"Ah . . ." said the priest. "I've heard about the business up in the Saskatchewan Territory. I told Riel he should just stay put, let the Indians sort out their own problems, but he said he had a calling."

"You were here when the men came to find him?"

"Yes, of course."

"Were there many who saw what went on?"

"Not so many. There are only about thirty souls who live in town. We serve the farms and ranches for fifty miles." The priest opened the door of the church, and he, Durrant, and Charlene stepped inside. The room was dark and warm. A woodstove rumbled in the corner. The priest walked to the front of the church.

"Father, did Riel attend your church?"

"Yes, he did."

"Was he a regular?"

"He was here every Sunday."

"And what did he do in Sun River?"

The priest had taken up a post at the front of the church before the altar. Durrant sat down in the front pew. Charlie sat down beside him.

"He taught school. He was a very well-educated man. He was very good with both the students and the parents."

"Did people know about his . . . past?"

"We did. Some of it. I imagine there are things in Riel's past that nobody knows for certain, but we knew enough."

"You knew that in 1874 Riel incited a revolution at Fort Garry, in what is now Manitoba, and a man, a Protestant named Thomas Scott, was murdered?"

"We knew this."

"You're a Jesuit."

"It's not about who follows which church, Mr. Wallace. It's about faith in Jesus Christ."

"Well, that may be so, Father, but for Mr. Scott it had everything to do with being a Protestant. There were many reasons why, in 1874, the Métis rose up, just as there are many reasons for the current resistance, now coming to an end in the North West Territories of the Dominion. One of them was the age-old quarrel between the interpretations of God's word that has formed the rift between Catholics and Protestants."

"Am I to take it you are not a God-fearing man?"

"I have seen too much of this world to fear anything but the frailty of the human spirit."

The church was quiet. Durrant could feel Charlene's eyes on him. The priest shifted. Durrant broke the silence. "I'm sorry, Father. We're here on urgent business. Riel's second rebellion is over. Many have been killed. I am investigating the death of one man who was murdered in our own compound. This man was despised by many, and it seems they were all converging on him to cause him harm. I am charged with bringing his killer to justice."

"What does that have to do with us?" The priest gestured as if his congregation was before him.

"I have it on good authority that the murdered man was in Sun River this past July. He came here under the pretext of being friend to Riel and the Métis. He travelled as part of the small company of men with Gabriel Dumont to try and entice Riel to return to Canada. His intent was not to help aid Riel's return, but to prevent it. He failed, and I don't know why. We hoped that by coming here we might learn what it was that happened, and how this may have led to his eventual murder."

"I remember the party of travellers, and I remember Dumont." The priest closed his eyes. "There were four men that came into town who approached Riel. Two men tended to the horses and camped up on the ridge."

"Two men?"

"Yes, there were two." The priest's eyes were still pressed shut.

"Did these men not come into town?"

"I don't believe so. As I recall, Dumont was very careful about this. He spent several days here to convince Riel that the time was right for his return."

"Father, I wonder if I might ask a favour of you. I wonder if you might recommend a place we can board ourselves tonight."

"Sun River doesn't have a hotel."

"Might we call on the grace of your church for shelter?"

"I suppose. Are you man and wife?"

"No, but I am this young woman's guardian," said Durrant. "I am charged with her safety." The priest nodded his agreement. Durrant continued, "In the morning, would you kindly take us to where these men were camped?"

TWENTY-FIVE
UNEARTHED REVELATIONS

JUNE 11, 1885. SUN RIVER, MONTANA.

Durrant lay awake, listening to the wind beat against the wooden walls of the church. Charlene was stretched out on the floor next to the stove, wrapped in a blanket. Several times he stoked the fire and Charlene opened her glacial-blue eyes and regarded him. In the early hours the wind died and Durrant began to drift toward sleep, but something jarred him awake. The fire in the stove was nearly out and the room was cool. Everything was dead still. Durrant shrugged off his blanket and struggled with his prosthetic. He stood up and looked to see that Charlene remained asleep. As carefully as his game leg would allow, he moved away from the stove and toward the centre aisle of the church. Using the silver-handled cane for support, he slowly went down the aisle.

He heard a clicking and the sound of wood creaking. Someone was opening the main door to the church. Durrant raised the Enfield. He realized he was holding his breath, and let it out. He took two more steps, stopped, and listened. The sound came again, louder this time and immediately in front of him. He moved to the left side of the double door and extended the Enfield before him. The door opened an inch and Durrant thumbed back the hammer on his pistol.

The moment was frozen. He aimed at what he imagined would be an intruder's head, his heart thumping in his chest, his hand sweating.

The door closed with a thud. The noise caused Durrant to step back, and he bumped the pew behind him; it made a scraping sound on the wooden floor.

"Durrant?" called Charlene.

"Quiet!" he whispered. He watched her rise silently and pick up the Remington shotgun from the floor next to her. He held up his right hand, the cane dangling awkwardly from his deformed fingers, and motioned for her to remain still, but she did not. She came up behind him, the shotgun pointed at the floor.

He turned to look at her and realized that she was not afraid. "There's someone outside the door." He advanced on the entrance and with his cane flipped the fastener and threw open the door. A gust of air entered the church and extinguished their only light. Pistol held at the ready, Durrant stepped out onto the top step, Charlene behind him. He scanned the area. The half moon resting on the western horizon provided enough light to see the country around them. Durrant heard horses running. He raised the pistol and saw, on the road a hundred yards away, two riders galloping away toward Fort Benton. He aimed the Enfield but knew at that distance, and with the riders' speed, he had no hope of finding a mark. And what if he did? Though it appeared the riders had come from behind the church, there was no way to tell. He lowered his pistol and looked at Charlene.

"Two men, both with broad-brimmed hats, dark horses," she said.

"Maybe they came to say confession."

"I'm all ears."

They stepped back into the church and together pushed a pew in front of the door. "That ought to do it. The father will be flummoxed to get inside come the morning, mind you."

"If he brings a coffee pot we might allow him in."

Durrant went back to their sleeping area, got a piece of cordwood, and opened the stove. Charlene rearranged their blankets, and Durrant imagined that she did it in a way that brought them closer together. He was about to put the wood in the stove when he was stopped in his tracks.

There would be no sleep that night: on top of the stove was a square of newspaper torn from the masthead of the *Calgary Daily Herald*. It was dated the day that Durrant and Charlene had left the city on their ride south. On it was a note scrawled in ink.

When you go to the ridge in the morning, bring the gravedigger.

THEY SEARCHED THE church and found the back door; Durrant cursed out loud at his own foolishness. "So while we were watching the front, someone snuck in and left this right under our noses."

Charlene was composed. She found an oil lamp and lit it. They sat by the stove with their backs to the wall. Durrant held his gun. "If they wanted to hurt us, why not just do it here?"

Durrant looked around. "It's a church."

"I think there have been more than a few murders in a church, have there not?"

Durrant looked at the note. "Let's go and find out."

THE PRIEST WAS shocked. "Who in the community knew we were here?" asked Durrant.

"I don't know. Maybe a few—"

"Who did you tell?"

"I told no one."

Durrant was silent a moment. Then he said, "There was a rider on the road—behind us, maybe a mile or two back." Charlene looked at him. "I think he might have followed us from Fort Benton. Maybe from before that. The *Calgary Daily Herald* suggests maybe *long* before that."

"What do you want to do, Sergeant?" the priest asked.

"Take us to the ridge where Reuben Wake was camped."

IT WAS A fine morning. It warmed quickly as the sun rose. Durrant and Charlene ate a meal the priest provided and then saddled their horses and rode north, out of town. When they were alone, Charlene asked, "Are you certain of this?"

"Yes," Durrant said quickly. "But if you wish to stay behind—"

"I just wonder if you trust this man."

"The priest? Of course not."

"What of the two riders on the road?"

"This priest may have been one of them." Durrant was watching the horizon. When they began up the hill, he mused, "I wonder who else was camped here with Reuben Wake."

The priest caught up to them, and Durrant and Charlene fell silent. They rode up the breaks above the Sun River. They were a few miles from town when the priest turned his mount. It was an open space with just a few cottonwood trees providing cover. "This is the place where Reuben Wake was camped, Sergeant."

Durrant rode a little and worked his way around the cottonwoods. There was a black spot on the ground indicating a fire pit, with dense clumps of vetch growing through bits of charred wood.

Durrant dismounted and walked stiffly around one of the trees. He kicked a few tin cans that were just starting to rust. Charlene dropped to the ground too.

"Reuben Wake was camped up here while Dumont and the others went into town to try and convince Riel to return to Canada? That was more than a year ago now."

"That's right. June of last year. We didn't see Wake come into town with Dumont. Only on his own."

"We know, Father, that Wake was here on very different business than he professed to be. Did Dumont know that?"

"All I know is that there was a row on the first night. Wake had come down into town and was spreading stories about Dumont and Riel. They got back to Dumont right quick. We all liked Mr. Riel. Nobody in town was going to listen to Wake tell his stories about Riel killing Thomas Scott in cold blood, that he wanted to start a war, or that Dumont was a murderer and a thief."

"If Wake was trying to come between Riel and his return to Canada, that seems a strange way to do it."

"I don't think he wanted to stop Riel's return. I think he wanted us to string these men up."

"You said Wake wasn't alone. Who was the other man?"

Durrant was about to press the priest when they heard Charlene cry out, "Over here!" Charlene was standing near the edge of an embankment that fell off onto the river's flood plain. When he arrived, Charlene was on her haunches, examining the ground. The earth had been turned over and new grass had started to grow in a rectangular shape. "It's a grave," she said.

THE PRIEST RETURNED with shovels and a man to help them dig. Durrant watched the priest from a long way off. "Is this the gravedigger you mentioned in your note, Father?"

"I didn't leave the note, Sergeant. This is Tom Scholl. He helps me around the church from time to time. He's got a strong back. He'll help us with the spadework."

"Mr. Scholl, did you meet Reuben Wake when he was in Sun River?"

Scholl was a broad-shouldered man, thick in the arms. He wore dusty canvas pants. Durrant noted that he wasn't armed. When he spoke, he seemed to draw out each word. "Met him once. He come into the stable to inquire about boarding the horses."

"He talk with you about Mr. Riel?"

"Sure did. Said he was a murdering man. Said we ought to run him out of town or string him up before he took after our children."

"Was he alone?"

"Yes, sir."

"Who do you think might be buried here?"

"Can't say. Should we get at this? I best return soon to tend to the horses."

Charlene, Scholl, and the priest started digging. Durrant felt his frustration growing, both with his physical ineptness and with the vagrancies of the investigation. While Wake's deception was now widely known, it didn't change the fact that he had won the confidence of the crafty and careful Dumont. Could he have managed to conceal an accomplice during the overland journey? And if so, how might this collaborator have aided Wake in his agitation of the Sun River community? Was it possible that someone had been helping Wake but not revealing themselves to Dumont's party? If Reuben Wake had met up with someone along their trail south, it would have aroused suspicion. Had someone been shadowing the party—some other member of the Regina Group—and joined Wake after he had arrived in Sun River?

"There's a body there." Scholl pointed. Durrant took one of the shovels and removed more dirt. He did this awkwardly with his left hand, but in a moment the ruined face was revealed.

"Oh Lord," said the priest, crossing himself.

"Blue Jesus," said Tom, and then added, "I'm sorry, Father."

Only Charlene remained silent.

The corpse was partially decomposed; the skin on the face was covered with a mass of carnivorous beetles and worms devouring the flesh. In places the skull showed through what remained of the skin. The eye sockets were empty, save for the wriggling of insects; the nose was missing. The hair fell in frayed strands and was caked with soil.

There was a neat hole in the skull along the ridge of the brow, directly between the eyes. Durrant stood up. "Let's uncover the rest of him."

Suppressing their nausea, the four dragged the dirt away from the rest of the corpse. The body's clothing was tattered but not yet completely decomposed. Soil clung to the fabric, but it was clear that this man had worn a heavy wool travelling suit. His riding boots were of fine leather, and almost perfectly preserved. A hand, where most of the flesh had been eaten by beetles, bore an expensive gold ring.

Durrant bent down as much as his prosthetic would allow. He went to reach for the man's coat.

"You ain't gonna touch him, are you?" asked Tom.

"Would *you* like to search his clothing?" Durrant snapped, and Tom backed away. "Let's go through his pockets and see if we can't find something that tells us who he is." Durrant carefully pulled open the man's coat. A piece of the fabric came off in his hand as he reached into the breast pocket. It was empty. He did the same on the other side. Nothing.

"Can't we let him rest in—?" started the priest.

"Peace? He's got all the peace he's going to find. This man is beyond care, but he may hold some secret that will help with my investigation, and therefore bring some rest to many others." Durrant continued with his gruesome task. The trousers were more difficult. Charlene stepped into the shallow grave and helped. They turned the body. Insects spilled from the man's flesh onto their boots.

"There's a billfold," said Durrant. The wallet was of fine leather and was snapped shut and lying in the soil under the body. "Charlene, would you grab that while I hold him?"

She retrieved the wallet and Durrant lowered the corpse. He was sweating. He felt bile rise in his throat and forced it down. When the body was prone once more, he and Charlene stepped from the grave.

"Would you like to do the honours?" he asked.

She opened the wallet. There was Dominion as well as American script, and several cards.

"Well, now," Durrant said, regarding the name on a pool-hall membership card. "It would appear that Reuben Wake had a brother. Or he could be a cousin. This man's name was Persimmon Wake."

"He's called Percy according this this." Charlene handed him a second card. It was a press-club membership. "It looks like he worked for *The Regina Examiner*," she said.

"That means he worked for Stanley Block. When we learn who killed Persimmon, we may also discover who killed Reuben Wake."

TWENTY-SIX

THE GINGER-HAIRED MAN

DURRANT AND CHARLENE RODE BACK into Sun River after refilling the shallow grave of Persimmon Wake. It was nearly noon and they were hungry and dirty, and Durrant was growing irritated with the tiny American town. They stopped at a saloon that advertised meals. The large windows that fronted the street filled the room with a warm light. There were men sitting at a table near the centre of the room; they looked up when the pair entered but quickly returned to their meals. Durrant and Charlene went to the bar, where a young man in a white shirt and black tie was standing with his arms crossed, looking bored.

"What can I do you for?" he asked.

"Like to ask you about Louis Riel." The men at the table behind them stopped talking. "Any of you know Mr. Riel when he was in Sun River?"

"He taught my children," said one of the men, pushing his chair back. "Who's asking?"

"I'm Durrant Wallace. I'm North West Mounted Police."

"You're a little ways from the Medicine Line, I'd say." The other men had gone back to eating.

"Yes, I am. Mr. Riel's rebellion has come to an end. He has been captured and will stand trial for treason. The penalty is death. There are some men, however, who aim to kill him before he can have his say in court. I'm trying to learn what I can to save his life. I wonder if any of you might tell me something about his time here in Sun River?"

The man at the table wiped his mouth with a handkerchief and stood up. One of his companions looked at him and shook his head. "It's all right," the man said. "I'll help Riel if I'm able."

"Red Coats want to hang him, Seth," said the second man.

"Maybe so. I don't know if what I have to say will make a difference one way or the other." He walked over and extended a hand. Durrant offered his left and they shook awkwardly.

"Care to sit?" Durrant asked.

"No, thanks. I'll tell you what I can, then it's back to the saddle."

"Very well. You were here when Dumont came to call Riel back to Canada?"

"Yes, sir. There was a real commotion. Dumont and them others rode into town and called on Mr. Riel and the next day there was a real uproar. We had a meeting down at the church about it."

"How many others were with Dumont?"

"There was three others with Dumont. And then there was the other who stirred up the hornet's nest."

"That would be Reuben Wake. I think a relation of his may also have been involved, a man named Percy."

"I believe I heard the name Wake. They come into town when Dumont was with Riel and his family discussing matters and tried to tell us that Riel was a murderer. Said we should hang him. We all knew about what happened back in '74. That's no big secret. There was a pair of them, going round to people and telling them. I heard about it after. I got a place a couple of miles outside of town and I was working my cattle that day. There were others in town, down from the Dominion country, and them I seen—"

"What others?"

"There were others in town at that time. Two other men."

"Not so unusual, is it?"

"No, it was only that they was from the Dominion Territory too. We get some, but not all at once, if you take my meaning."

"These others. Did you meet them?"

"Only in passing. They stayed out of town. My spread is east of here along the Sun, and I come upon them breaking camp one morning."

"How did you know they were from north of the border?"

"By the brand on their horses. They wore the Box D brand from a spread north of Outlook, Montana, up around your Fort Walsh. It's a big spread."

"I know it."

"That's how I knew they were Canadian."

"Did they associate with Dumont?"

"No, sir."

"What about with Wake?"

"They never seemed to be around town. It was as if they were just passing through, but I remember thinking it was odd that they was down at the same time as Dumont and the others."

"Can you tell me anything else about them? How they were dressed? What colour of hair?"

The man closed his eyes, straining to remember. "They was both about average, I'd say. One a little heavier than the other. The one fella had red hair. That I remember."

"I have reason to believe that a man was murdered here, in Sun River, about that time. Do you know anything about that?"

There was a long silence in the room. The man Durrant was questioning looked down at his boots, shaking his head. "I don't know nothing about that. Now, I reckon I ought to get back to my work."

"There *was* a man killed here, wasn't there?"

"This is the Montana Territory, Sergeant. People get themselves killed all the time. We don't go asking too many questions when it happens."

"He was a Canadian."

"Everybody bleeds the same."

Durrant accepted the statement of fact. "I appreciate your time."

"You know," Seth said, searching his memory, "there was something else you might find interesting. The one man was a ginger; the other fella, I think he might have been a Red Coat, or maybe a

179

former policeman. When I came up on them that morning when they was breaking camp, he had on one of them red shirts you wear."

"The serge?"

"If that's what you call it. He had it on under his coat. I didn't see him again, so I don't know if maybe I was mistaken."

"It wasn't the red-haired man who was wearing the serge?"

"Nope, the other."

"Can you tell me anything else?"

"He was the one who was a little bigger than the other fellow. I mean, around the waist. Looked like he ate real good, you know what I mean?"

"The men you saw down along the river. The man with the ginger hair—he killed Persimmon Wake, didn't he? And then buried him up on the bluffs."

"Sergeant, I guess folks just figured it weren't our problem if one of them killed another."

"Say that again?"

Seth looked at his table of friends. "I mean, it wasn't our business if one of them got killed. Not like he was American." Durrant could see that Seth's neck was red with embarrassment.

"You might be a marshal up in the Dominion, sir, but you ain't down here," said a second man, rising to his feet. "You leave well enough alone. You got what you come for. Now it's time for you to head north. Louis Riel might have been a revolutionary in the North West Territories, but down here he was just a schoolteacher. And a fine one at that."

Durrant watched the men. He could feel the eyes of the bartender on him. "You're right about one thing."

"And what's that?" asked Seth's friend.

"I got what I came for."

THEY HAD TO ride back through Fort Benton to send a series of urgent wires to Sam Steele, Leif Crozier, and Garnet Moberly.

Their task complete, and the day fading, Charlene urged Durrant to ride with her out of Benton, where Durrant's temptation to dig up the past would be too great to resist.

The next morning as they rode, Charlene asked, "Do you know who this red-haired man might be?"

Durrant was silent. They rode the broad back of the prairie, the sun cresting on the eastern horizon casting long shadows from solitary cottonwood trees across the flat expanse of earth. "Sub-Inspector Dickenson has red hair. It will be easy enough to tell if he was on leave from the Mounted Police during the time that Riel was being lured northward."

"We don't know that this ginger-haired man was the one who killed Percy Wake. We don't know that he is the same man who went to Batoche and killed Reuben Wake," said Charlene.

"We can say with some certainty that Sub-Inspector Dickenson did not kill Reuben Wake. I've checked with several of his compatriots, as well as with Major Boulton himself. He was charging into Batoche when Wake was murdered. That does not absolve him of conspiracy to commit murder, nor does it mean that he didn't travel to Sun River. When it comes down to it, Charlene, we really don't know anything," Durrant hissed between his teeth.

"In just a few weeks, Terrance La Biche will stand trial for the murder of Reuben Wake if I can't discover the man's true killer," he continued. "Whoever Reuben Wake was working with in this so-called Regina Group is still at large. We don't know who the Regina Group is, except for our errant Sub-Inspector Dickenson, and almost certainly Stanley Block. But who else in Regina wants Riel dead before he can take the stand in his own defence? And what are they willing to do to stop him? Many other lives hang in the balance!"

"Right now it seems most likely to me that someone within the conspiracy to free Riel learned that Wake intended to kill Riel should he be captured and did him in, but who?" asked Charlene.

"Now we learn that in addition to this ginger who was in Sun River at the same time as Wake, a man who dressed in the uniform of the Mounties was there as well."

"There may be a simple explanation for that, Durrant. How many former Mounted Police are there in the Dominion?"

"Too many." Durrant shook his head. "But there's nothing simple about it. It's entirely possible that this ginger-haired man riding the Box D brand was somehow associated with a man from Fort Walsh. It's possible, given that the Box D was so close to Walsh."

"Are any of our suspects former Mounted Police who served at Fort Walsh?"

Durrant considered. "I don't believe so." He slumped a little in the saddle.

"You know"—Charlene broke the silence—"there is a possibility that Stanley Block and Sub-Inspector Dickenson could have killed Wake. When men are entangled in a conspiracy to murder a man such as Riel, things go wrong. Wake sounds as if he were the sort of man who could arouse anger and resentment in even the gentlest soul. You told me yourself that even the priest Lefèbvre called him the devil. Maybe his fellow conspirators knew something that we do not. Maybe Wake had threatened them, or was going to spoil the chance to kill Riel, and they killed him and framed La Biche."

"That is a possibility, Charlene."

"And if Dickenson is involved, then there is nothing to say that other Mounted Police are not. Dickenson could have come to Sun River following the Wakes and when Persimmon stepped out of line, killed him. There's nothing to say that they didn't try and fail to kill Reuben then, too."

"We must sit this long time with all of these questions. It may be that Garnet and Saul have answers to them that we cannot know. This ride will be the longest."

"At least you have my charming company."

He looked at her. She was dressed as she might when masquerading as a stableboy, but she was smiling broadly, her hair touching her shoulders and the morning sun on her face. The light caught in the blue of her eyes was mesmerizing.

DURRANT WAS AWARE that they had been followed since leaving Sun River. In view of the note scrawled on the newspaper scrap, he suspected now that they had been since Fort Calgary. Somewhere, just past the curve of his vision, a rider had always been there. Durrant had caught glimpses from time to time of one and sometimes two horsemen on the distant southern horizon. Had he been alone, Durrant would have doubled back along one of the creeks that they forded and taken their shadow by surprise, but with Charlene with him, he dared not risk an open confrontation.

Instead, each night he lay down to rest with his armament at his side and waited in the dark for trouble. The shadow never grew closer; it was as if the riders following them were phantoms content to watch, wait, and trace their path across the plain.

FORT CALGARY EMERGED like a mirage in the desert. Durrant and Charlene were simultaneously hot and soaked to the skin when they finally reached their destination. The weather had alternated between sun, rain, and snow as they rode the Macleod Trail north into Canada to the confluence of the Bow and Elbow Rivers.

"Has it grown since we've been gone?" asked Charlene.

"I believe it has." Durrant rode with the Winchester across his lap.

They made the fort's parade ground by sundown. As they rode into town, the shadow that had drifted behind them seemed to evaporate into the business of the boom town. Durrant inquired with the fort's commander and secured the guest quarters for Charlene. He simply was not about to let her out of his sight while they were in the city. Next, he himself went to the non-commissioned officers' quarters, where he hadn't slept more than a night over the last two months, and washed, shaved, and found clean clothing. His face was white and raw after two months of whiskers were shorn, but he feared he had started to look like a ruffian.

The truth was, he wanted to do what little could be done to make his appearance more presentable. The scars from frostbite still cut across his cheeks and jaw, and there was no disguising the deep lines at the corners of his eyes, the result of riding into the sun all these years. His was a dishevelled face, but it would have to do.

He regarded himself in the mirror for a long moment. He looked at his hair, thick and dark and with a pronounced wave. He ran his left hand through it and then set his Stetson firmly on his head and went to the main hall, where the telegraph machine sat unattended.

Durrant found the strongbox located in Sub-Inspector Dewalt's office and opened it using the combination. He found a stack of correspondence intended for him in an envelope with his name on it. He sat down at Dewalt's desk and read.

> To Durrant Wallace.
> From Garnet Moberly.
> May 31, 1885. Arrived in Regina. La Biche safely in custody, as is Riel. Regina alive with rumour. Suspect that Regina Group has grip on city. Determining likely prospects for surveillance. Will keep you informed.

The next was from Saul Armatage. It was from the station in Prince Albert.

> Durrant: As feared. Farm of Terrance La Biche in ruins. Girl badly hurt. Passed on information to Crozier. Has ordered an investigation. Am proceeding to Regina to rendezvous with Moberly.

A week later there was another wire from Garnet.

> Located a cell of men from Regina Group. Keeping
> watchful eye. Am not only one. Others shadowing as
> well. Saul arrived and doing double duty.

Garnet's final correspondence was dated just a week previous.

> Now believe an attempt on Riel's life will be made
> when moved from NWMP barracks to courthouse.
> Guard has been doubled per Crozier's order. Regina
> Group has tentacles in ALL aspects of power here.
> Confirmed others are watching. No ginger-haired men
> seen. No sign of Dickenson. Come as soon as able.

The next wire was from Sam Steele.

> Durrant. Big Bear surrendered. Resistance is over.
> Proceed at once to Regina to aid in protection of
> Riel. Complete investigation into murder of Wake.
> Open fighting complete. Political fallout not done.
> Tread carefully.

Durrant folded the sheets of paper and, taking a box of matches
from his pocket, opened Dewalt's stove, set them afire, and closed
the door.

PART THREE
REGINA

TWENTY-SEVEN

THE FAMILIAR SENSE OF FALLING

JUNE 23, 1885. FORT CALGARY.

"You will come with me to Regina," he told her in the morning. They stood outside the fort commander's residence.

"Is that an order, Sergeant?" she asked with a wink.

"Ms. Mason, it is a request to be sure, an order if necessary."

"And what shall we do in Regina?"

"Catch a killer. Prevent another murder. Possibly keep the fragile peace."

"The usual fare. We shall have to get a change of clothing. I can't travel as your stableboy any longer. It simply won't do."

They caught a cab from the fort to the home of Charlene's employer. Durrant sat in the kitchen while Charlene prepared a travel bag. Before they left, she explained her situation to the Lloyds. "I don't know when I'll be able to return," she told them.

Durrant went out the back way and around to the front of the house to survey the scene on the street. He peered up and down but all seemed in order. The city was coming alive as men rode down the avenue toward work and children hurried to school. Durrant bid Charlene to hurry so they could catch the nine o'clock train for the east. They rode the cab down to the station with Durrant giving Charlene instructions as they went. "If he knows we're back in the city, then this is where he might try something."

Charlene was composed. "The station will be busy. He's a coward, Durrant, and must know that you will protect me. He's not like you at all. He'll avoid an open fight."

"We'll wait in the station master's office until the train is ready to depart. We should be safe enough there." They reached the station, and Durrant stepped out of the carriage and helped

Charlene down. She was dressed in a practical yet beautiful travelling dress and clutched a small bag. Durrant shouldered his satchel, his Winchester wrapped in burlap inside of it. Awkwardly, he clomped along the platform to the entrance to the station.

There were scores of people, and Durrant kept Charlene close at hand. "Do you see him?" he whispered as they entered the station.

"I don't."

Twenty minutes later, the train arrived from the west. Most of those who detrained in Calgary had been to the mountains to take refreshment and rejuvenation in the hot springs at Banff. Many more were boarding for the journey east. Just before the conductor blew his whistle, Durrant and Charlene made for the pullman car where they had purchased seats. Durrant scanned the platform as they went. Nobody barred their passage onto the train; nobody called out from the platform in anger. The whistle blew and the porter took their tickets and showed them to their seats. They sat side by side; two well-dressed men in beaver-felt hats across from them read newspapers. Charlene leaned close to Durrant and he could smell her delicate fragrance. "I think we've made a clean getaway," she said with a nudge.

He looked out the window at the platform as the train slipped out of the station. The city was soon speeding by. They crossed the Bow River and climbed up out of the valley and within a few minutes had left the shacks and tents of the sprawling city behind. The prairie stretched before them, long and slow and flat. Durrant breathed out heavily.

"All is well," Charlene said and patted his arm. The task of leaving Fort Calgary now safely behind them, Durrant turned his attention to what lay ahead. He thought of his two friends working together in Regina, and realized how much he was looking forward to sharing their company once more. It had been nearly a month since they had parted in Batoche. Durrant considered the content of the wires he had received at Fort Calgary. Garnet's principal responsibility over the last month had been to work with Tommy Provost to keep Terrance La Biche safe, and to watch the movements of the Regina Group. Garnet had suggested that he was not alone in this undertaking. Others appeared to be watching the Regina Group as well. Did members of the conspiracy to free Riel have the Regina Group in their sights even now?

With men like Stanley Block, owner of the most influential newspaper in the West, involved, this much was obvious. Durrant wondered if the murder of Wake might be attributed to something as simple as another member of the group wanting Wake dead. If this was the case, Durrant wondered why.

"You need some rest, Durrant," whispered Charlene. "I know how little you've slept these weeks."

"Someone may be watching us still," he said quietly.

"That may be so, but I think we're safe enough. Sleep a little."

He let his hands drop to his sides. "All right, for a moment. But stay close."

"I will venture only so far as the WC and then hurry right back."

Durrant glanced at her and then closed his eyes. Questions swirled in his mind. He leaned his head back against the well-appointed seat. The sound of the train and the rhythmic clack of the sleepers beneath hastened his slumber.

IN HIS DREAM he was in motion. It wasn't cross-ties creating the clatter beneath him but the cobblestone streets of Toronto. He was riding pell-mell through the city once more, his coattails flying behind him, the whip in his hand coaxing the horses on. But there was no thrill in this; he knew what fate awaited him. He drove up before the home and then was at the door and then the stairs. The world passed in a dull grey montage of images blurred at their edges. He was in the room; there was the iron smell of blood. Mary and the child lay motionless on the bed. They were both swaddled in white, their faces pale as ghosts.

HE AWOKE. HIS hand was on the Enfield, and he brought the pistol up to the face of a porter. The men across from him recoiled. Durrant struggled to get his bearings. Charlene was not beside him. He felt the uneasy motion of the train swaying on the tracks as it rounded the bend. Medicine Hat? Soon they were crossing the South Saskatchewan River far below. The porter swallowed. Durrant looked at his weapon, then lowered it. "What is it?" His voice was raw.

"Are you Durrant Wallace?"

"Yes, I am. Sergeant Durrant Wallace. North West Mounted Police," he said for the sake of his seatmates.

"Sir, would you come with me, please?" asked the porter.

The porter was sweating, and Durrant wondered if the beads of perspiration had been there before he drew his weapon on him. "What is it?"

"Would you accompany me to the front of the coach please, sir?"

Durrant holstered the Enfield and reached down for his cane. He followed the porter, who was already walking down the aisle. Durrant reached out and grabbed the man's left arm. "Where is my travelling companion?"

The porter looked around at the men and woman in the first-class car. "She's in the water closet," he whispered. "Please come this way." Durrant felt a sense of relief. He allowed himself to be led down the aisle of the car to where the WC was located. The porter pulled him in close to the luggage, a few feet from the head.

"Is there a problem?" asked Durrant.

The porter's eyes seemed much too large, and sweat still glistened on his ebony skin. "Sir, there is *some* trouble."

Durrant felt his pulse quicken. "What is it?" He looked around, his hand tightening on the handle of his cane.

"Well, you best be reading this." The porter handed him a piece of folded paper. Durrant opened it. It was written in Charlene's hand.

Durrant. He has me. We are in the WC. He wants to talk with you. He has a gun and will kill me if you try to come in.

TWENTY-EIGHT
SKILL OR BLIND LUCK

DURRANT TOOK THE ENFIELD IN his left hand and used the head of his cane to rap on the door. He tapped quietly and then quickly stepped to the side. The porter watched from behind the adjacent storage locker.

There was no sound. Durrant looked at the porter, who nodded to indicate that this was the right door. Durrant knocked again. "It's Durrant Wallace."

"Wallace," said a deep, angry voice from behind the door.

"That's right."

"I've got my wife in here."

"Has she been harmed?"

"Not yet."

"Will you let her go so you and I can talk?"

Durrant heard a laugh that sounded like the bark of a dog. "You must think I'm some kind of fool, Wallace. I ain't letting my wife out of my sight. Not ever again."

Durrant looked around him. The space was quite small: he estimated only two feet between the door of the WC and the outside wall of the train—not a big-enough space in the lavatory for Charlene and her abductor be confined without being on top of one another. "Mr. Mason, how do I know that Charlene is all right?"

"She's *my* wife, Wallace."

"How do I know that your wife is all right?"

The man laughed. "I'll let you say hello."

There was rustling, and then he heard Charlene say, "Durrant, I'm all right."

"Are you hurt?"

"I'm fine."

"See?" said the man. "She's fine. Now, you and me are going to have a talk."

"Charlene, do as he asks. Don't try to fight him."

"Sage advice, Red Coat. I've got my pistol pressed to her forehead. She fights, she dies."

"Why don't we put the pistol away?" said Durrant. "The train is liable to bump over a sleeper and you might make a terrible mistake." He felt his hand tightening on his own weapon.

Durrant looked up to see a man making his way down the aisle to retrieve something from the storage locker. He motioned to the porter to cut him off. As the porter did so, the gentleman looked alarmed to see Durrant, pistol drawn, talking to the lavatory door. Within minutes, thought Durrant, everybody on this train is going to know what is happening here. "So let's talk." His face was pressed close to the door.

"Why have you stolen my wife from me?"

"I haven't. Charlene and I are just friends, nothing more."

"That's hogwash!" shouted Mason, and several of the passengers now turned in their seats to look. Durrant motioned for the porter. "That's complete and utter bullcrap!" Mason yelled again.

"I tell you, it's true. I've never so much as laid a hand on her. She's still very much your wife."

"Then why she run off?" His voice was quieter now.

"I think you know why."

"What did she tell you?"

"She told me that you were too hard on her."

"That's a goddamned lie!" There was a sound like a fist hitting the door of the lavatory.

"Mr. Mason?" Durrant stepped back and raised his pistol.

"*What?*"

"We're just talking here. Have you hurt Charlene?"

There was a long silence. "No."

"Please don't, sir. If you do, it will make things very difficult."

"For who? For you?"

"And you, sir."

Durrant looked away from the lavatory door. There were two dozen people crowded around the storage locker, all pressed together and staring wide-eyed at him. Durrant motioned the porter over. "You've got to keep these people back. They may get hurt, and if they spook this man . . ."

The porter nodded and began warning people away. Durrant turned and spoke again to the man inside the WC.

"Sir, we're coming up on Medicine Hat. Why don't you let Charlene go? You and I can step off the train and discuss this."

"No goddamned way," yelled Mason.

"Then what are your intentions?"

"I'll get off in Swift Current and we're going to ride north again to our place."

"I don't think that's going to be such a good idea."

"Why the hell not?" he yelled.

"First off, there will be those who won't like what you've done here. We have laws in the Dominion of Canada against this sort of thing."

"You mean kidnapping?"

"Yes, that and other laws."

"It's not kidnapping if she is my wife." The train started to slow. "It's not kidnapping if I'm married to her."

"When you use a pistol and take her with force it is." Through the windows next to the lavatory door Durrant could see the town of Medicine Hat coming into view. He motioned for the porter and whispered to him, "When the train stops, go quickly to wire the Mounted Police detachment. Tell them what's happening. Tell them to send as many men as they can spare, but not to interfere. Do not let this train start again. Understood?" The man nodded his understanding.

"What's happening?" growled Mason from the lavatory.

"It's the Medicine Hat station. There's a thirty-minute stop here, then we'll be on our way."

"Are you going to try and take Charlene from me, Wallace?"

"No."

"I don't believe you!" the man roared, and the door to the WC took a tremendous thud. Durrant was afraid the door would split open and he would come face to face with whatever horror was behind it.

"You will simply have to, Mr. Mason. I have no improper intentions toward your wife."

"I'm getting off this train."

"You said you wanted to ride to Swift Current."

"I changed my goddamned mind!"

Durrant looked around. Every man and woman in the car had pressed again toward the WC, watching the drama unfold. Durrant whispered, "Push these people back to the other end of the car."

"What's happening?" barked Mason.

"I'm clearing a path for you. There are others in the car. I want them out of the way."

"You get those people back. They get in my way, they are going to get hurt!"

"I understand," said Durrant.

"Now you, you put your pistol on the floor where I can see it when I open this door. I don't see that pistol of yours, I'm going to kill her."

"I thought you loved her."

"I do ... I did ... but if I don't see that pistol ..."

Durrant laid the pistol down on the floor. The train's brakes began to squeal. He had to reach for the rail to keep from pitching forward.

"And the other," Mason instructed.

"What do you mean?"

"The other one. The little one you keep in your coat. Yes, I know all about you, Wallace. Read about you in the papers. Charlene here was most helpful when I asked her the right way."

Durrant drew out his snub-nosed British Bulldog and put it on the floor. "All right, you've got them both."

"Now get the hell back from the door. When this train comes to a stop, I'm going to open it. I see you standing right in front, I'll shoot you and then her."

"I'm back to the locker."

"I'm coming out."

Durrant stepped back. The train's brakes rattled as the train came to a halt. The porter reappeared and indicated that the message had been sent. Durrant held his breath as he heard the latch on the lavatory door being unclasped. He saw the door open a fraction of an inch and then close again. There was commotion on the platform, and Durrant could see porters from the Medicine Hat station herding passengers away from the car. The pullman porter had done his job.

Then door opened and Mason and Charlene were before him. Mason was immense. He stood over six feet tall and was broad and dark-skinned, with a thick head of greasy black hair that was combed back. He wore a dark suit coat and trousers and a grey waistcoat. Durrant could immediately smell the reek of sweat from him. Charlene looked tiny in his massive arms.

She was clearly terrified, but composed. Her mouth was gagged with a colourful handkerchief, and her hands were bound in front of her. Durrant could see that her left eye was bruised and swelling. He immediately felt a hot wave of fury wash through him and had to restrain himself from lunging at Mason.

Durrant saw the pistol raised to her temple. He locked eyes with Charlene and tried to communicate to her that everything would be all right. "So now what, Mr. Mason?"

"We get off this train."

"And then? I don't know how far you expect to get."

"If you come with me, we'll get farther."

"You want me to come with you?"

"I'm going to make sure no Red Coat takes a shot at me."

"Very well," said Durrant.

Mason quickly kicked Durrant's pistols into the WC and closed the door. "Get over here," he spat. Durrant walked toward them, leaning heavily on his cane. "Leave that," said Mason, pointing to the silver-handed walking stick.

"I do, and you're going to have to carry me." Durrant exaggerated his dependence on the cane.

"Blue Jesus, let's go!" said Mason. Durrant stepped forward. "Get in front of us!"

Durrant did as he was told. Through the train door's window he could see a crowd on the platform. "Let me clear these people," Durrant said. Mason kicked him in the back and Durrant jolted forward, slamming into the door. His face hit the window, and he felt the heat of his own blood there.

"Get out!" yelled Mason.

Righting himself, Durrant opened the door. He scanned the platform and was grateful that no Mounted Police had shown themselves.

He stepped down, holding the cane firmly in his left hand. When he reached the platform, he shifted it to his right, took two steps forward, and shouted, "All you people get back!"

Mason came to the door and waved his pistol. "You heard the Red Coat, get back!"

The crowd pushed back enough that there was a path that they might take to the station, which was nothing more than a boxcar set against the broad platform. Beyond, the boxcar opened onto a wide street.

Durrant headed for the temporary station, hobbling with the cane. Mason stepped onto the platform. His massive arm was around Charlene's throat. As Charlene struggled, Mason tightened his grip. Durrant reached the wooden doors set into the boxcar and with his left hand opened them. The space inside was largely empty; all of the onlookers were on the platform.

Durrant looked back. Mason was behind him, half pushing and half dragging Charlene. Durrant locked eyes with Charlene once more, and this time she closed her eyes and nodded.

Durrant took three quick steps into the room; it was dark in comparison to the bright afternoon sun, and the light from the opposite door, leading to the street, created a halo around him. As Mason pushed through the door, Durrant spun around, his left hand drawing the handle of the cane from its staff. In his hand was a small pistol that used the handle of the cane as its grip.

Mason drew up his Colt Peacemaker and tried to level it at Durrant, but Durrant pulled the trigger. The shot from the .22-calibre pistol was sharp and rattled in the confined space. A neat round hole appeared in Mason's forehead. He fell backwards toward the doors, Charlene still in his hold. Durrant reached for her but could not grab her arms, and she and Mason crashed through the doors, glass shattering around them. Mason hit the platform and Charlene landed on top of him, and a great cry went up from the people gathered there.

Durrant hurried through the doors, the tiny pistol still in his hands. Charlene struggled to stand. As she did, she turned over and beat her husband with her bound fists. Durrant reached for her. Several other men came forward. Durrant waved them back; Charlene hit Mason again and again. Finally Durrant took her, crying, in his arms. She buried her face in his shoulder and he put his right arm around her.

He looked down at the man beneath them, dead with a bullet hole squarely between his eyes.

TWENTY-NINE
THE THIRD CONSPIRACY REVEALED

JUNE 27, 1885. REGINA.

The couple's eastward progress was delayed several days in Medicine Hat while witnesses were interviewed and Durrant was debriefed by the local North West Mounted Police sub-inspector. Satisfied that the shooting had been in the line of duty and in self-defence, Durrant was allowed to leave, and he and Charlene resumed their journey.

The station in Regina sat against Broad Street, the city's main thoroughfare. When Durrant and Charlene stepped from the train through the veils of steam, Garnet Moberly appeared, along with Mr. Jimmy. "It has been much too long." Garnet embraced and then kissed Charlene on each cheek. To Durrant he said, "I understand that my gift of the cane has proven handy. Come, let's get your things to the hotel. Saul is awaiting us. There is a great deal we must discuss."

They made their way out of the station and onto Broad Street, where a buggy was waiting for them. Mr. Jimmy stowed their bags and took up the reins.

"You steal this?" asked Durrant, looking at Garnet.

"Goodness no. I bought it. I decided if we were to make Regina our home for some time, we had best have a means of transportation."

THE ONLY PROPER hotel in Regina was the Grand Saskatchewan. From what Durrant could see as the buggy angled up to its front door, it wasn't very grand. Two storeys tall and built from squared timber shipped from Winnipeg, it had the same appearance as nearly everything that sprang up along the main line of the CPR: temporary.

"It may not look like much"—Garnet read Durrant's mind— "but it's full. It would seem that the impending trial of Riel is causing quite the stir. I bought up a block of rooms for us for the

201

month." Garnet took Charlene's bag while Mr. Jimmy hoisted Durrant's, complete with Winchester rifle, out of the back of the carriage. "I figured better safe than sorry."

"Someday, Garnet, you will have to tell us the story behind your good fortune," said Durrant.

"Someday . . ." Garnet winked and bid them to follow him into the hotel.

Saul Armatage was waiting for them in the common room that served as lounge and dining area. He jumped to his feet when he saw them. He quickly shook hands with Durrant and then turned to Charlene. She graced him with a smile. "How are you?"

"I'm fine."

"Are you certain?"

"A little shaken, but well."

"All right then. Should you wish to talk, you'll let me know?"

"Is Evelyn here?"

"She is. She's putting the children to bed. She may make an appearance at some point."

"I should very much like to see her again."

"Then you shall."

"Very well, then," said Garnet. "Let's show the two of you to your rooms and arrange for some supper. Durrant, no doubt you have a great deal to tell, and Saul and I have stories of our own to inform you of. Let's meet back here in an hour?"

They agreed, and Mr. Jimmy took their bags to their rooms. The hotel was dark and shadowed but clean. The floors and walls smelled like the prairie dust. Durrant stopped outside of Charlene's room. "Will you be all right?" he asked after Mr. Jimmy had taken his leave.

"I will be."

"All right. I will see you at dinner."

She smiled at him. Then she reached out and touched the side of his face with a gloved hand. Her fingers rested there a moment on his scarred cheek. "Thank you, Durrant."

"No need to thank me."

"He would have killed me. He tried before. I knew he would try again."

"You are safe now."

"I know. I simply can't believe . . ." She stopped the words and began to cry.

"It's all right." He drew her to him and put his arms around her. She smelled of flowers.

OVER DINNER, THEY all talked about the current state of excitement in the territorial capital, the buzz about the upcoming trial, and the general state of agitation over territorial relations with Ottawa. But as supper ended, the talk became more serious. As the dining room cleared of other guests, Durrant broached the subject. "Tell us about this shadow group that the two of you have uncovered."

Garnet looked at Saul to offer him the chance to speak, but he merely shook his head. "I'm a doctor; you're the spy. It's your story to tell."

"There's really very little to tell, Durrant," said Garnet. "Our orders were to watch the members of the Regina Group. We've done that. I've got a list of more than half a dozen names for you." He patted the breast pocket of his jacket. "Besides your friend Stanley Block, we've got two prominent lawyers, a banker, a cattle rancher, a town councillor, and two men who own businesses here in town. I'm sure there are more, but these seem to be the ringleaders. They have been meeting nearly every night. They move around, but the town is yet small enough that finding them hasn't been too difficult. I suppose that is how we discovered their shadows."

"You keep referring to this group of men as shadows," said Durrant.

"They are! When I first spotted a fellow watching the Regina men, he was literally standing in the shadow of a mercantile, observing one of their meetings. For more than two weeks we've kept a nightly watch. Doctor Armatage, upon his return from Batoche, has joined Mr. Jimmy and myself in our nightly undertaking. We've located a series of what I'm certain the Regina Group must call shelters, where they hold near-nightly confabs. They seem very at ease. They post a guard most nights, but he is so obvious that it makes fooling him a simple matter of distraction or disguise. Several times I've been within listening distance, camouflaged as a lamplighter or some other creature of the night.

"This Regina Group is a powerful lot, making up the business elite of Regina. I believe, based on what I've overheard, that they also have connections in Ottawa. I suspect that somewhere within the ranks of Macdonald's party someone is giving the orders, but so far we haven't intercepted any correspondence."

"You've been looking into the wires?"

"I learned that trick from you, my good sergeant. So far, all we know is that Macdonald's people are truly concerned about what Mr. Riel will say on the stand about the state of the North West Territories, about the Indians and the Métis. This has been one cataclysmic foul-up, straight from the start, and it would seem that everybody in Macdonald's camp knows it."

Saul cleared his throat. "There is simply no getting around that the Dominion hasn't held up its end of the bargain with the Indians. Despite years of pleading, no good has come of it."

Durrant said, "That still doesn't justify taking up arms against the Crown."

"It doesn't justify it," said Saul, "but it does explain it."

"Did you happen to observe Sub-Inspector Dickenson in any of your travels?" asked Durrant.

"I did not. I most certainly had a lookout for him. Mr. Jimmy has spent some time at the Mounted Police barracks here in Regina, under the pretense of communications between myself and your colleagues, and has not seen him once."

"He seems to have gone underground," said Durrant.

"Or simply run off. You still don't believe that he was the one who pulled the trigger on Wake?" asked Garnet.

"He is the one man with a plain alibi. Unless General Middleton is in on this himself, and I do not believe that to be the case, then Dickenson is in the clear, at least for the murder. It doesn't absolve him of collusion if we learn that it was in fact Regina men who turned on Wake. It doesn't make me any less curious about his whereabouts. I don't think I could find a magistrate who would press charges for taking the Dakota Sioux's food and leaving Iron Crow to die, but there is a higher law."

"And just what might that be?" asked Garnet, smiling.

"I suppose it will have to be settled between us Red Coats." Durrant let out a long breath. "And given that he is the only ginger-haired person associated with this business, he might have been the man who surfaced in Sun River around the time that Dumont went there last spring." Durrant took a moment and told Saul and Garnet about his and Charlene's overland journey, about the discovery of Persimmon Wake's body, and about the mysterious rider who had shadowed them for much of their journey.

"I'll have to inquire with the commander at the Mounted Police barracks if our Sub-Inspector Dickenson was on leave during the time of Riel's return. We'll also need to look into Percy Wake's disappearance. If he was supposed to be in Minneapolis but was in Sun River instead, never to return, you would imagine someone might have taken notice. Tell me about these men you say are shadowing the Regina Group."

"A much more careful lot. I've yet to get a good look at a face, but they are always there."

"And what do you think this Shadow Conspiracy is after?"

"I simply can't say. They are very intent on watching the Regina men, and I can only surmise that their purpose is more than idle curiosity. We must be careful, as all of us are known to those who were in the zareba. If any of this shadow group was in Batoche, they will recognize us."

There was a long moment of silence. It was broken when Charlene slapped her hand down on the table, causing the coffee cups to jump. "What is it?" asked Durrant, his voice sharp.

"Oh, for the love of Job. Must I state the obvious? They won't know *me*! I can ask."

"I believe it might work," agreed Garnet. "I think a beautiful young woman might do the trick. We'll need a clever plan."

"We have a lot of police work to undertake first," conceded Durrant. "It will entail some risk. We can learn the nature of this Shadow Conspiracy and gain the identity of its followers through careful observation. This may well lead us to understanding which of these three conspiracies is responsible for the demise of Mr. Wake, and possibly his brother. But we'll have to work quickly. The trial of Riel could start any time, and with the judge and jury assembled, they may call the trial of La Biche any day."

"Durrant," asked Garnet, "what of the others? You feel very certain that this murder hinges on one of these conspiracies. Some of the conspirators are three hundred miles away."

"Are they?"

"Well, I assume—"

"I think if you were to check around town, you would see that our suspects have been called as witnesses for one trial or another, Mr. Moberly."

"What of Jasper Dire? We've looked in on him several times at his place of employ but have been told he is still away with the field force."

"Yes, Mr. Dire," said Durrant. "I should very much like to talk with him."

THIRTY
DIRE CIRCUMSTANCES

JULY 6, 1885.

Durrant stepped through the broad double doors of the carriage-manufacturing shop at the west end of Broad Street. He could smell machine oil, glue, the hot scent of metal, and the rich aroma of leather. The room was well lit with overhead lamps that glowed even at midday. Large windows along the rear of the two-storey building allowed abundant natural light to fall across the shop floor. A dozen men were working at the construction of half a dozen carriages. None looked up as he entered the shop. Jasper Dire was not among them.

Durrant walked through the shop to double doors with the letters OFFICE stencilled on them. He knocked and opened one. The clerk looked up as Durrant entered. "May I help you, sir?"

"I'm Sergeant Durrant Wallace of the North West Mounted Police. I am inquiring after one of your employees."

"No trouble, I hope?" The man stood and took off his glasses to give them a polish.

"It's to do with some business that took place in Batoche."

The clerk put the glasses back on his face. He tilted his head to the side a little, his mouth pursing. "Who is it that you are inquiring after?"

"A man named Jasper Dire." The clerk smiled. "What is it?" asked Durrant.

"Mr. Dire isn't an employee here—"

"He told me he was."

"Mr. Dire *owns* Broad Street Carriage, Sergeant."

"Is that so? Is the proprietor about today?" asked Durrant.

"Indeed he is," said a voice behind Durrant. He turned and saw Dire standing by the doors to the shop.

"Mr. Dire!" said the clerk. "Welcome back!"

"Thank you, Sam. It's fine to be back."

"You have just returned this very minute?" asked Durrant.

"Indeed, Sergeant, I have."

"I was told that Middleton's volunteers had been discharged more than a week ago."

"I was delayed. The business at Frenchman's Butte and across the narrows with Big Bear kept me longer than the others. Now, Sergeant, what can I do for you?"

"When we spoke, Mr. Dire, at Batoche, I was under the impression that you were an employee here. Now I learn that you are the proprietor."

Dire motioned toward the back of the office, where a glass-windowed door opened into another room. "Would you like to have a seat, Sergeant?"

Dire pointed to a chair. Durrant sat, and Dire followed him and sat down at a small desk. It was hot in the room; Dire went to the window and pulled it open, then sat back down.

"I had my reasons, Sergeant. I was in a company of men who are labourers—foremen at best. I didn't see the need to advertise that I was of the merchant class in Regina. This business is merely a hobby for me. I am a rancher at heart. I've only taken up in Regina in the last few years to take advantage of what I see as a trend across these territories."

"And what trend is that, Mr. Dire?"

"The expansion of commerce, of course, the growth of the city. Regina, Brandon, Winnipeg, your own newly minted City of Calgary."

"Do you maintain your ranch?"

"My family does. We have more than forty sections east of Fort Walsh."

"I know that country well," said Durrant, tapping his cane and pausing a long moment. "Tell me, Mr. Dire. Have you ever been to Fort Benton?"

"Yes, of course. Many times."

"When was the last time you were there?"

"I'd say two years ago, to buy horses and to secure goods for the manufacture of the carriages."

"You've not been back since?"

"There is no need now, Sergeant. The steel rail brings supplies from the east. The days of the Macleod Trail have passed."

"You weren't in Fort Benton last spring?"

"I just told you, Sergeant, it's been two years. I can have Samuel check the appointments calendar from then if you would like to know the exact dates."

"That won't be necessary."

"What is this all about?"

"It's about Reuben Wake."

"I understand from this morning's paper that Mr. La Biche is to stand trial as soon as the jury has been selected for Riel."

"Did you know Mr. Wake?"

"I told you I didn't. He was a businessman in Regina as I am, and as we both deal with horses, in a manner of speaking, we had occasion to cross each other's paths, but we were not personally acquainted."

"Do you hold with Macdonald's insistence that Riel must be tried as a traitor and hanged if found guilty?"

"What does that have to do with anything?"

"Just answer the question."

"If Riel hangs, it will be suicide for Macdonald. He will lose Quebec and Ontario. But we're a long way from Lower Canada, Sergeant. I don't really much care."

"Are you a Macdonald man or an Edward Blake?"

"I don't much know. I suppose neither, really."

"Come now, you must have some opinion."

"I told you, Sergeant, the business of government is so far removed from my dealings in Regina, and across the North West Territories, that I don't much pay attention to politics."

"Your ranch, Mr. Dire. Forty sections is a very large sum of land."

"It is. I assure you, that sort of undertaking doesn't happen overnight."

"Is that so?"

"No, it doesn't."

"And yet, I recall when I was stationed at Fort Walsh, up until five years ago, such large undertakings were an anomaly."

"You should check your memory, Sergeant. My family was granted this land in 1878."

"And what price did you have to pay?"

"I don't recall the exact figure."

"Do you have interests in the east, Mr. Dire?"

Dire shook his head. "Sergeant, I really don't understand the meaning of this interrogation."

"Surely your family must have started out someplace other than the bald edge of Saskatchewan?"

"We raised cattle in Ontario, what was then Upper Canada, the county of Lambton."

"Were you politically involved while you were there?"

"No more so than the next man."

"Lambton, on the St. Clair River, holds a special place in our nation's history, doesn't it, Mr. Dire."

"You'll have to educate me, Sergeant. I'm a rancher and a businessman."

"The second prime minister of Canada hails from the riding of Lambton."

"Alexander Mackenzie. Of course, I forgot."

"I don't think you forgot, Mr. Dire."

Dire laughed. "Sergeant, what does this have to do with Terrance La Biche and Reuben Wake, for heaven's sake?" The heat in the room was still stifling, and Dire took a handkerchief from his waistcoat and dabbed it along the edges of his slick, jet-black hair. He quickly tucked the cloth back into his pocket.

"This has been most helpful, Mr. Dire." Durrant stood and tapped his cane on the floor.

"I can't see how."

"In time you shall."

THIRTY-ONE

THE WATCH

JULY 7, 1885. REGINA.

They had been watching for a week. Each night after supper, they had split into two teams and gone out into the dirty streets to seek the Regina Group and their shadows. As June gave way to July, a heat wave struck the city and temperatures soared, baking the prairie town, wilting its inhabitants.

By the end of the first week of July, Durrant and his colleagues had identified and followed most of the members of the Regina Group and had a clear picture of what they had planned. The Shadow Conspiracy, as the team had begun to refer to them, remained a mystery.

During the day, Durrant hunted down and confronted his other suspects, all the while trying to tie each of them to what he had learned in Sun River but to no avail. On the evening of the seventh of July, they sat at supper and discussed their progress.

"Despite delays, Riel's trial starts in just a few days," said Saul Armatage.

"We can be reasonably confident that the Regina Group will make an attempt on Riel's life when he is moved to the courthouse," said Garnet Moberly.

"I've already notified the magistrate. They are working on a plan to ensure his safety. It's not what we know that concerns me, but what we don't yet know. Despite a week of this, we're no closer to having identified a single member of this Shadow Conspiracy, or understanding why they are so interested in the Regina men. There is something sinister at work here."

"Have you learned anything from the others? From Father Lefèbvre or Jacques Lambert?" asked Garnet.

"What I've learned only reinforces what we already knew. Lefèbvre and Lambert both seemed to have a clear reason for wanting Wake dead, and while both had the opportunity, I can't place either at the scene of the crime. Neither of them wears the scars of a man who has had a misfire of the sort we believe he must have experienced before shooting Wake. I can't connect either of them with Sun River."

"And Dire?" asked Garnet.

"There is much more to Jasper Dire than we can know. He may well be the key to understanding this Shadow Conspiracy, if only we can catch him in the act of espionage against the Regina men."

"You told us you learned something of his political affiliations," said Saul.

"They are only suspicions at present. I have sent wires to various stations to learn what I can." Durrant tapped his cane. "He has hidden his true nature from me more than once now, and I believe he is up to something; I simply can't say what."

Charlene was watching Durrant closely. He looked up at her as she spoke. "I wonder if maybe it's time for someone else to have a go at Mr. Dire."

"What do you suggest?"

"I might be able to get closer to him than you can. He will see you coming after your recent conversations and be on his guard."

"It's too dangerous." Durrant taped his cane on the table more aggressively.

"Durrant—" said Saul.

"Stay out of this, Doctor," Durrant barked, and the room fell silent.

Charlene spoke after a moment. "It's not too dangerous for you, but it's too dangerous for me. Is that what you are saying?"

"I'm glad for all your help, but I'm the law. It's my job to learn what motive, if any, Dire might have to be involved in this. I don't want to involve you, Charlene."

Charlene stood up, smoothed out her dress and fixed Durrant with her blue eyes. "As you wish, Sergeant. I know that the Mounted Police always get their man, but I didn't realize that they had to be horses' asses in order to do it. You can go and learn Dire's secret alone, if you wish. Be my guest. But sometimes help is what's needed. A new set of eyes might help see things you missed—like the fact that your man Jasper Dire dyes his hair. His natural hair colour is not black. I might be able to learn if this man is the ginger you have been searching for."

DURRANT SAT ALONE in his room in a leather chair, his prosthetic perched on an ottoman. He held the cane in his hand and was rhythmically tapping it on the floor. His face was slack, his eyes looking at nothing at all. In his right hand he held the locket. It was open, displaying the photo of Mary taken before she died. A knock at the door startled him, but he didn't reach for his weapon. "Who is it?" he asked, without getting up.

"It's Saul."

"Come in, Doctor, the door is unlocked."

Saul opened the door. He was dressed in a light cotton coat and wore a derby on his head. "Are you coming?" he asked. Durrant did not respond. The doctor entered, closed the door, and crossed the room to where Durrant was sitting.

"What are we doing, Saul?" Durrant asked.

"We're going to follow the Regina Group men. See if we can't uncover what this Shadow Conspiracy is all about."

"That's not what I mean and you bloody well know it." Durrant tapped his cane, his eyes narrowing. Saul pulled up a stool next to his friend's chair. He reached out and put his hand on Durrant's where it gripped the silver handle of the cane. "Did you know that you haven't stopped fiddling with that cane since you arrived here in Regina?"

"That's not true—"

"Oh, but it most certainly is. Driving me batty, to be honest. I'm surprised that Garnet hasn't rescinded his gift and discarded it in a rubbish bin. These Brits are simply much too tolerant."

Durrant looked at Saul's hand on his own. "What are we doing here, Saul?"

"Durrant, I swear with God as my witness, we're trying to catch a killer." Durrant let out a long sigh. "What is it, old friend?" asked Saul.

Saul moved his hand and Durrant shifted the cane to his right hand. With his able left, he grasped the handle and withdrew the slender, single-shot pistol. He sat looking at it in the dim light of the room.

"Is that what this is about?"

"She could have been killed, Saul."

"But she wasn't."

"*I* could have killed her. I'd never even shot this pistol before. I had no idea if its bore was straight. It might have exploded in my hand, and Mason would have killed her."

"But it didn't. He didn't. Your aim was true."

Durrant shook his head.

"Durrant," Saul said finally, looking at the locket in Durrant's hand. "Charlene is not Mary. You have suffered a terrible loss in your life. No man should have to lose both his wife and his child. And then to lose your leg, and use of your hand . . . It's simply too much. But Charlene is not Mary."

"What's to say she isn't?"

"First off, from what you've told me, Mary was as gentle as a lamb. Our Charlene is headstrong and bullish, if you ask me."

"There is nothing to say that she won't suffer the same fate, or some other terrible demise."

"You can't stop that. Only the Almighty has providence over such things."

"That's a load of horse manure, Saul. The benediction of the

Lord has nothing to do with such things. It's random and cruel, and if there was a God above, surely he would show some mercy from time to time."

"What's to say he doesn't? You're still alive."

"I can't lose her, Saul. I won't let it happen. Mason came this close." Durrant held up the thumb and forefinger of his game right hand. "It was all I could do to keep her alive. I don't know what I would have done without this," he said, holding up the pistol in his left hand.

"You didn't have to. Fate willed that weapon to your hand a year ago. It was there when you needed it, and true." Saul watched Durrant a moment. "Does she know?"

"Know what?"

"That you are in love with her?"

"She's a child, Saul."

"She is *not* a child. You continue to see her as the boy you rescued from the stables, and the helpless girl at the mercy of a deranged and brutal husband. If you look in your heart, old friend, and at her, you'll see a very competent and, I might say, beautiful young woman."

Durrant slipped the pistol back into the handle of the cane. He drew a deep breath and blew air out between his teeth. "Durrant," said Saul, "don't be afraid."

Durrant thought of the locket, the likeness of Mary forever remembered there. "Very well, then," Durrant said after a moment of silence that hung heavy in the room. "Let's go and see if we can find out what this Shadow Conspiracy is about."

Durrant stood and fixed his Enfield in its holster around his waist, and tucked the Bulldog into his boot. It was a warm evening, so he didn't bother with a coat. He put his bowler on his head and stepped out of the room. Together, he and Saul walked down the hall to Charlene's room.

"I suppose I will have to apologize."

"I expect you will."

Durrant knocked on the door and waited. "I hope she doesn't make this more difficult than it ought to be." There was no answer when he knocked again. He tried the doorknob; it was unlocked. He pushed the door open. The room was much like his own, except it had a delicate floral scent to it. The dress Charlene had worn at dinner was on the bed, and her boots were set on the floor. Durrant stepped into the room. On the bed, next to the dress, was Charlene's writing tablet, the one she had used in Holt City the year before. Durrant picked it up and read:

Gone to find out what Dire is up to.

"Blue Jesus." Durrant turned and went from the room as fast as he could.

THIRTY-TWO

IN THE SHADOWS

DURRANT, SAUL, AND GARNET SPLIT up, and each went to locations where Jasper Dire had been seen over the last week. They met again at eleven that evening, and none of them had seen either Dire or Charlene.

"Where the hell could she have gotten to?" Durrant's voice betrayed the panic rising in his chest.

Saul spoke up. "If you had killed Reuben Wake, and maybe his brother, you might well know that some of his old haunts were vacant, wouldn't you? Assuming for a moment that Dire is our man, and even if he's not, wouldn't Wake's stable be a good place to search for him, as it is now without a master?"

"Shall we go there?" asked Garnet.

"I will," said Durrant. "I want one of you to stake out the Regina Group, and the other, Dire's home. That way, we cover all the bases."

They agreed to meet again around one in the morning, and each set off for a different part of the town. The lamps on the main street had been lit as Durrant walked as quickly as he was able to Wake's stable. There were only so many places a group of men could meet to discuss their business in private. An abandoned barn would be one of them.

The night was warm and a wind blew in from the west, kicking up the dirt in the streets. He reached the crossroad near the Wake Stables and stood in the shadow of a general merchant's door. He watched to see if others were observing the space but could see no one. He crossed the road and walked quietly to the stable. It was a broad building, with grand double doors fronting onto Broad Street. A row of high windows allowed natural light into the building during the day. Durrant watched for any light coming from within and could see none. Unwilling to give up with Charlene missing, he found a narrow alley running the length of the barn. He carefully stepped around a stack of wooden crates and went to the back corner of the building. The rear of the barnlike structure was bordered by a laneway. He stopped and listened.

He could hear men's voices. Somewhere on the prairie there was a flash of lightning; a crack of thunder followed soon after. Heavy drops of rain began to fall, their sound quickly drowning out the voices. Durrant strained to hear the quiet talk somewhere close by. He couldn't tell if the voices were coming from within the stable or somewhere else on the street. He slowly looked around the corner to see if he could locate the men, and as he did the back door of the stable opened, just ten feet away. Jasper Dire, wearing a broad-brimmed hat, emerged and peered up and down the lane. Durrant was able to withdraw from view just in time to avoid detection.

Dire completed his scan and then stepped into the street. Half a dozen other men followed; Durrant recognized none of them. Each one had a hat pulled down low over his face, and the rain created a semi-translucent curtain through which little of each man's visage could be seen. The door was pushed shut after the final man stepped out, and the group wordlessly broke up. Durrant melted back into the shadows of the narrow passage between the mercantile and the stable. He watched as the clouded figure of Jasper Dire started down the street. A hand fell on Durrant's shoulder from behind.

Panicked, he wheeled and with his powerful left hand slammed the light body into the stable wall. It was Charlene, dressed in her disguise; her eyes registered something between amusement and terror.

"Blue Jesus . . ." muttered Durrant.

"Lovely to see you too, Durrant."

Durrant looked around the corner. The six men who had been in the stable were gone. "Well, now we've done it. I've lost track of them."

"It's all right—" Charlene began.

"Is it now?"

Charlene straightened and regarded him. "Yes, it is."

"And how might that be?"

"Because I know what they are up to, and what they have planned."

THEY SAT IN Garnet Moberly's room while Mr. Jimmy served them hot tea and cakes. Outside, the storm raged. Charlene had changed from her stableboy disguise into her blue travelling dress. She had let down her hair, and it fell in cascades around her face. She sipped her tea.

"I know it was all rather impulsive and, I suppose, a little hot-headed of me," Charlene said, "but after our row, I simply decided that there were places Charlie could go that the rest of us could not. A mute boy can find his way into places that a grown woman or three grown men cannot. I hurriedly got myself into my disguise and slipped out the rear of our accommodations. I first went to the newspaper office of Mr. Block, but that was too obvious. I also visited the Protestant church, but that too was a dead end. With Mr. Wake dead, I wondered who might be minding his business. We also now know that Wake's relative Percy is deceased. With both men out of the picture, it stood to reason that the place would be empty until the courts could arrange for its sale.

"When I arrived there was no one about, so I let myself in through one of the windows. I used some crates in the alley to hoist myself up. I nearly broke my neck trying to get down, but managed to land in a large pile of mouldering hay. The stable was completely empty of horses—probably they were taken off to be sold. I went about searching the place, but there was nothing to find. Either Wake had disposed of any written secrets before he joined up with Middleton or someone else had cleared them out. It was as I was preparing to leave that men suddenly appeared in the room."

"Suddenly appeared?" asked Saul.

"Yes, like vapour. I've never heard men move about as quietly as they did. Six of them, and our man Jasper Dire among them but by no means the leader."

"Did you recognize any of them?" asked Durrant.

"They struck no match, so it's hard to say. The only light was from the street lamps outside. I secreted myself in one of the stalls and listened as they whispered their plans. They aim to ensure that Riel lives to testify at trial, and they are willing to kill every member of the Regina Group if that's what it takes."

THIRTY-THREE

SETTING THE TRAP

THE ROOM WAS SILENT AS Charlene revealed her news. Finally Durrant broke the hush. "Dire killed Reuben Wake. I should have seen it from the start. He was at La Jolie Prairie, and his presence behind the field force's lines would not have aroused suspicion of any kind. He could easily have fired the shot that wounded Wake, and then, when the bullet missed its mark, lay in wait for him on the final day of the battle."

"It would have been a simple matter for Dire to seek out the man's own pistol and use it to dispatch him," said Garnet.

"I'll need to examine his hand, but I suspect any burns left two months ago will have healed," said Saul.

"There were black marks on his hands when I met him on the road the day before he left for Fort Pitt, or wherever he was off to," said Durrant. "I was led to believe that they were caused by his work staining carriages, but, as I have since learned, Mr. Dire pushes paper at his carriage shop."

"Black walnuts." All three men turned to look at Charlene. She held her cup close to her lips, her eyes shining in the dark room.

"Pardon me?" asked Saul.

"Yes, of course—" Garnet snapped his fingers.

"Excuse me, Garnet, but do you know what she is talking about?"

"I should have figured it. He uses black-walnut dye in his hair. The tannins provide an excellent dye, while the mordant found in the husk makes the dye semi-permanent."

"That's right," said Charlene. "It also stained his hands."

"In Sun River, we discovered that a ginger-haired man had been seen about town around the time of Riel's return. When he returned from Sun River last year, he would have changed his appearance. If word got out that he had been south of the Medicine Line while Dumont was luring Riel back to the territories, he would not have been placed at the scene."

"He killed Percy Wake too, and buried him on that hillside," said Charlene.

"So we know what this Shadow Conspiracy is up to but aren't much closer to knowing their motivation," Saul added.

"I may be able to fill in some of the gaps there," said Durrant.

"Do tell," said Garnet, leaning forward in his chair.

"Politics, with a healthy dose of religion and a fair apportion-ment of greed, just to make things more interesting. Dire is a Catholic Liberal. He is the son of the patriarch of the Box D Ranch, a vast holding of land that was deeded to his family in 1878. It was one of the first such parcels granted in the Saskatchewan Territory. Dire Sr. came west overland from Sarnia and held the deed to most of the country east of the Cypress Hills. He didn't do much with it until he knew the railway would provide an opportunity to move his cattle east."

"1878 . . . Sarnia . . ." Saul mused.

"Yes, that's right. The Dire family backed Prime Minister Alexander Mackenzie and helped ensure his election in 1873. When the family decided to strike out for the west, they were handsomely rewarded. Ironically, it was Macdonald who made the venture profitable by returning to power in '78 and resuming his drive to connect the country with the railway.

"The aim of the Shadow Conspiracy must be to ensure that the trial of Louis Riel does the maximum damage to Macdonald's Conservatives, and their supporters in English, Protestant Ontario. We know that the Regina Group wants to kill Riel to save Macdonald the double embarrassment of both the trial and the execution that will almost certainly follow. If Riel is killed before he can stand trial, the government doesn't have to be the executioner. We also know that Riel's supporters want to free him before he hangs. This Shadow Conspiracy hopes only to keep Riel alive long enough to embarrass Macdonald, so that Edward Blake might win the next election and secure power for the Liberals again."

"It's quite the audacious plan," conceded Garnet.

"Do we ride over to Dire's home and arrest him now?" asked Saul.

"We wait. There is so much more to this than the simple murder of Reuben Wake and his kin."

Charlene added, "In overhearing the plans, we've also learned what the Regina Group aims to do. When Riel is moved to the courthouse, they plan on striking."

"But the Mounted Police will use a decoy," said Garnet.

"Of course they will, but the Regina Group has infiltrated the North West Mounted Police, I'm sorry to say. Our Sub-Inspector Dickenson is yet unaccounted for, and my bet is that others within the force are sympathetic to their aims. No, the Regina men will know about the decoy, and they will move on Riel."

"And at the same time, the Shadow Conspiracy will move on them," said Charlene.

"Someone associated with the force was with Dire in Sun River last year," Durrant added. "We still don't know who that is."

"All the while good Father Lefèbvre will be plotting to free Riel and spirit him back to Montana," said Garnet.

"If we simply arrest Dire, the Shadow Conspiracy will replace him, and we will be no closer to catching the rest of his lot. We have no actual evidence of any of this. Whispers overheard in the night won't stand up in court. I don't want to simply stop this from happening. I want to arrest those responsible for the death of at least two men, and the conspirators of these various plots. To do that, we need to trap them."

"Trap who, Durrant?" asked Garnet.

"Trap them all."

ASSISTANT COMMISSIONER LEIF Crozier sat silently behind a desk at the NWMP headquarters. Beyond his window, the parade ground was steaming as the morning sun warmed the rain-soaked earth. He tapped his fingers on the table, considering all he had just been told.

"It's a risk," he finally said.

"Yes, sir." For the first time in more than a year, Durrant was dressed in his scarlet serge, three golden chevrons on his sleeve above the wrist, his gleaming white helmet under his left arm.

"You understand what's at stake if you fail?"

"Yes, sir."

"There's a lot on the line." Crozier stood and straightened his uniform before turning to the window. Durrant remained motionless. "We can't take any risk with the prisoner."

"I believe to do nothing would put him at additional risk, sir."

"Yes, I believe you are right." Crozier rose up on his toes and then rocked backwards on his heels. "Very well, Sergeant. I will speak to the magistrate, and to the defence. You know they've brought in a police officer all the way from Hamilton to handle the evidence for the prosecution? Bloody insult to the force, if you ask me." Durrant nodded his agreement. "There is a lot more on the line if this trap of yours fails. There are lives on the line, and your future with the North West Mounted Police too. Is that understood?"

"Yes, sir, it is."

"Very well. Pick your team, report to me, and let's catch these conspirators. All of them. And no newspapers. One way or the other, this must remain utterly secret."

"ALL RIGHT." DURRANT faced his three friends. "You each know what must be done. This is the last moment where we might turn back. After this, we're committed, and we will have to follow through." They were sitting in Garnet's room. They had taken their meal there, prepared by Mr. Jimmy, to ensure secrecy. "I know I am

224

asking a great deal of each of you. You all know I consider you my very best friends and colleagues at arms."

Garnet looked at the others. He picked up a small glass of sherry and raised it. "For the Dominion!" he said, beaming.

"For the Dominion and for Riel." Durrant raised his cup of tea.

SAUL ARMATAGE FOUND his way to the Roman Catholic church, its whitewashed exterior gleaming in the moonlit night. He knew he would find who he was looking for in the rectory.

The door swung open silently. He closed it behind him, shifting his medical bag to his left hand as he did. He heard a voice at the front of the sanctuary. "Father Lefèbvre, it's Doctor Armatage." Saul still could not see the man. "I've come to check on Mr. Lambert. I wish to check to see if his wounds are healing. I am worried about infection."

There was a long silence in the dark sanctuary. The priest stepped out into the gloom from behind the pulpit. "How do you know that Lambert is here?" he asked, closing the distance.

"I saw him here two days ago. I heard that he has been called as a witness. I was passing by on the street and saw him come into the church. He looked a little grey. This was the first opportunity I have had—"

The priest raised his hand. He was now standing before the doctor. He peered behind him. "Your friend, the policeman. He is not here?"

"He has been reassigned to Fort Calgary."

"The Red Coats will let La Biche stand trial?"

"I don't know." Saul shook his head convincingly.

"And Riel—?"

"I understand his trial is to begin tomorrow."

"Have you seen him?"

"No. I have not yet." The priest hung his head. His hands were folded before him as if in prayer. "May I see Lambert?"

"Yes, certainly." Lefèbvre turned and walked toward the front of the church. Saul followed. Soon they had passed through the portico and were in the rectory of the building.

"Where is the priest who normally attends Mass in this location?" asked Saul.

"He is in Winnipeg. I asked to be moved here from the North so I could attend the trial of Riel. He will need our prayers." They stopped in front of a door near the back of the rectory and the father knocked. A voice responded, and soon the door opened. Lefèbvre spoke. "Doctor Armatage has come to call. He wishes to ensure your wounds are healing."

"They are fine, merci."

"May I have a look?" asked Saul over the priest's shoulder.

"Very well." Lambert stepped from the room and closed the door. The three of them sat down at a table and chairs in the middle of the room. Lambert put his arms, palms up, on the table for Saul to examine.

"They appear to be healing well," said the doctor. "Sometimes with this sort of . . . self-inflicted wound, there can be trouble. You're doing well."

Saul stood and Lefèbvre placed his hand on the doctor's arm. "You said you hadn't seen Riel, not *yet* . . ."

"Yes, that's right."

"But you will see him?"

"I have been asked to see him tomorrow morning before the trial to ensure that he is physically up to the rigors."

"I would like for you to pass on my blessing. Are you meeting at the courthouse?"

"Oh, no. For the man's safety, he's not being moved there." Saul made as if to rearrange items in his bag.

"Ah, yes, of course . . . those rumours of a conspiracy to cause him some harm."

"That's right. I'll be seeing him at the police barracks, in the infirmary, at nine in the morning."

"Doctor?"

Saul turned to Lefèbvre.

"Please tell Riel when you see him that soon his soul shall be free."

GARNET MOBERLY WALKED straight into the offices of *The Regina Examiner*. There were half a dozen men standing around the layout table in the middle of the small press room. Several smoked pipes, and a haze of tobacco smoke drifted like clouds above them. "Office is closed," one of them said, and they all returned to examining the front page for the following day's paper.

"Very good, then. I've got a news tip," said Garnet.

The same man looked up. "We're open at nine in the morning. The paper's put to bed."

"Very well," said Garnet again. "I suppose it can wait until tomorrow. Riel's trial is not to start until latter in the morning."

"Did you say it was about Riel's trial?" Stanley Block stood up behind his colleagues.

"Indeed, sir."

"Come in," Block said.

Garnet stepped toward the cluster of newspapermen. Block extended his hand and Garnet shook it. "Garnet Moberly, sir. I was at Batoche. I was with Wheeler's Survey Corps."

Block led Garnet to his office. It was panelled in rich wood and lined with bookshelves. There was an ornate lamp on his broad desk, which he lit when they entered. Block sat down in his chair and motioned for Garnet to sit opposite his desk.

"Now, what news?"

"Well, sir, it would seem that there is a plan afoot to free Riel."

"What of it? There've been rumours of this since before he was captured."

"As fate would have it, I have overheard that tomorrow at ten the Red Coats will be moving Riel in secret. I have come to learn that he will be examined by a medical doctor before the trial to ensure that he is fit to take the stand. The Red Coats will be moving him from his cell to a doctor's examining room at their barracks at nine. I believe that a gang of men will try to free him then."

"And how did you come by this information?"

"I'd rather not say—"

"But you must, sir."

"The doctor is a friend. I'm afraid that he sympathizes with Riel. The doctor has fallen under this madman's spell," Garnet moved his hands before him as if conjuring magic, "and has told that he won't resist should men try to free Riel. I suspect that these men will try to spirit Riel back to Montana by the fastest road possible."

"How can I know it's the truth?"

"Well, you might take my word as a Scot."

"I'm not sure that's going to be good enough, Mr.—"

"Moberly. In addition to being a proud Scot, I'm also an ardent supporter of our dear prime minister. John A. could use a break. If Riel takes the stand and things go as expected—" Garnet put his hands around his own neck and made an exaggerated choking motion.

Block considered Moberly for a long moment. "Leave this with me. I'll see that I have a reporter on the scene to cover this suspicious turn." Garnet stood and extended his hand. Block shook it. "All right. I've got a paper to print."

"Indeed." Garnet left and walked out onto the street.

CHARLENE MASON WAS dressed in her one and only fine dress as she stepped into the street and made her way toward Reuben Wake's empty stable. She had no doubt that Durrant would follow her. She reached the stable in ten minutes and stopped in front of its broad double doors. She could see no lights in the building but guessed that the Shadow Conspiracy men would be there as they had been the previous night. She stepped up to the doors, opened them, and entered the gloom. "Mr. Wake?" she called out.

There was no sound. She could tell, however, that there were men there. Something shifted toward the back of the barn, where the light of a street lamp seeped in through the high windows.

"Mr. Wake? Mr. Wake, I have important news." Stillness. She turned, left the stable, and hurried down the street. When she passed the town hall, she glanced at the clock. She had just a few minutes to reach the newspaper office. She didn't look back over her shoulder, and though the temptation was nearly overwhelming, she resisted the urge to stop and tie her boots and peer behind her. She reached the newspaper office in time to see a well-dressed man confidently stride out of the false-fronted building and wink at her.

DURRANT WALLACE WATCHED as Charlene entered the stable, called out twice, and then turned and walked down the street. He waited, almost without breathing, until a man emerged from between the buildings. The figure moved deftly up the street, pausing in the doorways of shops along the way. Durrant observed as Charlene and her follower turned the corner at the town hall, then made his way along the avenue. He checked over his shoulder to ensure that no other member of the Shadow Conspiracy was following. The man tailing Charlene stopped before she got to the newspaper office and slipped between two buildings. Shortly after, Durrant saw Charlene leave the newspaper and head back toward the hotel.

Durrant wished he could catch up to her to inquire as to Block's reaction but instead went through the dark to the rear of the newspaper building. He carefully crept through the bleakness until he could observe the member of the Shadow Conspiracy, who was standing outside the open window of Stanley Block's office, listening attentively. Durrant secreted himself among a stack of crates.

"Well, we're going to have to do something, and fast," said a voice inside the office. Durrant glanced toward the newspaper building. The Shadow Conspiracy agent was concealed there by a large crate of newsprint.

"Goddamned right we'll have to do something. This changes all of our plans. This notion that Riel is to be examined is just another ruse by his sympathizers to play to his insanity defence. It's not going to work," Durrant heard Block say.

"What do you want to do?"

"Let's wait until after he leaves the NWMP barracks. It will be easier to take him on the outskirts of town, between the barracks and the courthouse. He'll be too heavily guarded once he gets to the magistrate's. Same plan as before. Just a different location. Are you up for it?"

"I haven't had time to scout the location."

"Then you had better go now."

"Very well."

The conversation ended abruptly. The man listening beneath the window moved quickly away from his hiding place and directly toward Durrant. Durrant held his breath as he passed. It was Jasper Dire.

Dire paused at the mouth of the narrow passage between buildings, his jet-black hair gleaming in the light of the street lamp. And then he was gone.

"YOU KNOW I'M going to get fired if I get caught," said Saul.

"You can tell them that I ordered you to do this," said Durrant.

"Why could we not simply ask?"

"That would mean more people would have to know about our plan. I simply don't know who to trust. With the Regina Group and their shadows firmly rooted in all aspects of the North West Territories, I would prefer that we keep as small as possible."

"So we're going to steal the mannequin from the I.G. Baker store?"

"That's right. Technically, it's not stealing. I'm a sergeant in the North West Mounted Police, you'll recall. I am merely drafting it for official duties."

"How could I forget?"

"HOW IS IT that we ended up with a glamorous job like this?" asked Charlene. She was hiking up her skirt and preparing to climb onto a crate next to a rubbish bin behind a barbershop on Broad Street.

"I'd say it's a true sign of our good sergeant's affection for the both of us that we've been sent to perform this task," Garnet laughed.

THE SUN WAS nearly up when Durrant Wallace walked into the courthouse. The wooden two-storey structure at the corner of Victoria Avenue and Scrath Street had been rented two years earlier by the federal government, and come the morrow it would see the start of its most famous trial to date. Durrant opened the door to the magistrate's office with the key he had been given, stepped inside, and closed the door behind him.

"Up we go, lads." Durrant tapped the floor with his cane.

The sound of grumbling could be heard in the darkness. Then a lamp was lit. Five men were asleep on the floor of the magistrate's office. A sixth slept on the fine leather couch.

"Let's rouse these men, Tommy." The man on the couch sat up. "You've done a fine job with La Biche since Batoche. Now we have one last bit of business before we can finish this affair with Riel. You and these lads have been selected for a special assignment."

"Does it involve coffee?" asked one of the men.

"Private, it does indeed. First you need to be briefed. And then you're for the trail. We have a trap to set."

THIRTY-FOUR

THE HAMMER IS RELEASED

THE POST WAS QUIET. A wagon hitched to a pair of stout quarter horses rested in front of a long, low building that doubled as the infirmary and bunkhouse for the post's doctor. Next to the wagon were two members of the North West Mounted Police, dressed in serge, white helmets gleaming in the sun, and standing at the ready with their Winchesters. They watched the road that led from Regina to the barracks.

While most of the barracks' constables were stationed at the courthouse for the trial, the labourers and non-commissioned members of the force went about their work. A young man pushed a heavily loaded hand truck the size of a wheelbarrow from the quartermaster's store toward the stables. The Mounted Police standing guard eyed him warily. The truck passed out of sight, momentarily eclipsed by the infirmary. Silently it came to rest near the back of the building. The young man pushing it stopped and scanned the yard. It appeared deserted. He reached down and uncovered his load: a man unfolded himself from the hand truck and stood up. He was dressed in a long black robe, and his head was covered in a hood. At the end of the building was a single door, and the labourer reached into his pockets to retrieve a set of heavy keys. He fumbled nervously and looked at his companion, whose face was hidden by the hood. The young man inserted a key into the sturdy Yale lock. The man in the robe took a canvas bag from the truck, and they passed out of the glare of the sun and into the building.

Father Lefèbvre pulled back his hood. "Quickly now. We don't have a moment to lose." He handed the bag to his companion. The man put on a Red Serge. He strapped on a gun belt and awkwardly checked that the Enfield pistol it held was loaded. He looked up at the priest. He was sweating profusely.

"It will be all right, Private," said the priest.

"I'll hang if we get caught. It's treason." The young constable had a thick French accent.

"The force owes you nothing," whispered Lefèbvre. "They declared war on your people, and on your religion." The young man nodded. "Good. Let's free the prophet."

The constable took a pair of manacles from his tunic and placed them on the priest's wrists without fastening them. He drew his Enfield, and the priest walked ahead of him. They made their way out of the storeroom and entered a long hallway that ran the length of the building. It was dark even at midday.

"Which room will they be examining him in?" asked Lefèbvre in a whisper.

"Likely the last room at the end of the hall," said the constable. "It's the largest, and closest to the exit."

"Very well. Let's go." They reached the door to the infirmary. "Are you ready?" the priest asked.

The constable nodded and knocked on the door. Stepping back, pistol in hand, he held on to Lefèbvre's manacled arms as Saul Armatage opened the door. "What is it?" asked the doctor.

Behind his shoulder stood a bearded man, his head bowed low and his back to the door. The constable said, "This prisoner was caught trying to reach the courthouse. He was injured. My orders were to bring him here."

Saul looked skeptical. "Is that so? It's most unusual. I have . . . a delicate examination under way."

"May I bring him in? He's been shot in the arm."

Saul stepped aside. The constable guided the priest into the room and then closed the door behind him. "Put him there, on that gurney for now." Saul pointed.

"Riel!" cried the priest, as he shed his manacles and reached into his robes, drawing forth a small, double-barrelled derringer pistol. He pointed the gun at Saul. Saul immediately put his hands up.

"Come, Riel, we have a truck awaiting you!" The priest drew close to his prophet. "Do you not recognize me?"

The man in the beard looked up. "Of course I recognize you, Father," said Durrant Wallace. At that moment, the young constable turned his pistol from Saul to the priest. Father Lefèbvre gasped in surprise. "Put the gun down, Father. You are under arrest."

"You have betrayed me!" the priest shouted at the constable.

He shook his head. "It is you who has betrayed your country, Father."

"All right," said Durrant. "Let's get this man locked away." He turned to the constable. "Well done, Private Norman. Crozier will hear of your good work. Now, follow through and get the father here under wraps. Father, I will need your robe."

SAUL ARMATAGE STEPPED out of the infirmary and shielded his eyes from the glare of the noonday sun. He addressed the two policemen standing guard. "The prisoner is ready." They entered the building, and as they did, Durrant Wallace, having shed his fake beard and dressed himself in the robes of Father Lefèbvre, quickly exited from the back of the building, Private Norman with him. A third man was thrown over Norman's shoulder. He was dressed in common clothing—tan slacks and tunic, and a wide-brimmed hat—and wore a thick beard. When they reached a waiting wagon, the man was gently lowered into it. Durrant got in with him, while Norman mounted the wagon's spring-loaded seat and quickly snapped the reins. As they drove off, the policemen rushed from the building, their rifles in their hands, and shouted after the escaping prisoner. One of the men levered a cartridge and, taking careful aim, fired twenty feet over the driver's head.

Saul appeared behind them. "Well done, lads. Now, make haste to your next post." The men ran for their horses, tethered at the stable.

THE ROAD BETWEEN the NWMP barracks and the town of Regina ran alongside the banks of Wascana Creek and through a narrow draw and then emerged along the flats, where it dissected the town. It was little more than a mile in distance and provided very few places for cover. Jasper Dire knew that the escaping prisoner would not pass this way. If they were headed for the US border, one hundred and twenty miles to the south, they would not risk the passage through Regina proper but instead would cut west and circle the town and then ride hard for the Medicine Line. Dire had set his trap where an old cattle trail passed between a pair of low sod buildings that had been abandoned by homesteaders.

He had been patient, and it had paid off. Now the final payment would come, when he recaptured the recently freed Riel. God have mercy on any man who stood in his way. He looked across the open prairie. A telling rooster tail of dust could be seen on the horizon. As the wagon drew near, Dire gave his signal, and a man hidden behind a low shed heaved a handcart into the road just as the wagon rounded the bend. The driver pulled up hard on the reins. The horses reared and kicked, and the man in the serge stood to try and rein them in. Behind the driver, Jasper Dire saw the priest clutch at his hat; he seemed to be supporting Riel, as if he had been injured.

As the wagon came to a violent stop, Riel appeared to fall to the floor of the wagon bed. Dire rushed from the hut, his Webley pistol in his hand, and shouted, "Stand to! Stand to! Put your hands in the air and I won't have to shoot!" Another man from the sod hut opposite came forward with a shotgun. The man who had pushed the handcart reached into it for a Winchester. The constable at the reins stood and raised his hands high into the air.

Dire approached, holding his pistol straight in front of him. "Stand, priest." He aimed his weapon at the back of the black-robed man. The priest stood, his cloak concealing his face. "Now you"— Dire turned to the constable—"unholster that sidearm, carefully, and toss it into the road." The young constable did as he was told. "Priest, step down from the wagon and turn so I can see you." Dire noted that the priest seemed to have injured his leg, because he walked with a limp. As he approached, he looked up. "Mr. Dire" —he removed his habit, revealing the face of North West Mounted Police Sergeant Durrant Wallace—"you are under arrest for the murder of Reuben Wake."

For a moment Dire seemed frozen. He raised his pistol but collapsed forward as he did so, falling into the dust. The man with the shotgun spun to take aim at Durrant, but he too fell forward, clutching his chest. No shots had rung out.

The third man, Winchester in hand, turned as if to run but tripped in the dirt and also fell forward, clutching his leg. He crawled a few feet, clawing at his thigh, where a small spot of blood was emerging, and then lay still. Durrant reached down and picked up the pistol Dire had dropped. He threw it to Private Norman. Garnet rose up from the sod next to the hut. He was covered in dirt and grass. He was smiling broadly and had a long wooden tube in his hands. He came forward quickly.

"Well done, Mr. Moberly," Durrant said.

"Likewise, Sergeant, Private."

"Nice choice of weapons." Durrant pointed to the blowgun in Garnet's hands.

"Ah, yes, a relic from my time among the Dyaks of Borneo. Very effective. The serum that Doctor Armatage concocted last night should keep these men asleep for several hours. One would hope . . ."

"There will be a company along within a few moments to take care of these prisoners. Now, we must make haste." Durrant bent down to unbutton Dire's tunic.

STANLEY BLOCK STOOD in the shadow of a doorway on the main street of Regina. He checked his watch. Soon they would ride into town triumphant. He would have his day, and it would come with great reward: in time, Macdonald might even appoint him to the Senate. Of course, the mumbling drunk must never know the lengths his faithful supporters had gone to in order to shield him from the embarrassment of this trial, but Macdonald's keepers in Ottawa would know.

Block waited. He checked his watch. He looked up the road, and as he did, the woman appeared on horseback as she had promised the night before. She slowed her horse to a canter and rode past the storefronts, looking for him. He stepped forward, and she drew the sweating horse up alongside him. "You bring good news, I hope?" he asked, and she smiled. "You've been most helpful. Tell me, was Dire successful?"

"He was."

"Are you sure you won't stay and celebrate with us tonight? I may have to insist . . ."

"I cannot," she said. "Once Riel is done for, I must take the train for Winnipeg and report our success. The family of Thomas Scott will have some peace, at long last."

"How is it you have come to be so helpful to us so late in the day?"

The young woman with the icy blue eyes laughed. "Someone is always watching." She pressed her heels into the horse. As if on cue, the wagon being driven by Jasper Dire rounded the corner and entered the town. He sat erect at the reins. In the back sat a man with a Winchester and another with a shotgun. Between them was the bearded Riel, his hat pulled down low, obscuring his face. Block faded back into the shadows.

From down the street came a shout, and several Mounted Police on horseback began to ride toward the wagon. Dire drew up on the reins; as he did, Block looked to the window of a building across from him, raised his hand, and then quickly drew it down.

A shot, clean and crisp, rang out. The driver of the wagon jumped down, landing hard in the road. The two men in the back with Riel dove for cover. A second shot was fired, and the hat on the prophet Riel disappeared and the head of the man seemed to disintegrate. His body slumped into the wagon. The constables rode up hard, their pistols drawn, as passersby in the street screamed and ran for cover.

Dire hobbled to the back of the wagon, his leg obviously damaged from his fall, and yelled, "He's dead! They have killed him!" The constables dismounted and descended on the building where the shot had been fired as Stanley Block opened the door behind him and disappeared. He knew the shooter would already be gone.

THIRTY-FIVE

SMOKE AND MIRRORS

AS DURRANT SHOUTED, "HE'S DEAD! They have killed him!" he noticed the dark shape of Stanley Block fade back and disappear. The four policemen dropped from their horses and rushed toward the building the shots had been fired from. Durrant reached down and touched the shoulder of Private Norman. He whispered, "You all right, son?"

"Yes, Sergeant."

"Okay, you know what to do."

The lad sat up and, with his shotgun in hand, quickly dismounted from the wagon.

"You there, Staff Sergeant Provost? Planning on taking a nap?" asked Durrant. Provost was dressed as one of the men from the ambush.

"No, Durrant, just making a good show of it."

"Show's over. I need you with me."

Provost stood up, pushing down hard on the "corpse" next to him.

"Easy now Tommy, got to keep up the façade," cautioned Durrant.

"I'd say he's lost his stuffing," said Provost. Next to him were the scattered remains of the mannequin's head and the false beard that had been glued to it.

"Yes, I fear that the good doctor will be none too pleased. Hell of a shot." Durrant snatched his cane from the bed of the wagon.

"It's a good thing. At that distance, one of us might have been zipped," said Provost.

"All right, let's get a move on. He'll be halfway to the stable by now." They mounted the buckboard, and Durrant cracked the reins and drove it hard down Broad Street. People pressed to the windows of the shops to see them ride by.

They rounded a sharp corner onto Victoria Street, and Wake's stable came into view. "How do you know he's got a horse stashed here?" asked Provost.

"There was fresh hay here last night when Charlene was snooping around. There was tack laid out by the door. When she was there the night before, there was nothing. It's a good bet this is where he's stashed his mount."

They stopped two buildings away from the stable, and Durrant motioned for Provost to cover the front of the building while he slipped into the alley between the stable and the adjacent structure. Though Provost outranked Durrant, they had come to the understanding that Durrant was in charge of this undertaking. Durrant reached the place where the crates were stacked and carefully climbed onto them. He put his cane down and reached up to open one of the windows, just as Charlene had several nights before. Then he hoisted himself up and quickly slipped inside.

The stable was dark, but Durrant knew at once that there was a horse there. He could hear it breathing. Steadying himself with his left hand, he lowered himself down to a carefully placed box and waited for his eyes to adjust to the dimness. As he did, he quietly drew his Enfield and held it at his side.

There was a noise, and it wasn't the horse. Durrant could hear wooden wall boards being pried open. He crouched next to one of the empty stalls and watched one of the boards at the back of the stable being dismantled. The assassin would have made this preparation beforehand, ensuring that he had a way to get into the barn unseen. A dark shape moved through the opening in the wall. The boards were left open, allowing some light into the room. Durrant could easily see the figure move through the darkness.

The man found his horse saddled and waiting near the front of the barn. Durrant stopped when he was just one stall away from the horse. He raised his pistol and waited. The moment would come when the shooter opened the door to make his escape. Tommy

Provost would bear down on him, Durrant would catch him by surprise, and the final trap would be sprung.

The horse didn't move. Durrant began to feel uneasy. Then the barrel of a pistol pressed into the back of his head. "Sergeant Wallace."

"Mr. Dickenson," said Durrant.

"It's still Sub-Inspector to you."

Durrant straightened. "You're not fit to wear the serge."

Dickenson laughed. "No, but then neither are you. I could hear you clomping along with that peg leg of yours the moment I walked in here. Toss your pistol."

Durrant threw the Enfield, too hard, and it skidded across the floor and hit the stable doors with a dull thud. "You'll not ride out of here alive," he said.

"Who says I'm to ride?" asked Dickenson, and Durrant was silent. "Let's go. Back the way I came."

Dickenson guided Durrant toward the opening in the rear wall. Durrant said, "So, you have been part of this Regina Group since the beginning. Holding La Biche was merely a ploy to stay close to the prisoner. You knew that sooner or later Riel would come, and you would have your shot."

Dickenson laughed, and Durrant felt the barrel of the pistol clip the side of his head. His ear burned with the pain of it. "If you think you're going to get any sort of explanation from me, Wallace, you're a bigger fool than I imagined."

They reached the back of the stable, and Dickenson pressed the pistol hard into Wallace's back. "You first. If you try to run with that gimp leg, I'll cut you down. Killing you would make no difference to me." He shoved Durrant, and as he did Durrant tripped on the floor joist. He tumbled through the opening and landed in the dirt in the back alley. The sun blinded him, but he managed to turn as Dickenson came through the opening, his pistol held out before him. It was the missing Colt .45, the one that had been planted on Terrance La Biche.

"The great Durrant Wallace, lying in the dirt like a dog." Dickenson carefully stepped closer and extended his pistol toward Durrant. He thumbed the hammer.

"Drop it," said Tommy Provost. He stepped into the alley and held a Remington shotgun just a foot from Dickenson's head.

Dickenson wheeled on the man and the shotgun exploded, the blast blowing a hole in the side of the stable. He grappled with Provost for the weapon, the two men careening into the wall. From his prone position Durrant reached for his British Bulldog. He fired as the two men before him struggled to take aim at each other.

Dickenson wheeled against the stable, spinning and collapsing, his face twisted in agony. His pistol landed in the dirt, and he clutched at his leg. "You shot my goddamned knee off!" he screamed. Provost was breathing hard beside him, his gun aimed at Dickenson.

Durrant struggled to his feet, the Bulldog still trained on Dickenson. "We'll see if we can't get you fitted with a stump, Mr. Dickenson. See how *you* enjoy it." He bent down and picked up the Colt and put it in his pocket. "Evidence," he said, patting his coat.

TOMMY PROVOST HAD turned the wounded Dickenson over to Saul Armatage. Now Provost and Private Norman stood with Durrant behind the newspaper office.

"All right, lads. I don't know what we should expect here, but let's go and find out." They stepped through the back door of the two-storey building and went up the stairs to the large copy desk. The room was empty. All of the reporters were chasing the various story-lines of the day. They made their way to Block's office and stopped outside the door. Durrant counted in a whisper, "One, two, three!"

Provost kicked in the door, and with guns drawn the three men stormed the room. Block was behind his desk. His mouth was gagged and his hands were bound in front of him with a white lace scarf. Durrant saw him first. "What the Blue Jesus . . . ?"

"Hello, Durrant." Charlene was standing against the wall, Block's four-barrelled pistol in her hand and aimed casually at the man at the desk.

"Charlene! What in God's name are you doing?"

"He caught up with me and insisted that I join him for a celebratory drink. I thought I'd save you the trouble."

Durrant looked at the others and back at Charlene. He shook his head. "All right, lads . . . and lady. Let's wrap this up and deliver this fellow to the magistrate."

THERE WAS A line of NWMP officers around the courthouse. On the street, a crowd stood in the afternoon heat, awaiting some word on the opening day of the trial of Louis Riel.

Durrant, Norman, and Provost ushered a shackled Stanley Block to the back door of the courthouse in time for the first recess of the day. There was some hullabaloo out front as reporters came to the door to share the news of the trial's first hours. Durrant, taking pains not to be seen by the crowd of scribes, approached a familiar-looking constable and identified himself and the others. He asked that they be allowed to escort the prisoner to his appearance before the magistrate and then to the town's makeshift jail in the building's basement.

The four men were granted access through the courthouse's rear doors, and Durrant led them into the vestibule at the back of the judge's chambers. They sat on a bench, awaiting the opportunity to present the prisoner. Durrant caught Block regarding him scornfully.

"You have something to say?" Durrant asked him. Private Norman looked from Block to Wallace.

"You seem to have found yourself on the wrong side of history, Sergeant," sneered Block.

"I'm a North West Mounted Police officer, Mr. Block. I don't have a role in history. My only aim is to ensure justice is delivered."

"Time will tell, Sergeant, but I can say with certainty one thing."

"And what is that?"

"That your so-called justice won't be delivered anytime soon."

Provost jumped to his feet, drew his pistol, and pushed it into the stomach of Private Norman. He pulled the trigger. The explosion was muffled by the constable's serge; he fell forward onto the floor. Provost then turned the gun on Durrant, who had begun to stand, and held it to his forehead.

"Tommy, don't do this."

Block stood up behind him. "Shoot him, Mr. Provost."

"That wasn't part of the plan, Block," protested Provost.

"He knows too much. He's seen all of our faces. Shoot him. We can say it was Norman."

"Tommy, why are you doing this?" asked Durrant.

"He can't get away with it," said Provost.

"Riel? He's going to go to trial. That's the way we do it in Canada."

"Yes, he is. He'll create sympathy in the press for his cause. He'll make Macdonald look like the killer when he himself is a homicidal maniac."

"Tommy, it's not our job to pass judgment. Our job is to uphold the law."

"Still believe all that tripe that Sam Steele has been feeding you, Durrant?"

"You believed it too. You saved my life on the Cypress Hills."

"Yes, Durrant, but that was long ago. Much has changed quickly in this young nation."

Durrant leaned forward as he spoke his next words, his forehead pushing the pistol back toward Provost, who took a step back. "Nothing has changed, Tommy. We're still Mounted Police." Provost backed into Block, and flinched. Durrant seized the moment and swung his cane for Provost's hand. The pistol clattered to the ground. Provost lunged for Durrant, who stepped aside and used his cane to spear his attacker in the neck. Provost dropped to the floor, his hands on his throat, his face turning red as he gasped for breath.

Durrant scrambled for the Enfield pistol, but Block, his hands manacled before him, dove for him, and Durrant's prosthetic gave way. They crashed to the floor. Block sat astride Durrant and pressed the shackles of his bound hands into Durrant's neck. Durrant reached for his cane with his right hand as he felt the chains cutting into his windpipe. He started to gasp for breath.

"All of this," grunted Block, "for a goddamned half-breed!" Durrant pressed his left leg into the floor and gave a tremendous push, leveraging his body just enough to free his left hand. As he did, the Enfield came out from under him, and he felt it catch in the soft fabric of a body beside him. He had little time to look, but with his strained peripheral vision he could see the barrel pressed into the side of Tommy Provost, who was clutching at his shattered windpipe. He struggled to free it. Then Provost seemed to roll away, and the weapon came up in a neat arc and connected with Block's temple.

Block's grip on Durrant's throat slackened a moment, and oxygen once again found its way into Durrant's lungs. Block struggled to renew his grip. Durrant swung his pistol and the butt of it connected with his assailant's temple again. There was a cracking sound, and Block's eyes went glassy but his chains remained tight against Durrant's throat. Durrant hit him a third time. This time, Block's body turned and his hands fell to the floor. He lay motionless on his side.

The door burst open and he heard a voice. "What in the name of God is . . . Blue Jesus!"

Durrant awkwardly stood up, using the wall for support, and faced the judge. His leg was askew and he had the blood of Private Norman on his waistcoat and face. His own throat was red from where Block's chains had cut into it. There were three bodies on the floor at his feet.

"Sergeant Durrant Wallace, sir, of the North West Mounted Police," he sputtered.

The judge was in his robes. His mouth opened and closed twice before he found the words he was searching for. "What has happened here?"

Durrant looked around at the three bodies on the floor. "I think it's time my commanding officer, Sam Steele, and I explained things to you, sir."

THIRTY-SIX

THE FINAL BETRAYAL

TOMMY PROVOST DIED THAT NIGHT. Durrant sat next to him in the infirmary at the North West Mounted Police barracks. Saul Armatage had performed surgery to repair the man's windpipe, but by the time he had completed the task, Provost was dead. Durrant never got to ask him the questions that burned at him nor did he tell him how grateful he was that Provost had once saved him. He would never understand how it was that such a good man had come to deceive him. When Saul told him it was over, Durrant simply got up and walked out of the barracks and out onto the dry prairie, where he watched as the sun sank low in the west. The long, slanting rays of light coloured the rough grass with streaks of red and gold and then, as the sun was eclipsed by night, a deep blue.

For Durrant, Provost's disloyalty and death was the final betrayal in the third Riel conspiracy. In the wink of an eye the sun disappeared, and the world plunged back into night. Too brief was the day, thought Durrant, and so long the endless sleep.

Then Charlene was beside him. She put her hand on his arm, and he didn't withdraw it. "You might consider getting yourself cleaned up." Durrant realized he was still dressed in Dire's clothing, and it was caked with dust and dried blood. He looked down at himself and shook his head and wondered what was to become of this new world.

HE WORE HIS scarlet serge, as the uniform was the only article of clothing he had in Regina that was not bloody. He walked to the magistrate's private chamber via the courtroom, unable or unwilling to face the antechamber where he had been betrayed by and then killed his long-time friend. The judge's chamber was the only place where they could be assured of privacy.

The court was empty at 10:00 PM, but Durrant could feel the tension still in the room. The first day of Riel's trial had electrified the new nation. Reporters from as far away as England were in Regina to cover the events.

Durrant knocked on the magistrate's door. When the door opened, Sam Steele stood before him. "Good to see you, Durrant."

"Likewise, sir."

"Come in."

Durrant stepped into the chamber. It was a small, unpretentious office. There were several men seated there. "Of course you know Assistant Commissioner Crozier," said Steele. Leif Crozier stood to shake Durrant's hand.

"And this is Sir Edgar Dewdney, lieutenant-governor of the North West Territories." Dewdney was seated in an overstuffed chair. He had wavy grey hair and thick chops and wore a stern expression.

Durrant stood at attention and said, "It's an honour to meet you, sir."

"Yes, yes," said the lieutenant-governor. "Sit, and let's hear what you have to say."

"As you know, sir, I was originally called to Batoche to help with peacemaking after the conflict. With the murder of Reuben Wake and the incarceration of Terrance La Biche, my efforts took a different direction. Mr. La Biche had every motive to commit the murder of Mr. Wake, but he was not the only one. Others also had cause. I felt it was simply too convenient that La Biche should be found with the dead man's pistol in his pocket and arrested for the crime. What I did not grasp from the start, though he was always a suspect, was that the man who claimed to have found the pistol and arrested La Biche was in fact Wake's killer."

"That would be Jasper Dire," said Crozier.

"Yes, sir."

"And what motive did he have?"

"Well, sir, that's where things get complicated."

"Make it simple for us, would you, Sergeant? It's late and I still must inform Ottawa of this debacle," said Dewdney.

"Very well, sir. It seems as if there were layers of conspiracy in this case. The most elemental conspiracy was that of Father Lefèbvre, who was caught today at the North West Mounted Police barracks trying to free Riel. He has held since the start that should the effort at Batoche go poorly for the Métis, they would not rest until Riel was freed and returned safely to Montana.

"The second conspiracy involved Stanley Block, Sub-Inspector Dickenson, Reuben Wake, Tommy Provost, and others. They called themselves the Regina Group. They wanted Riel dead before he could be given his day in court."

"Why kill Riel now? He is going to hang." Dewdney spoke matter-of-factly.

"To protect Macdonald, sir."

"That is Prime Minister Macdonald to you, sir."

Durrant continued, "They feared what he will say on the stand. Riel uses words as a mighty weapon. Their belief is that Macdonald will suffer terribly when Riel has his say in court. The handling of the complaints of the Métis and the Indians has been a catastrophe. If Riel testifies in his own defence, and then hangs for his crimes, a schism will be driven into this young country that will further divide French and English, Catholic and Protestant, east and west. It might take generations to heal, if at all."

"I think you overestimate both the power of Riel and the memory of the inhabitants of Ontario and Quebec, Sergeant," said Dewdney.

"This was the belief of the Regina Group. My colleagues and I have made extensive notes on the others involved in this conspiracy, and we will be turning them over to Superintendent Crozier to follow up on. I believe arrests can be made of a good number of men involved with the conspiracy to commit murder."

"And you think this is why Wake was killed?"

"While I have no proof, I believe it's why the man we have discovered to be his brother was murdered as well. The body we found in Sun River had been shot in the head. I believe that Jasper Dire followed Wake when he went with Gabriel Dumont to Sun River last year, surprised the Wakes when they were camped above the river, and killed Percy. We have a witness that says a man riding a horse bearing the Box D brand was in that country at that time. That's Dire's brand. Dire may have tried to kill Reuben Wake as well."

"What for?" asked Steele.

"To ensure that if Wake got close to Riel, he would not succeed in his effort."

"And what was that?"

"At that time, I believe Wake's purpose was to disrupt the effort to return Riel to the North West Territories. He was to sow seeds of doubt in the community and spread rumours. When that failed, and he was faced with an angry Gabriel Dumont, he likely decided to take a more direct route and lie in wait for them, and that's when Jasper Dire got to Wake's brother."

"And why not Wake himself?" asked Crozier.

"Maybe Dire tried but failed. In any case, at that point he would have been known to Wake, so he assumed a disguise. He dyed his hair black to cover up his ginger locks and returned to Canada."

"Sergeant, you reported to me that there was another man with Jasper Dire when he went to Sun River. You told me he wore a Mounted Police uniform," said Crozier.

"That's right. I've had time to check the record at the barracks, sir. I believe it was Staff Sergeant Provost. He was on extended leave at the time Dire went to Sun River. I believe Mr. Provost was the cleverest of the lot. He managed to infiltrate his enemy's ranks and was trusted among them. He was able to convince Dire to allow him to travel to Sun River, and went so far as conspiring to kill the Wake brothers just to get close to Dire and the others. We'll never know. Dire and Provost are both dead."

"This so-called Shadow Conspiracy. What was its role in all of this?" asked Crozier.

"Should Riel be captured, the Shadow Conspiracy's purpose was to ensure that he would stand trial. To ensure that whatever the outcome of the Northwest Rebellion, Riel's story should cause the most harm to Prime Minister Macdonald."

"Are you saying, sir, that Edward Blake's Liberals are behind this?" Dewdney sounded incredulous.

"I'm not willing to speculate, sir. I doubt very much that any of our political leaders would admit direct involvement of any kind—"

"I should say not!"

"What I can say with some certainly is that Jasper Dire and his colleagues intended to kill as many members of the Regina Group as necessary to keep Riel alive long enough to stand trial. When Dire saw the chance to eliminate Wake, first at La Jolie Prairie and then again in the zareba, he took it."

"Do you think it was Dire who took a shot at you when you were on the Humboldt Trail?" asked Steele.

"I suspect as much," said Durrant. "And it was likely he who followed me to Sun River and back. I think the Humboldt Trail incident was intended as a warning, as was the note left in the church in Sun River. If he wanted to kill me, he could have. I believe that his following me to Sun River was to see just how much I had learned about these conspiracies."

Edward Dewdney stood up, as did the other men in the room. Dewdney came toward Durrant. "Sergeant, you will turn your notes on the Regina Group over to me. I will supervise the investigation personally." Durrant looked askance, and the lieutenant-governor demanded, "Is that a problem, Sergeant?"

Durrant caught Sam Steele's eye. "No, sir, that won't be a problem."

"Very well, then. Good work, Sergeant, in bringing this matter to a conclusion." And he left.

The room was silent. "You don't think—?" began Durrant when the silence had hung long enough.

Crozier cut him off with a raised hand. "Don't even ask that question, Sergeant. This country isn't ready for it."

"THAT WAS IT? 'Good work in bringing this matter to a conclusion?'" asked Saul.

"That was all," said Durrant.

"And do you suppose that Dewdney will be opening his investigation tomorrow?" asked Saul with a wry smile.

"I suspect that he will spend some time first considering the notes with great care."

"That is, as soon as we are able to make a copy of them," said Charlene.

"Mr. Jimmy has set about that task already," said Garnet. They were seated in his room. A pot of tea was set in the middle of the table. "I am very sorry for the loss of your friend."

"His death stings, Garnet, but it is his betrayal that burns the most."

"There is no doubt that this was a nasty piece of business. I fear it will leave a scar long after that wound on your neck has healed."

"It's best not to think too much on it," said Charlene. "We are among the living."

"Yes, we are," said Durrant. "And I am grateful for all that you have done."

"Where to next, Durrant?" asked Saul.

"Steele wants me back at Fort Calgary as soon as I can. The railway is making its final push toward completion at Rogers Pass, and he is in need of my particular brand of policing elsewhere along the line."

"You're not going straight away, are you?" asked Garnet.

"No. No, I'm not. There is yet unfinished business. Somewhere in the dale of the Saskatchewan around Batoche is the body of the teamster who was supposed to accompany Dumont to Sun River. Reuben Wake murdered him and took his place. I can't let that stand. More work needs to be done to uncover the circumstances around the demise of Wake's brother, Percy. I have questions that need answering, and they may well take me back across the Medicine Line. Who knows? I may yet make it into the Kootenay country to look in on my old friends Jeb and Bud Ensley."

"I suppose you'll be gone come the morning then, won't you?" asked Charlene.

"I will. I could use a hand, if you're up for it."

"When do we leave?" Charlene beamed.

"For Queen and country," said Garnet, raising his cup of tea.

"And for friendship. Long may it last," said Durrant.

THE RESISTANCE OF LOUIS RIEL

NOVEMBER 16, 1885.

THE CROWD THAT WAS ASSEMBLED outside the barracks of the North West Mounted Police seemed to include half the population of the North West Territories. The day was icy cold, with a bitter wind from the north. Despite that, people had been arriving by train and wagon for the two days since the last appeal of Louis Riel had been dismissed.

Inside the barracks, Lieutenant-Governor Dewdney and other politicians, the senior brass of the North West Mounted Police, and handpicked members of the eastern media had gathered for the event.

Stanley Block was not among them. Though he had begun to make a recovery from the cracked skull he had suffered at the hands of Durrant Wallace, he had not regained his power of speech. His conspiracy trial had been postponed until he regained his faculties, but there was no indication of when that would be.

Jasper Dire and Sub-Inspector Dickenson had both been found guilty of conspiracy and attempted murder, and were now awaiting sentencing. Father Lefèbvre and Jacques Lambert had been returned to the northern communities after serving three months each for their roles in the attempted prison break.

Charlene Louise stood next to Durrant. She had convinced a Justice of the Peace to posthumously annul her marriage to Mason and had dropped his last name. She wore a heavy coat and stylish cap and was pressed in close to Durrant as they stood waiting. Durrant wore his sealskin cap and greatcoat and heavy woollen gauntlets.

Durrant felt a body brush against his in the crowd and turned to see Saul Armatage smiling at him. "Hello, Durrant, welcome back. How was Craigellachie?"

"Mostly pomp and ceremony but dignified, I suppose."

"Can you be seen in the tintype of the driving of the last spike?"

"I should hope not. I managed to get in behind Donald Smith, who nearly blocked out the sun with his girth. No, this visage won't stain the nation's memory of that event."

"I understand that you've been given a promotion?"

"Pardon me?" Charlene looked at Saul, then back at Durrant. "Why didn't you say so?"

"It didn't seem appropriate, given these dour circumstances."

"Word has it that Mr. Wallace here is now a full inspector in the North West Mounted Police," said Saul.

"It would seem so."

"Does that mean you can pull rank on Sub-Inspector Dewalt?" asked Charlene.

"I suppose it does." Durrant looked pleased. "Steele felt that if I was to remain clandestine in my investigations, I would have to report directly to him and not be held to account by the likes of Dewalt. It seems that Ottawa doesn't want there to be an investigative branch of the force, but Steele has found a way to circumnavigate that." Durrant faced Saul. "I had hoped that Garnet would be here too."

"He wanted to be, and sent a dispatch from somewhere in the Far East to say so. He's off on another one of his adventures, but he'll be back. Any word on Riel?" asked Saul.

"None, yet," said Durrant. What seemed like an eternity passed, and then the judge exited the barracks and a hush fell over the crowd. He stood for a moment and then cleared his throat. "For the crime of treason against the Crown and the Dominion of Canada, Mr. Louis Riel was hanged from the neck until dead."

For a moment the crowd was silent. The prairie wind blew hard, and it seemed to freeze those in attendance. Then a ripple went through the mass, and some people clapped while others yelled. Someone threw a rock, and in a moment they were on the brink of pandemonium. Durrant steered his friends away from the melee.

When they were away from the crowd, he said quietly, "The Riel Resistance ends." He pressed close to Charlene.

She reached for his left hand and squeezed it, and he did not pull away. "But the story just begins," she said.

"Yes," said Durrant. "Long live Riel."

"Long live Riel," she echoed, and all three of them walked away.

ACKNOWLEDGMENTS

MY SINCERE GRATITUDE GOES OUT to the many people who have helped me with the historical research that underlies this novel. The Parks Canada staff at Batoche National Historical Site in Saskatchewan have provided ongoing information as I've undertaken the writing of this novel. Shari Colliness of the City of Regina Archives provided information on the early history of that city and direction on the real-life conspiracies that surrounded the trial of Louis Riel. Jo-Anne Colby and Nick Richbell, archivists with the Canadian Pacific Railway, once again came to my rescue, providing the earliest map of the City of Regina that I have found, along with valuable diagrams of early CPR railcars. Author Sharon Wildwind provided plenty of leads for my research. My appreciation to Stephen Maly, a historian with Helena Civic TV, who filled in the gaps about Riel's time in Sun River. Miranda Grol, the archivist at the Fort Macleod Museum, helped me with research on that critical piece of the story. Fellow TouchWood author Bill Gallaher provided important feedback on the North West Mounted Police, and Dr. Bill Waiser, A.S. Morton Distinguished Research Chair at the University of Saskatchewan, took the time to first read the manuscript and then discuss the critical events surrounding the Northwest Rebellion with me. It was a pleasure.

As always, I am indebted to TouchWood Editions: Ruth Linka, Emily Shorthouse, Pete Kohut, Cailey Cavallin, and the rest of the staff make it possible for me to worry only about writing as best I can, and they take care of the rest. Frances Thorsen, who is my story editor, is an extraordinary help in bringing these novels to life. I suppose I could do this without her, but the final product wouldn't be much good. Thanks also to Vivian Sinclair for her work as copy editor; she kept me from embarrassing myself too much.

My thanks go out to all of the booksellers, big and small, who have stocked my books. Each and every day I say thanks for making it possible for me to continue writing.

But above all else, I am grateful for my wife, Jenn, who supports me and gives me everything I need to make an investment in the writing process. Together we travelled to Saskatchewan when I was researching this book, and for two years she gave me the time and space needed to rise early each morning and create this novel. I am deeply appreciative of her love and support.

STEPHEN LEGAULT is an author, consultant, conservationist, and photographer who lives in Canmore, Alberta. He is the author of six other books, including the first three installments in the Cole Blackwater mystery series, *The Vanishing Track, The Cardinal Divide*, and *The Darkening Archipelago*, as well as *The Slickrock Paradox*, the first book in the Red Rock Canyon mystery series, and *The End of the Line*, the first book in the Durrant Wallace mystery series. Please visit Stephen online at stephenlegault.com or follow him on Twitter at @stephenlegault.

Other books by Stephen Legault
Carry Tiger to Mountain: The Tao of Activism and Leadership (2006)

THE DURRANT WALLACE SERIES
The End of the Line (2011)
The Third Riel Conspiracy (2013)

THE RED ROCK CANYON SERIES
The Slickrock Paradox (2012)

THE COLE BLACKWATER SERIES
The Cardinal Divide (2008)
The Darkening Archipelago (2010)
The Vanishing Track (2012)